Sanctuary in Providence Ridge

Historical Christian Romance

Vivian Belle

Sterling Ridge Press LLC

Dedication

For those who are still waiting for the storm to pass.

And for those who have learned that sometimes the storm is what carries you to the place you were always meant to be.

Love Always,
Vivian Belle

"He maketh the storm a calm, so that the waves thereof are still. Then are they glad because they be quiet; so He bringeth them unto their desired haven." — Psalm 107:29–30

Contents

Chapter 1

The rain came sideways, heavy and cold, and Clair Whitmore moved through it with her carpetbag pressed tightly against her chest. The road south of Livingston had been packed earth that morning, but hours of rain had turned it into a shallow creek, water running brown through the wagon ruts and pulling at her boots with each step.

Her horse had gone lame several miles back, before the storm clouds broke. She had crouched beside him in the dry grass and run her hand down his foreleg and felt the heat gathered in the tendon like a warning. No riding left in him, she had loosened the girth, pulled the saddle, and left it beside the road where a traveler might find it useful. The horse she turned loose. She'd taken her canteen and carpetbag, and she had walked south.

The mud pulled at her boots with a wet, sucking grip, and her calves burned. She could feel raw places brewing on her feet with every step, bright specific points of pain that kept time with her walking like a metronome she couldn't silence.

The wind shifted, the rain drove harder, and Clair stopped in the middle of the road and looked south. The road was barely visible. A thin wash of moonlight filtered through the edges of the storm clouds, enough to make out shapes for maybe thirty yards. Beyond that, the valley dissolved into rain and the blackness of night. The foothills she'd been using to orient herself were gone. She didn't know where she was and just assumed she was still south of Livingston. Somewhere in the wide ranch country between the Absaroka Mountain Range and the road to Yellowstone. The specifics had stopped mattering. She needed to get out of the rain and close her eyes for a few hours. If she didn't, her body would make the decision for her, and she'd drop wherever she stood.

Lightning came and cracked across the sky to the southeast, and the world turned white, and in those few frozen seconds of light, Clair saw them. A barn, dark against the foothills, sat on a rise. Beside it and to the left was the shape of a house. Two stories. A wide porch. A stone chimney. No lamps in any window.

Clair turned and started moving in that direction. The tall grass pulled at her skirt with every stride, heavy with water, tangling around her ankles and pulling like hands trying to slow her down. She kept her eyes on the place where the barn had been, waiting for the next flash of lightning. It came thirty seconds later, closer; the thunder rolling in so fast after the lightning that the ground seemed to shake with it. She could make out the pitch of the roof, the broad face of a sliding door, and the dark lines of fence rails running into the grass.

Her boots slid on the slope where cattle had churned the ground to slick mud, and she went down hard on one knee. The impact jarred through her leg and up into her hip. For a moment she stayed there, kneeling in the mud with rain beating on her back, her carpetbag clutched against her chest. Her arms were shaking from exhaustion, though the cold had done its own work, settling into her bones hours ago. Six days of moving had stripped her down to whatever was left beneath endurance, and what was left wasn't much.

She got up, planted the bag against her side, and pushed herself through the last twenty yards of churned ground.

The barn door was a heavy wooden slider and well-built. She set her carpetbag in the narrow shelter of the roofline where the eave kept the ground almost dry, braced her boots against the mud, and pulled. The door resisted at first, then finally gave. She grabbed her bag, stepped inside, and pulled the door shut behind her.

The roar of the storm dropped to a muffled drum. Rain hammered the roof in heavy sheets, and somewhere above her head a loose board tapped in a steady rhythm. Clair stood just inside the door with water running off her in thin streams, pooling around her boots. The air inside was warm and thick. After hours in the chilly rain, it felt like stepping into a room where someone had kept a fire burning.

She moved forward carefully with one hand extended, letting her eyes adjust. Thin lines of moonlight showed between the wallboards, and a faint wash of light came from a high window at the far end of the barn. Tack hung from hooks on the near wall, and tools stood upright in a rack beside the door. Everything organized, everything in its place. Whoever kept this barn was particular about it. Stalls were along the right wall, two horses standing quietly with their heads turned toward her, watching.

To her left, hay bales were stacked against the wall in neat rows, shoulder height. Beyond them, a ladder leaned against the wall, leading up to the hayloft. The loft ran the length of the barn's left side, a raised platform built over the hay storage below. From up there, she'd be above the sightline of anyone entering at ground level.

She climbed the ladder with her carpetbag strap hooked over her shoulder. Her arms shook on every rung as her boots, slick with mud, slipped on the worn wood. She pulled herself up one rung at a time, her breath coming hard, until she got her knees onto the loft floor and crawled forward. Hay bales filled the space, stacked in tight, orderly rows that ran the length of the loft. She worked her fingers under the twine of the nearest bale and pulled until the binding gave and the bale broke apart in her hands. Clair spread the loose hay into a thick layer against the wall, far from the ladder's edge. She repeated the same process with a second bale of hay, creating a deep bedding.

Clair dropped into the hay she'd spread, and for a moment she just sat there with her eyes closed and her hands pressed against her thighs. Her whole body was trembling in fine, continuous shudders.

Thank you, Lord, for guiding me here.

She opened her eyes and began working on her boots. Her laces were swollen tight with water; her fingers stiff and clumsy. It took her longer than it should have to work each knot loose. She pulled the first boot free and set it upright at the edge of the hay. The second came off more easily. Her stockings were soaked through, and she peeled them away, wrung them out, and draped them over the boot tops. Her feet were puckered and raw, and she had blisters along both heels that were open and weeping. She tucked her feet into the loose hay where it was warm and reached for her carpetbag.

She pulled her carpetbag onto her lap and ran her fingers along the inside of the lining. The oilskin packet was where she'd sewn it, flat and stiff against the bag's frame. She'd stitched it in herself the night she'd fled Helena. Her fingers moved to the small inner pocket where her folded money was tucked away.

Satisfied and too tired to worry about much else, she curled onto her side in the hay with her carpetbag pressed against her stomach. The hay was deep, and she burrowed into it until it rose around her, holding the warmth her body was starting to give back.

For six days she'd been on the move. Four on horseback, sleeping in stands of timber and once in an abandoned line shack east of Helena where mice had chewed through the flour sacks and left their tracks in the dust. Two days on foot because her horse went lame. The sunburn she'd gotten crossing the open country was peeling along the back of her neck where the rain had found it and turned it to fire.

She hadn't spoken to another person in two days. Not since the boardinghouse in Livingston, where she'd paid for one night and had left before dawn.

Her stomach ached with hunger. She'd eaten the last of her dried meat this morning. Tomorrow she'd have to solve that problem. Tonight she was too tired to care.

She could feel sleep pulling at her, heavy and irresistible, settling into her limbs. Her shivering was easing as the hay insulated the warmth her body was finally producing. The rain on the roof had steadied into a deep, constant drum that her heartbeat was slowing to match.

She thought about the dark house she'd seen through the lightning with its wide porch and stone chimney. This barn was stocked and held horses. Whoever lived here on this property would be up before dawn, most likely, crossing from the house to the barn to check stock and start chores. If she was still here when that door slid open, she might have to explain herself if she was discovered.

She'd rest for a few hours and then slip out before dawn. She'd find the road and keep walking south. Deeper into the valley.

Lord, hold me. Keep me safe tonight. Let me sleep. Give my body enough to carry me for a few more days. Wake me before anyone finds me here.

Chapter 2

Adam Dawson buttoned his shirt and tucked the hem into his trousers. He struck a match from the tin on his dresser and lit the candle beside it. He crossed to the washstand and poured water into the basin.

The shock of the cold water against his face and the back of his neck helped to wake him further. He dried with a cloth hanging from a hook on the wall and ran his fingers through his hair to push it flat. He buckled his belt, pulled his suspenders up over his shoulders, then took the candle from the dresser, crossed his room, and stepped out into the hallway. His daughter's bedroom door was directly across from his, and he eased it open.

Emma was curled on her side with a thin cotton blanket pulled to her chin and one bare foot sticking out from beneath it. She was six years old and small for her age, and in the candlelight, she looked even smaller. Her breathing was slow and even, and Adam stood for a moment, watching the steady rise and fall of her body beneath the blanket.

He went downstairs; the candle lighting his way on the stairs and followed the sound of iron on iron that meant his mother was already at the cookstove. The lamp on the sideboard was lit, and the kitchen was bright enough to work in, so he blew out the candle and set it on the end of the counter as he passed.

Lydia Dawson stood with her back to him, working a spatula beneath something in the skillet. She was forty-eight years old and ran this kitchen and home with hands that had started refusing to work a few years back and had gotten steadily worse. She was a testament to the kind of stubbornness her son had inherited.

Lydia turned when she heard him and smiled. "Storm took a branch off the cottonwood in the yard," she said. "Woke me up in the middle of the night; sounded like a rifle shot."

"I heard it." Adam said as he crossed to the stove where the coffeepot sat on the back plate. He took it by the handle and poured two cups. He set one near his mother's elbow where she could reach it and carried the other to the table. He placed the pot on an iron trivet on the table, where it would stay warm enough for a second cup without Lydia having to get up and fetch it.

Lydia brought the skillet to the table and slid eggs and sliced ham onto both plates with the edge of the spatula, her swollen knuckles bearing the work. She set the skillet back on the stove and then brought the biscuit basket from the warming shelf. She settled into her chair across from Adam with the careful, staged lowering of a woman whose joints made sitting down a negotiation rather than a single motion.

Adam had watched his mother's health decline slowly for the past several years. Each month brought some small new concession—a jar she needed him to open, a kettle she gripped differently, a morning where the swelling in her knuckles was visible from across the room. He couldn't fix this for her. He was unable to slow the progression. All he could do was help her with the things that were becoming more and more difficult for her to do, carry the heavy things, make adjustments to the way their home and lives functioned, carry more of the burden of keeping a ranch running, and pretend, when she needed him to, that he hadn't noticed the latest thing that her hands had stopped allowing her to do.

Lydia bowed her head, and Adam followed. Her prayer was short and direct; she spoke to God the same way she spoke to everyone, as if He were standing in the next room and could hear her perfectly well without formality. She thanked Him for the food. She thanked Him for the roof that held through the storm. She asked for hands sufficient for the work of the day and for protection over them all. She said amen and reached for a biscuit, breaking it open with her thumbs pressed flat against the bread rather than pulling it apart with her fingertips.

"I intend to check on the mare before I start on the south fence work this morning," Adam said, cutting into his eggs. "She was restless yesterday."

"She's been restless for a week. That foal's coming whether you've decided you're ready or not."

"The foal, I'm ready for. It's the mare I'm watching. She's carrying high, and she doesn't like being stalled."

"She doesn't like being stalled because she's got more sense than the man who stalled her. Let her into the paddock, Adam. She'll tell you when it's time."

He didn't argue. His mother had been right about horses more often than he'd been willing to admit, and the mare was her horse before it was his.

They ate without rushing; the kitchen was quiet except for the low tick of the mantel clock in the sitting room and the occasional pop from the cookstove as the firebox settled. Adam finished his eggs and ham and took a second biscuit. Lydia wrapped both hands around her coffee cup and drank with the slow, deliberate satisfaction of a woman who considered the first cup a duty and the second one a pleasure.

"The garden probably took a beating last night," she said. "I'll check the beans once there's enough light to see what's standing and what isn't."

"I'll check the fences near the creek. The hard rain we got yesterday evening could have pushed the creek bank a bit."

Adam got up and carried his plate and hers to the dry sink. Then he crossed to the front door, sat down on the low bench beside it, and pulled his boots on, lacing each one snug and double-knotting them the way his father had taught him when he was a young boy. He took his hat from the peg on the wall, lit a lantern, adjusted the wick until the flame drew steady, and stepped out into the morning.

The fresh morning air hit him clean and sharp, carrying the particular clarity that follows a storm that has wrung everything out of the sky and left nothing behind. The yard between the house and the barn was soaked, and there was water standing in the low spots. The ground was soft enough that his boots pressed full prints into the mud with each stride. Puddles caught the gray half-light of dawn and held it flat like tin laid across the earth. The grass lay beaten sideways, heavy with water.

Adam crossed the yard to the barn with the lantern swinging at his side, its flame throwing a small, shifting circle of yellow light.

He pulled the barn door open and stepped inside. The mare heard him and stamped once, a solid strike of hoof against packed earth that echoed off the stall boards. He went to her first, setting his hand on her neck and running it down along the heavy swell of her barrel. She was warm, her coat damp with the close air of a barn that had been shut tight through a summer storm. She turned her head and pushed her nose against his chest with the blunt insistence of a horse that wanted to be acknowledged before it wanted anything else. He felt along her flanks, noting the way she shifted from one hind foot to the other. Close, but not tonight. Maybe not this week. He gave her neck a final rub and stepped back from the stall.

He turned toward the hay storage, and that was when he saw the muddy footprints.

A trail of it crossed the barn floor from the main door toward the far wall, where a ladder leaned against the edge of the hayloft. The prints were small, too small for a man's boot, and they tracked in a slight weave. Dried mud clung to the rungs of the ladder.

He walked to the ladder and tested the first rung with his boot, then climbed with the lantern held out to one side and his free hand on the rail. At the top, he lifted the lantern above the loft floor and let the light reach into the depth of the space.

A figure lay curled in loose hay. A woman, and she appeared to be close to his age or near it. Her clothing was muddied and creased, a dress of fabric finer than anything worn in this valley, dark with water stains along the hem and sleeves and road dirt ground into the folds. Her boots stood upright at the edge of the hay with her stockings draped over the tops, and her bare feet were tucked into the loose hay. Her hands were locked around the straps of a carpetbag pressed tight against her stomach.

Adam stepped off the ladder onto the loft floor and held the lantern steady, studying her, letting the details tell him what they could before he decided what to do. The mud on her boots was layered. Her dress, even soiled, had the cut and stitching of city work, tailored seams and covered buttons, a quality of cloth that didn't come off any mercantile shelf in a valley town like Providence Ridge. And her face in sleep held a fineness, a calming stillness in her features. Her hair had come loose from whatever arrangement had held it and lay across her shoulder in a fall of light brown that caught the lantern glow.

"Ma'am."

She didn't stir. Her breathing held the same deep, even rhythm, the kind of sleep that comes only when the body has spent everything it owns and has nothing left to give to wakefulness.

"Ma'am." he said it louder, and the woman came awake as if she'd been pulled up from under deep water. Her eyes opened, and her whole body tightened at once. Her arms drawing the carpetbag up tighter against her chest and her knees pulling in. For a moment she looked at him with the wide, fixed stare of someone who didn't know where she was or who was standing over her with a light.

Within a few seconds, she gathered herself into something that looked remarkably like calm. Considering she'd woken to a stranger standing over her in a hayloft with a lantern, her quick composure was something to admire.

"I was caught in the storm last night and took shelter in your barn. I apologize for entering without your permission. I meant no harm," she said.

"Where did you come from?" Adam asked.

"A ways away from here, my horse went lame, and I continued on foot."

"Where are you headed?"

She paused, and that pause told him more than any answer would have. "South."

"South is a great deal of territory, ma'am. You have people expecting you?"

"I'd rather not trouble you with the particulars, Mr. —"

"Dawson. Adam Dawson."

"Mr. Dawson. I'm Clair Whitmore, and I'm grateful for the shelter your barn provided. I apologize again for the intrusion. If you'll allow me just a moment, I'll gather my things and go."

She was already reaching for her stockings, pulling them on with fingers that moved quickly but not steadily; the fine tremor was visible in the way she fumbled the fabric over her toes and had to try again. She tugged her boots on next, working the laces with the kind of haste that had nothing to do with modesty and everything to do with wanting to be upright and moving before he asked another question.

Adam stayed where he was and let the details accumulate the way fence posts accumulate in a line, one after another, each one confirming the direction of the run. He'd noticed that her feet were rubbed raw and blistered along both heels. Her fingers shook with the sustained tremor of a body that had been running on less than it needed. Her dress carried wear that didn't come from a single day of travel; the hem stiff with mud, the cuffs beginning to fray where they'd caught on brush or branch or rock. This woman had been on the move for days.

She got her boots laced, picked up her carpetbag, and stood.

Her legs straightened beneath her, one hand white-knuckled on the carpetbag strap, and then her knees folded and her body pitched forward. Adam's hand closed around her upper arm. His grip held her upright long enough to keep her from going down, and then he guided her back to sitting with a firmness that left no room for negotiation.

"Stay here," he said. "My mother has breakfast made in the house. Let me bring you a biscuit and a cup of coffee before you try going anywhere."

"That isn't necessary, Mr. Dawson. I don't want to be a bother to you or your family."

"It's a biscuit and a cup of coffee. Not a bother. Stay put."

"I assure you I'm quite capable of —"

"Ma'am, your legs just told you differently. Give me five minutes."

He set the lantern on the loft floor near the ladder, where it would give her light. Then he descended the ladder, crossed the barn floor, and went out through the door.

He walked toward the house with his hands loose at his sides and his mind working through everything he'd just seen, sorting it the way he sorted any problem that showed up uninvited on his land. A young woman in city clothes and blisters on her feet. A carpetbag she'd clutched to her chest before her eyes had finished opening. A woman who spoke with the precision of someone educated in a proper household and the careful evasion of someone who was hiding something. A woman who had been traveling on foot for days, from the looks of her, and wouldn't say from where or to what end. Her every instinct upon waking had been to protect that bag before she thought to protect herself.

She was on the run; that much was as plain as day. He didn't want to know what she was running from or to. Knowing would make it his concern, and he had enough of those to fill every hour from first light to last. He'd bring her food and drink, then he'd point her toward the road. He'd go back to his mare and his fence line, and the morning would go the way mornings were supposed to go.

The kitchen was warm and bright when he came through the front door. His mother stood at the stove, making another pot of coffee.

"Is the mare all right?" She asked.

"The mare's fine." He pulled his hat off and held it against his leg. "There's a woman in the barn, Ma."

Lydia turned to face him.

"I found her sleeping in the hayloft." He rubbed his thumb along the brim of his hat, a gesture his father used to make and that Adam had never managed to stop repeating. "A young woman. She gave me her name, Clair, and nothing much beyond that. Her clothes aren't from around here, city-made, and she speaks like it. She's been traveling for some time, is my guess. Her boots are caked with mud, and her feet are torn up. Blistered raw. She tried to stand and couldn't hold herself up."

"Is she hurt?"

"Worn through, more than hurt. She looks as if she hasn't had a proper night's rest or a good meal in a long while."

"How old?"

"Near my age. Thereabouts."

Lydia drew a deep breath and looked toward the ceiling as if searching for an answer to their dilemma.

"I told her I'd bring her a biscuit and some coffee," he said. "Then I intend to send her on her way."

She looked at her son. "Bring me to her."

Chapter 3

Clair stood at the stall door with her carpetbag tucked under her arm and her right hand extended over the rail. The mare's muzzle rested in Clair's palm, her dark eyes half-closed, and her ears tipped forward with the lazy confidence of an animal that had been handled gently its whole life.

"You're a patient one," Clair said. "A patient one and a pretty one. You've got a kind owner, I think."

The mare blew a soft breath through her nostrils and shifted on her front feet. Clair could see the heavy swell of her belly in the lantern light. The surrounding barn was orderly in a way that went past cleanliness into something closer to philosophy—every tool returned to its hook, every bridle hung at the same height on the tack wall, the hay bales stacked in rows so precise they could have been measured with a ruler. Whoever maintained this barn didn't tolerate loose ends. He didn't leave things undone or out of place, or unaccounted for.

She had come down from the hayloft while Adam was in the house, and the descent had cost her more than she wanted to admit. Each rung of the ladder had sent a fresh jolt through her feet. By the time she reached the barn floor, her legs were shaking badly enough that she had to stand still with both hands on the ladder rails, breathing through the pain until the trembling settled into something she could walk on.

The barn door slid open, and the light of early morning pushed across the floor in a wide stripe. She turned from the mare and saw Adam Dawson step inside.

The woman behind him was shorter by half a foot, with greying brown hair pinned back in a knot. She wore a cotton dress covered by a work apron, and she moved with a careful, deliberate gait. Her eyes went to Clair and stayed there with a steadiness that held no judgment.

Adam stood near the door with his hat in his hand. "This is my mother, Lydia Dawson," he said.

Lydia crossed the barn floor and stopped a few feet from Clair and studied her the way a woman studies a child who has come in from the cold and won't say where she's been.

"I apologize for the trouble I've caused. I only meant to shelter for the night, and I'll be happy to—" Clair said.

"Are you hurt?" Lydia interrupted.

"No, ma'am. I'm quite all right."

"You look like you haven't sat at a proper table in a week."

The accuracy of it caught Clair, and she felt her composure slip.

"I've been traveling," Clair said. "A few days now. I was caught in the storm last night, and your barn was the nearest shelter I could find. I'm grateful for it, and I don't intend to impose further."

"You're not imposing." Lydia took another step closer. "You're standing in a barn looking like the last thing between you and the floor is stubbornness. You need a good meal and rest."

"Mrs. Dawson, I truly don't want to —"

"Lydia. And you'll come inside and sit down and eat something, and that will be that."

There was no sharpness in her words. The tone carried the settled quality of a decision already made and a woman who didn't plan to revisit it. Clair looked at her for a long moment and found in Lydia Dawson's face the quiet, direct look of a woman who saw a younger woman in trouble and had already decided what she was going to do about it. The kind of look Clair hadn't received from anyone since her mother had died.

Clair pressed her tongue against the roof of her mouth and held it there until the sting behind her eyes retreated.

"Thank you," she said. "That's very kind."

Lydia nodded once and turned toward the barn door. "Come along."

They crossed the yard with Lydia walking at a pace that was measured and purposeful. The ground between the barn and the house was soft with storm water, the mud pulling gently at Clair's boots with each stride.

Clair's eyes moved across the property as they walked. She could see a garden behind the house, surrounded by a split-rail fence. The beanstalks were leaning at odd angles where the storm had pushed them, a few rows of turned earth that had been started and left unfinished, and weeds standing tall between the vegetable plants.

The porch ran the full length of the house, wide and solid, with three chairs. The stone chimney rose square and plumb against the roofline. Everything she could see had been built with care and maintained with discipline, but the garden told a different story.

She glanced back once before they reached the porch. Adam stood in the barn doorway, one hand on the frame, watching them cross the yard. His posture held a rigid stillness.

Lydia led her up the porch steps and through the front door, and Clair stepped into the kitchen behind Lydia and paused just inside the doorway, reading the room.

The kitchen was clean and orderly. The cast-iron cookstove dominated one wall. A dry sink stood beneath the window. Shelves lined the far wall and held crockery, tins, and a row of canning jars arranged by height.

The sitting room just off the kitchen held a settee facing the fireplace. Two chairs were along the back wall with a small table between them. A basket of mending sat nearby. A family Bible sat on a shelf, its spine cracked and softened from use. Beside it, several other books were stacked, neat and orderly.

"Sit down," Lydia said, pulling a chair back from the table for her. "I have eggs and ham left from breakfast, and I just made a fresh pot of coffee."

"Please let me help," Clair said.

"Nonsense. You're a guest in my home." Lydia moved to the stove and took the coffeepot by its handle, struggling a bit to grip it. She carried it to the table and poured a cup for Clair. Then she brought a plate to the table with eggs, ham, and a biscuit from the warming shelf and set it in front of her.

"Thank you," Clair said as she picked up the fork and cut into the eggs. They were good, cooked through, and seasoned with salt and pepper; the ham alongside them sliced thick and browned at the edges. She ate slowly because the alternative was to abandon every piece of table manners her mother had taught her and clear the plate in thirty seconds. The discipline of eating at a civilized pace when her stomach was clenching with hunger was its own small act of control.

"How long have you been on foot?" Lydia asked as she slowly lowered herself into the chair across from Clair.

Clair set her fork down and took a sip of coffee. "Two days. My horse went lame south of Livingston, and I couldn't ride him any further."

"Two days of walking in this country?"

"Yes, ma'am."

"And before your horse went lame?"

Clair paused. "A few days on horseback before that."

Lydia reached for her coffee cup and drank from it before continuing.

"Do you have family expecting you somewhere?"

"No," Clair said as she picked up her fork and took another bite.

Lydia didn't press, and after a moment she said, "I assume you've come a long way, then."

"I have."

"And do you know where you're headed?"

"I haven't settled on a destination exactly. South, for the time being."

"South for the time being," Lydia said. "That sounds like a woman who's moving first and planning second."

Clair looked at her. Lydia's gaze was direct and friendly and carried no edge of accusation. Suspicion Clair could handle. Interrogation she had prepared for when she walked into this house.

What she hadn't prepared for was kindness, the steady, unflinching regard of a woman who was choosing to see a tired girl rather than a stranger with secrets.

"I suppose that's a fair description," Clair said.

"Well," Lydia set her cup down. "You're getting a good, solid meal in your belly. Now here's what I'd like you to consider, and I ask that you hear me out before you start telling me it isn't necessary. You need a bath, and you need rest. You've been traveling for several days, and on foot for two of those days. Whatever is ahead of you down that road south will still be there after you've had a chance to regain some strength."

"Mrs. Dawson —"

"Lydia."

"Lydia. You've already done more than I had any right to expect. A meal and a cup of coffee are one thing. I can't ask you to —"

"You're not asking. I'm offering. Do you have a clean dress to change into?"

"No. I had a second bag that held my clothes, but I had to leave it behind when my horse went lame."

Lydia absorbed this without surprise. "I have a dress that will do for now. It'll be large on you, but it will be clean and dry. I can wash yours today, as I have washing to do, regardless."

"I can't take your dress."

"You're not taking it. You're wearing it while yours gets clean and then dries on the line. Please stay with us. Rest here for a bit, get your strength back, and then you can be on your way."

Then you can be on your way. An exit. A door left open. The offer wasn't a trap, and it wasn't a cage. It was shelter with a boundary Clair could see and a departure she could name. She could rest here. She could leave when she was able.

"All right," she said. "Thank you. I'll stay long enough to rest, and then I'll go."

Lydia stood. "Come. I'll show you where you can change out of that dress and where you can lie down to rest."

She led Clair into a bedroom on the first floor. The room was modestly sized and simply furnished: a bed with a quilt folded at the foot, a washstand with a ceramic pitcher and basin, and a dresser. A pair of reading spectacles sat on the bedside table along with a folded handkerchief, a kerosene lamp, and a Bible.

"Lydia, I assume this is your room... I can't—."

"Hush, child. We'll make up a pallet on the floor for you to rest on." Lydia said as she opened the small wardrobe beside the washstand and pulled out a folded quilt and a pillow that had been stored on the top shelf. "Here. Help me lay this out along the wall, if you would."

Clair set her carpetbag on the floor and knelt beside Lydia, spreading the quilt along the floor between the bed and the window. She folded it double for thickness and set the pillow at the head.

"My granddaughter, Adam's child, will be up soon," Lydia said. "She's six, and she sleeps like the dead until she doesn't, and then she's wide awake like a barn cat in a thunderstorm. So, let's get you a bath right quick. I'll have Adam bring in the tub you can use to bathe in."

"Let me help," Clair said. "I can carry the buckets of water and heat them on the stove. If you'll just tell me where the washing tub is, I can get it and bring it in... there's no reason to bother your son."

Lydia nodded. "Follow me then; we store the washtub on the back porch. There are buckets there as well for water. The well is just outside the back door."

Clair followed Lydia out of the bedroom, and as they walked to the back door, she sent up a silent prayer.

"Thank you, Lord, for kind people. Please watch over me, help me to rest, and if it's your will, lead me to safety once I leave this home."

Chapter 4

The borrowed dress smelled of cedar and lavender sachets, and the fabric hung from Clair's shoulders with the loose, unfamiliar weight of clothing that had been made for a fuller frame. She had pinned it at the waist with two of Lydia's sewing pins and folded the cuffs back twice, and the result was serviceable. Her hair was damp against the back of her neck, pinned in a low chignon.

She stood in the doorway of Lydia's room with her dress bundled under her arm, the mud-stiffened fabric folded inward so the worst of the dirt wouldn't transfer onto her clean clothing. Her feet were wrapped in clean stockings Lydia had given her, and the raw blisters along both heels throbbed with the sting of wounds that had been scrubbed clean and were now making their displeasure known. She could feel every mile she had walked in those blisters.

A girl sat at the table in the kitchen with a biscuit in one hand and a cup of milk in front of her. Her brown hair fell past her shoulders in a tangle of sleep-loosened waves. Her bare feet hung above the floor, swinging in a slow rhythm.

"Oh," the girl said. Her eyes went wide with interest and the frank appraisal of a child encountering someone new. She looked at Clair's face, then at the dress, then back at her face. "You're wearing Grandma's dress."

"I am," Clair said. "She was kind enough to lend it to me while mine dries."

"Grandma said you slept in the barn and that your name is Clair." Emma set her biscuit on the table and leaned forward. "Did you sleep in the hay? Was it scratchy? The hay in our barn is timothy, and Papa says it's the best hay in the valley, but I think it's scratchy."

Lydia stood at the stove with a cloth in her hand, and she turned to watch the exchange.

"It was a little scratchy," Clair said. "But I was so tired I didn't mind."

"I'm Emma. Emma Louise Dawson. I'm six." She said as she held up six fingers. "And you're Clair. Clair what?"

"Clair Whitmore."

"Emma, now that we know Clair's last name, you will address her as Miss Whitmore, understood?" Lydia said.

"Miss Whitmore," Emma repeated. "Did you come from far away? You talk different."

Emma looked at Clair the way she probably looked at a new calf in the barn or a bird she hadn't seen before—with the bright, uncomplicated interest of a person who assumed that new things were worth investigating.

"I came from Helena," Clair said. "It's a city quite a long way from here."

"Is it big?"

"Quite big."

"Bigger than here?"

"I'm not certain, but I assume it's a good deal bigger."

"Do they have horses there?"

"They do."

"Do they have mountains?"

"They have mountains nearby, but the city sits in a valley. You can see the mountains from almost anywhere in town, but they aren't as close as yours are here."

Emma considered this with the gravity of a six-year-old processing geography. Then she picked up her biscuit and took a large bite and said, "I like our mountains."

"Emma, don't speak with food in your mouth," Lydia said.

Clair set her bundled dress on the floor by the back door and then stood at the edge of the kitchen.

"Come sit and have a cup of coffee with me," Lydia said.

"Let me pour it for us," Clair said. She crossed to the stove and took the coffeepot by its handle, carried it to the table, and filled two cups. She set the pot on the iron trivet at the center of the table and pulled out the chair Lydia had sat in before.

Lydia lowered herself into her chair with the careful, staged descent Clair had watched her perform earlier—one hand on the table edge, a pause at the midpoint, and the slow release of weight into the seat.

"Emma, sweetheart, we haven't done your hair yet this morning," Lydia said. "Come here and let me work through those tangles while Miss Whitmore and I talk."

Emma slid off her chair and came to stand beside Lydia. Lydia reached into her apron pocket for a comb and began working it through the lower ends of Emma's hair. The motion was slow, and Clair watched Lydia adjust her grip on the comb twice in the first few passes, her fingers repositioning around the handle.

"May I?" Clair said.

Lydia looked at Clair across the table and smiled as she handed her the comb. "Bless your heart, these fingers of mine are not working so well today."

Clair rose and moved behind Emma. She started combing at the ends, the way her mother had taught her, working the tangles loose in small sections before moving higher.

"You're gentle," Emma said. "Grandma tries to be gentle, but sometimes it pulls."

"Hair is easier when you start from the bottom and work up," Clair said. "My mother taught me that."

"Does your mother have pretty hair?"

"She did," Clair said. "She had hair like mine, only darker. And she wore it in a braid sometimes, the same kind I'm going to do for you."

"I want a tight braid," Emma said. "The kind that doesn't come out. Grandma's come out, and then my hair gets in everything."

Clair separated Emma's hair into three even sections, her fingers pulling the strands taut the way her mother's had—firm enough to hold through a full day of climbing and running and whatever else a six-year-old on a cattle ranch found to do with her hours. She worked the sections over and under, each pass snug against the last.

Emma stood still for the braiding and only tilted her head once to look up at Clair, a quick glance with a smile at the corner of her mouth, and then faced forward again.

Clair tied a short length of ribbon at the bottom of the braid that Lydia had handed her.

"There," Clair said. "That should hold."

Emma reached back and felt the braid with both hands, running her fingers down its length and testing the tightness at the nape. Her face broke into a wide, unguarded smile. "It's tight and won't come out."

"Most likely not," Clair agreed.

"Will you do it tomorrow too?"

"We'll see," Clair said.

Emma accepted this and went back to her chair and her biscuit, her new braid swinging between her shoulder blades with each step.

Lydia took a drink of her coffee and set the cup down. "Emma, take your milk and your biscuit and go sort through my button tin for me. I need the brown ones and the bone-colored ones separated from the rest. Can you do that?"

"Yes, ma'am." Emma collected her breakfast with the efficiency of a child who had been given a task she considered important, and she carried the cup and the biscuit to the sitting room. Clair watched as she settled onto the floor near the sewing basket.

Lydia folded her hands on the table. "I'm not a foolish woman, Clair."

"No, ma'am. I don't believe you are," Clair said as she sat down across from her.

"I've noticed the way you speak and the way you carry yourself. The way you ate breakfast this morning—with manners that came from a table with standards, even when you were hungry enough to forget them." Lydia paused. "The dress you arrived in was city-made. Tailored seams, covered buttons, and fabric that is quite fine. And those boots by the door are not the boots of a woman who has spent her life walking dirt roads in ranch country."

Clair wrapped both hands around her coffee cup and said nothing.

"A woman of your evident upbringing and education doesn't end up walking alone through a thunderstorm in the Montana foothills with no destination in mind unless something has gone very wrong in the life she left behind. I don't need every detail. But I need enough to understand what I have invited into my home."

The kitchen was quiet except for the soft tick of the mantel clock in the next room and the click of buttons as Emma sorted through the tin. Clair looked at Lydia across the table and measured the question against the answer the way she measured everything—carefully.

Lydia had given her a bath, a dress, and a meal. She had walked into a barn and looked at a stranger and decided to help before she knew a single thing about her beyond what exhaustion and mud could tell. She had earned more than evasion.

"My mother died when I was sixteen," Clair said. "My father raised me after that. He was a businessman in Helena, and I assisted him in his work. He died four months ago. After his death, I discovered circumstances involving his business that put me in danger. I would rather not go into the particulars, if you'll allow me that. The details are complicated. But I will tell you this much honestly: I left home because I no longer felt safe there."

"And is trouble following you?"

"I don't believe so. I didn't travel in a straight line, but I cannot say with certainty that no one is looking for me."

Lydia studied her for a long moment.

"You're an only child," Lydia said.

"Yes."

"And there is no one else. No husband, no intended, and no family you can go to."

"No one. My mother's and father's families live out east, and I've never met any of them."

Lydia picked up her coffee and drank, and when she set the cup down, she kept both hands around it.

"I'm going to tell you something about this household," Lydia said, "and I ask that you hear me without polite objection, because I have thought about it since the moment I saw you standing in my barn, and I have not arrived at this lightly."

Clair straightened in her chair.

"My body has been giving me trouble for some time now. It started slowly—stiffness in the mornings, days when my hands wouldn't cooperate with what I asked of them. For a while, I managed well enough that no one needed to worry. But it has gotten worse, and I'd be lying to you and to myself if I pretended I didn't know which direction it's heading." Lydia flexed her right hand slowly, opening and closing the fingers with the deliberate attention of someone testing a mechanism she no longer fully trusted. "Some days I can do everything this house requires. Other days I cannot open a jar or grip a coffeepot without spilling. The garden is half-tended because there are days when my knees and my hands won't both cooperate at the same time. The mending is behind because the needle is harder to hold than it was a year ago. And Emma—sweet Emma deserves better than what I can give her alone."

Lydia paused. "I have been praying for help, Clair. I have been praying for it specifically and by name—help with this house, help with my granddaughter, help for my son who carries more than any man should carry alone and will not admit it. I've been asking the Lord to send what this family needs, and I have been trusting that He would answer in His time and in whatever form He chose." She looked at Clair with steady, unhurried eyes. "I am not so proud that I cannot recognize that you are an answer to my prayers."

Clair held Lydia's gaze as she pressed her thumbnail into the pad of her forefinger beneath the table and held it there until the sting behind her eyes retreated.

"What I'd like to propose," Lydia continued, "is an arrangement that I believe would serve us both. You need a roof over your head and food in your belly while you figure out what comes next. I need help with this house, our garden, and my grandchild. You stay here with us, eat our food, and sleep in my room. And in exchange, you help me with the work of keeping this household together."

"Lydia —"

"I'm not finished. I can hear in your speech that you've received a proper education. Am I right?"

"You are."

"Providence Ridge has no schoolhouse and no teacher. Emma is six years old, bright as a new penny, and curious about everything that crosses her path. I have a primer, a few children's books, and a Bible. My eyes tire faster than they used to. Would you be willing to teach her while you're here? Reading, arithmetic, whatever you're able. She deserves that, and I cannot give it to her the way it ought to be given."

Clair looked toward the sitting room, where the soft click of buttons continued in its steady rhythm.

"I should tell you honestly," Clair said, turning back to Lydia, "that my skills may not be what you're accustomed to. I had a maid, a housekeeper, and a cook in the home I left. I know the fundamentals of keeping a kitchen and a home. My mother taught me to sew and to cook a few basics before she died. But gardening, outdoor work, and the physical demands of a household such as this—I have very little experience with any of it. I would rather not misrepresent what I'm able to offer."

"Then you will learn," Lydia said, "and I will be glad to teach you. Every woman who has ever kept a house in this territory learned by doing, not by knowing beforehand. These are skills you can take with you into whatever life you build next, whether you decide to return to Helena or build something new somewhere else."

Clair turned her coffee cup slowly on the table, her thumb tracing the rim.

She was a considerable distance from Helena. This ranch was remote. This arrangement could give her time. Time to rest, time to think, time to consider how the ledger pages and other evidence sewn into the lining of her carpetbag could reach the right hands without putting her in the path of the wrong ones.

"Would your son be agreeable to this?" she asked. "He didn't seem pleased this morning after we left the barn."

"Adam runs this ranch," Lydia said. "He runs it well, and he has earned every right to the decisions he makes about it. But this house is mine too, and I still have a voice in the matters that concern it. I will speak with Adam this evening. You let me manage that conversation."

"I would rather not create difficulty between you and your son."

"You won't. Adam is a good man who has forgotten what it looks like when God provides. I intend to remind him."

Clair looked at her across the table. This kind woman, with her swollen knuckles and steady gaze and her faith that spoke in the language of daily bread rather than Sunday sermon, had given her an opportunity.

"I'll stay," she said. "Until I've rested and sorted out where I'm going and what comes next. I'll earn my keep while I'm here. And I'll teach Emma whatever I'm able to teach her."

Lydia nodded as small footsteps crossed the floor. Emma walked to Clair and held a book out to her.

"I know some letters, but I get stuck on some. Will you help me?"

Clair looked at the primer in Emma's outstretched hands. "I believe that sounds like a fine idea."

Chapter 5

Adam came through the front door after his day's work was complete. What he found stopped him two steps inside the threshold.

The kitchen table was set for four.

His mother sat in her usual chair, watching him with her coffee in front of her and both arms resting on the table.

At the stove, Clair moved a pot off the heat. She wore his mother's dress, the gray cotton with the small blue flowers along the collar, and it hung from her shoulders.

Emma sat on the floor in the sitting room with a book open across her knees. Her braid, the one that was usually half-undone by mid-afternoon and trailing loose ends by supper, hung in a single tight rope between her shoulder blades.

"Come sit down, Adam," Lydia said.

Adam pulled his hat from his head, hung it on the peg beside the door, and stayed where he was. "She's still here."

"She is."

"I assumed you would feed her and then send her on her way."

"I've had a conversation with her since then, which I'd like to tell you about, if you'll come away from that door and sit at this table like a civil man who intends to listen before he rashly decides."

Adam crossed the kitchen and pulled his chair out and sat. He rested his forearms on the table and looked at his mother. "I'm listening."

Lydia took a deep breath and told him what she had proposed to Clair that morning. She told him the terms: Clair would stay at the ranch, sleep in her room, and in exchange she would help with the house, the garden, and Emma's care and education. She would learn what she didn't already know. The arrangement was temporary. Clair would remain until she had determined her next course, and then she would go.

Adam listened without interrupting, and when she finished, he said, "You made this decision without asking me."

"I did."

"This is my ranch, Ma."

"It is, but this is my home as well, and that child in the next room is my granddaughter, and I'm telling you what I need." Lydia's voice didn't rise. "Dr. Porter confirmed what I already suspected. The rheumatism in my joints is the kind that doesn't improve. You know this. I told you when I came home from that visit, and you nodded, and then we both went back to pretending I could manage. I have been grateful for that pretending, because it let me keep my dignity. But dignity is a luxury I can't afford at the cost of this household."

She paused. "I cannot do what I did a year ago. I cannot do what I did six months ago. There are mornings when I can't grip the coffeepot without it shaking so hard I have to set it down and try again. The garden is a mess. My mending basket is full, and I haven't touched it lately because I can't hold the needle long enough to finish a seam. Your daughter's hair." Lydia glanced toward the sitting room, where Emma was tracing a letter in the primer with her fingertip. "You've seen the braids I send her out with in the morning. You've seen them by supper. That child has been wearing her hair half-done because I cannot manage a braid that holds, and I have been too proud to say so."

Adam sat still as his chest tightened like a rope tightens around a post when the animal on the other end pulls against it.

"This young woman walked into our barn during a storm seeking shelter," Lydia said, "and I believe God put her there. I have been praying for help. I have been asking specifically, and I have been trusting that the answer would come in whatever form He chose. And I'm not so proud that I will refuse the answer because it arrived in a way I could have never imagined."

Adam looked down at the table and ran his thumb along the edge of his plate in a slow half-circle.

"We don't know her," he said.

"I know enough, and I'm trusting my judgment. Clair is a young woman alone, educated, willing to work, and in need of shelter. She is safer under our roof than on the road by herself. This household needs her help, Adam. I need her."

Adam looked at Clair as she stood by the stove. Her attention was on him with the steady quality of a woman who had been listening to every word that had been said and hadn't tried to make herself smaller or invisible during the hearing of it.

"You left Helena, and there was trouble with your father's business after he died, and you didn't feel safe. Is there more to it than that?"

"Yes," Clair said. "There is more to it."

"Are you going to tell me what it is?"

"I would rather not go into the full particulars tonight, Mr. Dawson. Not because I intend to deceive you, but because some of the details are complicated, and I'd like to earn a measure of your trust before I ask you to carry them. I will tell you what I told your mother. I didn't travel a direct route, and I do not believe anyone followed me. But I will not lie to you and tell you there is no possibility that someone is looking for me."

Adam noticed she hadn't flinched and didn't oversell herself. People who had something to hide tended to talk too much. They explained when they hadn't been asked to. They softened their answers with reassurances designed to make the listener comfortable rather than informed. This woman did none of those things. She said what she was willing to say.

"If you stay, you work," he said. "You earn your keep, and when you've gotten yourself sorted out, you move on. This isn't a permanent arrangement, and I won't have Emma thinking it is. Are we clear on that?"

"We are, Mr. Dawson. I understand completely, and I'm grateful. I promise I will not be a burden to your household."

"See that you're not." His words came out harsher than they should have, and from the corner of his eye he saw his mother's chin lift a fraction.

"With everything the day has brought, supper will be simple tonight. Cold ham, bread, and stewed beans. Nothing that required much fuss," Lydia said.

Adam pushed his chair back from the table and stood. "I'll wash up."

He went out the back door, where a washstand stood on the porch. The evening air was still warm with July heat. He poured water into the basin and scrubbed his face, neck, and forearms. He worked the day's grit from his skin with a roughness that had more to do with his state of mind than with the dirt. He dried his hands on the towel that hung from the nail beside the basin and stood for a moment looking west.

The sky above the ridgeline had turned the color of old brass. From inside the house, he could hear his mother's voice and the higher, quicker notes of Emma's, along with the new sound of the woman who was now their houseguest for the foreseeable future.

He went back inside as Clair was bringing bread to the table, a loaf cut into thick slices and arranged on the board his mother used for serving. She set it near the center and stepped back to the stove. Emma had migrated from the sitting room to her chair at the table and was sitting with her feet swinging and her attention tracking Clair's movements.

Adam took his chair as Clair brought the beans to the table and set the pot on the iron trivet, and then she sat down and folded her hands in her lap.

Lydia bowed her head. Adam followed, but he kept his eyes on the table and listened to his mother's prayer. She thanked Him for the food on the table, the roof overhead, and the day that had brought more than they expected. She asked for wisdom to receive what He provided, and she said, Amen.

Adam lifted his head and reached for the bread; he took a slice and passed the board to his mother.

The first few minutes of the meal passed in the weighted quiet of four people sitting at a table where three of them knew the rhythms and the fourth was learning them in real time. Adam ate steadily with the focus of a man who regarded meals as fuel rather than an occasion. Lydia ate slowly, cutting her ham into small pieces. Clair ate with the measured pace of someone who was conscious of being watched.

Emma broke the silence. "Papa, did you fix the fence today?"

"Started on it."

"Was the creek high from the storm?"

"Some."

"Did you see any deer? I saw a deer in the backyard this morning, but Grandma said it was probably just a pronghorn."

"Might have been either one."

Emma considered this and apparently found it insufficient, because she turned to Clair and said, "Miss Whitmore, did you know that pronghorns aren't really deer? Papa told me that. They look like deer, but they aren't."

"I didn't know that," Clair said. "What makes them different?"

"Their horns and they're faster. Papa says they're the fastest animal in the whole valley."

"I imagine your father knows a great deal about this land," Clair said.

"He knows everything about the ranch," Emma said. "He knows where the creek goes fastest and where the best grass is and which horses are mean, and which ones are nice."

"Emma, eat your supper," Adam said.

"How's the mare, Adam?" Lydia asked.

"Close, but not tonight. I'll check her again before I turn in."

"She's been restless. She's due to foal soon," Lydia said to Clair.

"Is it her first?" Clair asked.

"Second. She foaled two years ago without trouble. This one's sitting higher than the last," Adam said. He took another bite of bread and didn't offer anything further.

"Mr. Dawson," Clair said. "I'd like to know what time your morning begins so that I can have coffee ready. And whether you take anything with you to eat while you're working through the day. Your mother mentioned the general shape of things, but I'd rather hear the particulars from you so that I'm sure of what to expect."

Adam looked at her. "I'm up before first light," he said. "Coffee should be on when I come down. I eat before I go out. Eggs, biscuits, or whatever's simple. I take bread and cold meat or a biscuit with me on days when I'll be working farther from home with the herd. I'll let you know when those days will be; otherwise, I normally take the midday meal here at home with Ma and Emma. Supper when the work's done for the day, which depends on the light and the season. This time of year, the light holds longer."

"And the stove. Does it need to be stoked from the night before, or do you bank it, and I'll need to rebuild the fire?"

"I bank it. The coals hold if the damper's set right. My mother can show you in the morning."

Clair nodded, and Adam continued to eat. He watched his plate, he chewed his bread, and he told himself that the arrangement was simple, functional, and temporary. A woman who needed shelter. A household that needed help. Terms agreed to. Problem managed.

"Papa," Emma said. "I'm finished with dinner. Can Miss Whitmore help me with my letters?"

Adam looked at his daughter, and then he looked at Clair.

She was looking back at him, and he held her look for a moment, and then he nodded.

Clair turned to Emma. "Go get your primer, and we'll sit here at the table and work."

Emma slid from her chair and crossed into the sitting room to find the primer, her braid swinging behind her.

Chapter 6

Clair crouched in front of the cookstove in her stockinged feet, the kitchen floor cool through the thin cotton where her knees pressed against it. Ash grit worked into the pads of her fingers as she felt along the damper lever, trying to position it the way she imagined it should go. She'd been up for ten minutes and had accomplished nothing beyond getting dressed in the dark and making her way from Lydia's room to the stove without waking anyone.

Adam had told her last night that coffee should be on when he came downstairs. She intended to have it on.

She adjusted the lever on the stove and pulled it. It resisted, then gave with a low scrape of iron on iron that sounded enormous in the quiet house.

She started a fire and fed kindling into the stove, three thin sticks of split pine laid crosswise over the coals the way she'd watched the cook in her Helena home do it. The wood caught in under a minute, and she added two larger pieces and closed the stove door, adjusting the damper again until the draft pulled evenly and the fire settled into a low, steady burn. She rose from the floor and brushed the front of Lydia's dress where ash had gathered in the folds of the skirt.

While the stove heated, she removed the flour bin that was in the lower cabinet beside the stove, a lidded tin with a scoop nested inside. Lard in a crock on the shelf above it, beside a smaller tin of baking soda and a jar of salt with a wooden spoon stuck in the top. Coffee was in a tin with a hinged lid. She opened it and spooned grounds into the coffeepot. She filled the pot with water and positioned it on the stove.

The shelves along the far wall held crockery in mismatched sets: cups, saucers, plates, and bowls. Canning jars lined the upper shelf, their contents dark and indistinguishable in the low light. A row of tins with hand-lettered labels: sugar, tea, and dried beans. Everything had a place. The organization wasn't decorative; it was functional, the kind of system a woman built when she needed the most used items readily at hand.

The coffeepot began to tremble against the stovetop as the water heated, and Clair positioned it more squarely on the plate when the bedroom door opened.

Lydia was dressed, her hair pinned up in a knot. She stopped when she saw Clair at the stove with the kitchen already warming and the coffeepot beginning to steam.

"Well," Lydia said. She looked at the stove, then at Clair, and a small, pleased expression settled across her face. "I'm impressed."

"I hope you don't mind," Clair said. "I wanted to have the coffee started before Mr. Dawson came down. I fiddled with the stove until I figured it out. I wasn't certain I had it right, but the fire seems to be drawing."

Lydia crossed to the stove and looked at the firebox through the vent slots. "You have it right. The trick is to pull the lever all the way to the left notch before you open the door so the draft catches the coals from underneath. Most people set it to the middle and wonder why the fire takes so long." She glanced at Clair with an expression that was equal parts approval and amusement. "Our stove has opinions. You'll learn them."

"I'm looking forward to it," Clair said.

"Did you sleep well?" Lydia asked.

"I did, yes. Quite well." It wasn't entirely true. She had slept in stretches, waking twice to the unfamiliar sounds of the house and the distant call of something in the pasture. But she had slept more than she had on any of the six nights before this one, and the difference was enough to count.

Lydia lowered herself into her chair at the table and began working her fingers, pressing each knuckle with the opposite thumb in a slow, deliberate rotation. The joints of her right hand were visibly swollen this morning, the skin taut across the knuckles. She flexed and released, flexed and released, with the patience of a woman performing a task she had performed every morning for longer than she cared to remember.

"Biscuits," Lydia said. "Do you know how to make them?"

"My mother taught me when I was younger. I haven't made them in months, actually, since my father passed. I had gotten quite lax and let the cooks at home make whatever they wanted and rarely participated in the kitchen as of late, but I believe I remember the proportions."

"Good. Flour, lard, a pinch of salt, and buttermilk from the crock on the bottom shelf. If the buttermilk's turned, use water with a splash of vinegar. Work the dough with your hands, not a spoon. And don't overwork it, or they'll come out like stones."

Clair mixed the biscuits at the counter beside the dry sink. The buttermilk was still good, tangy, and thick when she poured it into the well she'd made in the flour. She quickly remembered the way dough should feel when it was ready: slightly tacky, holding its shape without sticking to her palms. She cut rounds with the rim of a cup and laid them on the baking tin Lydia pointed her toward, then slid the tin into the oven beside the firebox.

"Your mother taught you well," Lydia said.

"She taught me most of what I know. She insisted I knew how to cook the basics and use a cookstove. She raised me with the knowledge that just because we had a cook in our home, that didn't mean we should take her for granted. More often than not, she would be in the kitchen working right alongside our cook. I have wonderful memories from my childhood of sitting and watching the two of them work side by side. They were the best of friends," Clair said. "The rest I learned from watching our cook, a woman named Mrs. Berger, who helped run our household in Helena after Mother passed."

"Was she a good cook?"

"She was excellent and patient with me. I was eager to learn everything at once and couldn't stop asking questions about why the bread rose some mornings and not others."

"That's the best kind of student. Emma's the same way. She'll wear you out with questions." Lydia smiled and then nodded toward the shelf. "The eggs are in the basket there. The skillets are on the hooks beside the stove. Use lard, not butter, to cook the eggs and meat. Butter's for the table."

Clair found the basket and counted out six eggs, cradling them against her waist as she carried them to the counter beside the stove. The skillets were heavy, black cast iron, worn smooth on the cooking surface. She set them on the stovetop and spooned a measure of lard from the crock into each. It began to melt almost immediately, spreading in a thin sheen.

"I'll show you where the root cellar is today," Lydia said. "I brought slices of ham up last evening and wrapped them in the cloth. Look up on the second shelf."

Clair found the wrapped ham and laid the slices in the melting lard. They began to sizzle right away. She cracked the eggs into the rendered fat in the other skillet, and they spread and whitened immediately, the edges crisping against the hot iron.

"I'll take mine with the yolks broken, if you please," Lydia said. "Adam takes his over easy, but don't fuss about it. He'll eat them however they come."

Clair noted this and cooked accordingly.

She turned when Adam entered the kitchen; his shirt was tucked, his sleeves were rolled to mid-forearm, and his hair was damp at the temples. He looked at the stove, at the coffeepot, and then at Clair.

"Morning," he said.

"Good morning, Mr. Dawson."

He crossed toward the stove, and Clair was standing directly in its path. He reached past her, and his hand stopped when hers closed around the coffeepot handle first.

"Let me," she said, and took a cup from the shelf and poured.

"Thank you," he said, and carried the cup to the table.

He set it at his place, then turned and came back to the stove. He took a second cup from the shelf, filled it, and carried it to Lydia.

Clair pulled the biscuits from the oven, golden across the tops and firm when she tapped them, and arranged them on a plate. She carried the food to the table in two trips: eggs and ham first, then the biscuits and the butter dish. She set the coffeepot on the iron trivet between the place settings.

Clair sat in the chair that had been hers last night, across from Adam, with Lydia between them at the end. The plates steamed, and the kitchen smelled of rendered fat, hot biscuits, and strong coffee. The first real light of the July morning had begun to press against the window above the dry sink, turning the glass from black to a pale, steel gray.

"Mrs. Dawson," Clair said. "Would you mind if I said the morning prayer?"

Lydia looked at her and smiled. "I would welcome that."

Clair bowed her head and folded her hands in her lap.

"Lord, we thank You for the shelter of this home and for the kindness of the people at this table. We are grateful for the food before us and for the hands that provided it. Give us strength for the work ahead and let Your provision rest upon this household today and in the days to come. Amen."

"Amen," Lydia said.

Clair served herself some food and began to eat. The biscuits were good. Not as fine as Mrs. Berger's, but hers were solid enough to hold butter without crumbling. Lydia ate hers in small bites, tearing pieces from the edge. Adam ate steadily, the way he had at supper, with the concentration of a man who treated meals as a task to be completed rather than a pleasure to be extended.

The silence between them held its own character, different from last night's. At supper, there had been a child's voice filling the spaces.

Clair set her fork down and looked at Lydia. "How far is town from here?"

"Three miles by the wagon road," Adam said before Lydia could answer.

"And what is this town like?"

Lydia wiped her fingers on her napkin. "Providence Ridge is small. Smaller than you're used to, I'm sure. There's a mercantile, Pemberton's, which is where we get most everything that doesn't come from the garden or the smokehouse. A clean boarding house run by Leora Hanscombe. We have a livery, a blacksmith, and a new doctor who just arrived early last month. Marshal Tom Callahan has an office, but spends more time sorting disputes about fence lines than chasing outlaws."

"How many people?" Clair asked.

"The last count I heard was two hundred and fifty."

Helena had thousands, and the streets had been packed with wagons and foot traffic and the noise of commerce from early morning until the lamps came on. Two hundred and fifty people spread across an entire valley. The contrast must have shown on her face, because Lydia tilted her head and the corner of her mouth turned up.

"I imagine it'll take you some time getting used to the slower pace and wide-open spaces here," Lydia said.

"I assume it will," Clair said. "Helena was rather larger."

"Helena is a city with ambitions," Lydia said. "Providence Ridge is a town with a creek and a mercantile and enough stubborn people to keep it standing and steadily growing."

"Is there a church?" Clair asked.

Lydia shook her head. "Not a proper building, not yet. There's been talk for two years about building a proper schoolhouse that could serve for Sunday worship as well, but the plans, lumber, and labor haven't come together quite yet. For now, we meet in the boarding house dining room. Leora pushes the tables back and sets up chairs, and we gather there."

"Who leads the service?"

"Reverend Webb Hale. He's a retired circuit rider who settled in the valley some years back. He comes every other Sunday and leads us through Scripture and prayer, and he preaches a message that sticks to the bones without a lot of polish on it. The weeks he's not here, someone reads from the Word, and we sing hymns. Margaret Pemberton leads those singing normally."

"And on fair-weather Sundays?" Clair asked. "Does the gathering ever meet outdoors?"

"Occasionally. If someone offers their home or their yard, and the weather cooperates, we've held services outside. Last month Webb preached from the Pembertons' front porch with the congregation sitting in the grass. It was pleasant enough until the wind came up and took his Bible clean off the rail."

Clair smiled. "When is the next service?"

"This coming Sunday. Reverend Webb will be here, and he'll be glad to see a new face. Did you attend services regularly in Helena?" Lydia asked.

"Yes," Clair said. "My mother took me from the time I was small. First Presbyterian on Warren Street. We went every Sunday morning, and she taught me the Psalms at home during the week from the family Bible. After she died, I continued. My father came with me when his work allowed, which was most Sundays. He wasn't a man who spoke much about his faith, but he was faithful in his attendance, and he read from the Scriptures in the evenings after supper."

"That's a good inheritance," Lydia said. "A mother's faith carried into a daughter's life. It's the kind that lasts."

"It has," Clair said. "Through everything that's come since."

Lydia picked up her coffee and drank, and the kitchen was quiet for a moment except for the tick of Adam's fork against his plate and the low murmur of the fire behind the stove door.

"The nearest ranch," Clair said, turning to Adam. "How far is it?"

"South of here is the Hargrove place, and that's a fair ride away," he said. "West of here is the Mayhew ranch, and to the east sits the Stackhouse ranch. Either one of those takes a bit to get to, just under an hour on horseback either way."

"So this ranch is quite isolated."

"It's private," he said as he pushed his chair back from the table and stood. He carried his plate to the dry sink and set it down, then crossed back and took Lydia's plate from in front of her and carried that to the sink as well. He crossed to the hook beside the front door, took his hat, and turned to look at Clair.

"The mare in the barn is close to her time," he said. "If you have a mind to wander and go into the barn and she's restless, stay out of that stall. Come find me if you need anything."

Chapter 7

C lair knelt between two rows of bean plants with her sleeves pushed past her elbows and her fingers buried to the second knuckle, working a clump of pigweed free from the ground. She pulled until the weed came loose with a soft tearing sound and a shower of dry soil across her wrist. She tossed it into the pile growing at the end of the row and moved to the next one.

"Not that," Lydia said from behind her. "That's a bean seedling. The leaves are broader, and they come in pairs. You see how they open like two hands facing each other?"

Clair sat back on her heels and looked at the plant she'd been about to pull. The leaves were broader, paired along the stem in a pattern distinct from the narrower, irregular leaves of the weeds surrounding it.

"I see it," Clair said.

"If you follow the bean stem down, you'll feel it's rooted deeper than most of the weeds. Weeds tend to sit close to the surface."

Clair pressed her thumb against the base of the next plant and felt the difference immediately. The weed beside it gave at the slightest pressure, its root system shallow and spreading.

Lydia stood with a hoe in both hands, her grip wrapped high on the handle where it gave her the most leverage with the least demand on her fingers. She paused every few strokes to adjust her hold, rotating her wrists the way a person rotates a key that has stuck in a lock.

The garden sat behind the house inside a split-rail fence; the rails silvered and cracked from seasons of weather. The rows ran east to west, organized with the same plain logic as the kitchen shelves: beans on their stakes nearest the house, then the lower plants extending outward in order of height. Squash vines sprawled in the farthest row, their broad leaves covering the ground like overturned plates. Potatoes occupied the center rows, their leafy tops thick and tangled; the surrounding soil mounded in ridges that had flattened since the storm. The tomato plants stood along the south-facing fence, tied to stakes with strips of cloth, their branches heavy with hard green fruit no bigger than crab apples. Corn in the far corner stood knee-high, the stalks bending slightly toward the light.

"Emma," Lydia called. "Come here and let me show you something."

Emma trotted over from the edge of the garden, where she had been crouched, inspecting something on a leaf. Her braid swung between her shoulder blades, and her pinafore was already streaked with garden dirt at the knees.

"Yes, ma'am?"

"Do you see these fat green caterpillars on the tomato leaves? The ones with the white stripes on their sides?"

Emma leaned in and studied the leaf Lydia was pointing toward. Her face scrunched in concentration. "That one's as big as my finger."

"It is. Those are tomato worms, and they'll eat a plant down to the stem if you let them. Your job this afternoon is to pick every one you find off the tomato plants and the bean leaves and drop them in that pail. Can you do that?"

Emma peered into the bucket Lydia had set beside the row. "What happens to them afterwards?"

"The chickens will be grateful for them."

"That's awful, Grandma," Emma said as she picked the first caterpillar off a leaf with two fingers, holding it at arm's length while its body curled and flexed, then dropped it into the pail with a soft thud.

"There's two more on this plant alone," she said. "They're hiding under the leaves."

"That's good, child," Lydia said. "Check every plant. Both sides of every leaf."

Emma moved from plant to plant along the tomato row, lifting each leaf with careful fingers, narrating her progress as she went to no one in particular.

"Found one. Found another one. This one's really small, Grandma. Do the small ones count?"

"They all count," Lydia said.

"Even the tiny ones?"

"Especially the tiny ones. They're the ones that grow up and eat the most."

Emma considered this and resumed her work with renewed purpose.

Clair moved to the next section and began pulling weeds from around the base of the potato plants. The mounded soil was warm under her hands, and the July sun pressed against her back through the cotton of Lydia's dress. At five thousand feet, the heat carried a different quality than Helena's. It sat on her shoulders and her forearms, but left the air itself dry and moving. A faint current coming down from the mountains kept the afternoon from settling into the thick, breathless warmth she remembered from summers in the city.

"These potato hills need building up," Lydia said, working her hoe along the far side of the row. "You pull the soil up around the stems, like this." She demonstrated with the hoe blade, scraping loose soil toward the base of the nearest plant and mounding it in a ridge around the stem. "Any potato that sits above the soil line will turn green from the sun. Green potatoes are bitter and not fit for eating."

Clair cupped her hands and drew the soil upward, packing it against the stems the way Lydia had shown her. The work required a kind of careful, repetitive pressure that made her forearms burn. She'd used her hands for ledger work, for pen and paper, and for the precise task of copying columns of figures. Garden work asked something different from the same muscles, and they registered the complaint in a dull ache that ran from her wrists to her elbows.

"You're a quick study," Lydia said. "Most people hill potatoes too high or too shallow the first time."

"I'm measuring by the stem," Clair said. "Enough soil to cover the base by two or three inches, high enough to keep the sunlight off but low enough that the leaves have room."

Lydia looked at her with an expression that was part amusement and part recognition. "You think like a woman who's used to reading instructions."

"I think like a woman who's used to reading ledgers," Clair said. "Everything has an entry and a corresponding balance. If the soil is the entry, the plant is the return."

Lydia laughed, a short, warm sound. "Well, the garden doesn't always balance the way a ledger does. Some years the beans come in thick, and the tomatoes rot on the vine. Some years it's the opposite, and there's no accounting for why. But the work is the same, regardless. You put in what you can and trust the Lord with the rest."

"That sounds like a sermon," Clair said.

"It sounds like forty years of gardening," Lydia said.

Emma appeared at the end of the row, her pail held out in front of her with both hands. "I found eleven," she said. "Eleven tomato worms. One of them is so fat it didn't even try to hold on. It just fell right off the leaf when I touched it."

"Good," Lydia said. "Now check the beans. The worms like them almost as much."

"Do the beans have different bugs?"

"Some, but they have the same appetite."

Emma carried her pail toward the bean rows with the purposeful stride of a girl who had been promoted.

"Miss Whitmore, are your hands dirty?" Emma asked.

Clair held them up. Her fingers were caked with soil to the knuckles, dark lines of grit pressed into every crease. "Thoroughly."

Emma studied them with approval. "Good. Grandma says clean hands in a garden means you aren't working hard enough."

"Your grandmother is a wise woman."

"I know," Emma said, and continued down the row.

Clair watched her go, this small, brown-haired girl with her braid and her bucket of caterpillars, crouching among the bean plants with her face inches from the leaves, completely absorbed. The earnestness of it pulled something loose inside Clair's chest, a feeling she hadn't expected from the simple image of a child doing garden chores. She turned back to the potatoes and continued hilling.

They worked for a while without talking. Lydia worked the hoe where the weeds were thickest, her strokes measured, her pauses growing slightly longer as the afternoon wore on. Clair cleared the rows Lydia had loosened, pulling weeds and hilling soil, and learning by repetition which plants to spare and which to pull. Emma moved between the rows with her pail, calling out each find with the delight of discovery.

"Found a beetle," she called from somewhere near the squash. "It's green and shiny, and it's eating a hole in the leaf. Do beetles go in the pail too?"

"If it's eating the plants, it goes in the pail," Lydia said.

"What if it's pretty?"

"Pretty beetles eat just as much as ugly ones."

Emma dropped the beetle into the pail. "Grandma, do toads eat beetles?"

"They do. And caterpillars and slugs and just about anything else that moves and fits in their mouths."

"Then the toad is on our side."

"The toad has always been on our side," Lydia said. "Your grand-father used to say a garden with a toad in it was a garden that didn't need watching."

"I wish he were still here," Emma said. "He could have helped with the weeds."

"He could have," Lydia said. "He was an excellent weeder. He always said weeding was the only honest argument a man could have with the ground."

Emma laughed, a bright, clear sound that carried across the garden.

Lydia paused in her work and pressed her right hand flat against her thigh, rolling her knuckles against the muscle there. The gesture was quick, performed with the kind of precision that comes from habit. She adjusted her grip on the hoe, resettling her fingers higher on the handle, and resumed her short, scraping strokes.

Clair had been watching Lydia's hands since the morning. The swelling in her knuckles was visible even from several feet away; the joints thick and slightly angled where the bones had begun to shift beneath the skin. Her fingers curled inward at rest, a slow, involuntary closing that Lydia tried to correct by pressing them flat against whatever surface was nearest. Occasionally she worked each finger individually, bending and straightening with the delib-erate patience of a woman coaxing a rusted hinge.

Clair sat back and brushed the soil from her hands. "Lydia, may I ask you something?"

Lydia stopped her hoe and looked at her. "You may."

"Your hands. You mentioned the other morning that some days are harder than others. I'd like to understand better what helps and what worsens it so that I know what to watch for. I don't want to wait until you have to ask me. I'd rather see it coming and step in before it gets to that point."

Lydia was quiet for a moment, her gaze on Clair steady and measuring. Then she nodded once and lowered herself onto the wide rail of the garden fence. She set the hoe against the rail and rested her hands in her lap.

"This arthritis started in my fingers," she said. "I woke up one morning about six years ago, and my right hand wouldn't close. I thought I'd slept on it wrong. I shook it out and went about my day, and by noon it was fine. But it came back the next week, and then the week after that, and so on until one day it didn't leave."

"Both hands?"

"The right one first. The left followed about a year later. My wrists came next, and then my knees. Cold mornings are the worst. Damp weather is nearly as bad. A good day means I can button my dress and hold a cup without thinking about it. A bad day means I can't close my fist around a spoon."

"And the days in between?"

"The days in between are most days now," Lydia said. "I can manage more than you might think, but it takes me longer than it used to, and there are some things I've stopped being able to do at all. Braiding Emma's hair decently. Lifting the cast-iron skillet with one hand. Opening jars. Wringing laundry properly." She glanced at her fingers where they rested against the fabric of her skirt, the knuckles swollen and the joints pulling her fingers into a slow, inward curve. "Some mornings I sit on the edge of the bed and work my fingers for ten minutes before I can trust them to hold anything."

"What helps?" Clair asked.

"Warmth. If I soak my hands in warm water before I start the day, the stiffness eases some. Movement helps too at times. Dr. Porter gave me a salve, a liniment that smells like something died in it, but it takes the edge off the worst swelling."

"Dr. Porter. He's the doctor in Providence Ridge?"

"He is. He came to town only this past June. Before him, we had to ride to Livingston for anything more than folk remedies and prayer. He's young, but he's careful, and he doesn't pretend to know more than he does, which I consider a virtue in a physician."

"What has he told you about what's ahead?" Clair asked.

Lydia looked at her for a long moment. "He told me the truth, which I appreciated. The condition is progressive. It won't reverse. The swelling will worsen over time, and my joints will continue to stiffen. Eventually my hands may not open fully. My knees and my wrists will follow the same course. He said some people progress slowly and manage well for years. Others lose function faster. There's no predicting which way it will go, and there is no cure."

"I think about it the way I think about weather," Lydia continued. "It's coming whether I prepare for it or not, so I prepare for it. I do what my hands allow today. Tomorrow they may allow less. The Lord gave me this body, and it has carried me through a great deal already. When it can no longer carry me, He will carry me instead. I don't say that to be pious, Clair. I say it because I have buried a husband and watched my son bury a wife and helped raise a granddaughter from the day she was born. Every one of those things required more than my body had to give, and the Lord provided anyway."

She said it without performance, the way she said everything, as though stating the weather or the time of day. It was the voice of a woman who had tested her faith against the hardest losses life could deliver and found it sufficient.

"I believe that," Clair said.

From the bean rows, Emma called out. "Miss Whitmore, I found a caterpillar that's a different color. It's brown instead of green. Is it still a tomato worm?"

"Bring it here and let your grandmother look," Clair said.

Emma trotted over with the caterpillar balanced on a leaf, holding it out for Lydia's inspection. Lydia leaned forward and studied it.

"That's a cutworm," she said. "They hide in the soil during the day and come out at night to eat the stems. You found it early. Put it in the pail."

"The chickens are going to have the best supper of their lives."

"They've earned it by giving us eggs every morning," Lydia said.

Emma deposited the cutworm and carried her pail back toward the tomatoes. A jackrabbit appeared at the far corner of the garden fence, its tall ears swiveling, its body frozen in the half-crouch of an animal deciding whether to stay or bolt. Emma spotted it and went still.

"Grandma," she whispered, loud enough that neither the whisper nor the intent behind it was subtle. "There's a rabbit."

"I see it," Lydia said.

"Can I go look at it?"

"Just stay where I can see you."

Emma set her pail down at the end of the row and moved toward the rabbit with the exaggerated care of a child who has been told not to run but whose legs have not received the message. The rabbit watched her approach for three seconds, then bolted through the fence rails and across the grass in long, bounding leaps. Emma followed to the fence and leaned over the top rail, watching it go.

"It's so fast," she said. "It's faster than the pronghorn. I think it's faster than Papa's horse."

"It is not faster than your father's horse," Lydia said.

"It might be," Emma said, and climbed through the fence rails to follow its path a few yards into the grass, where a cluster of butterflies scattered from a patch of wild clover. She forgot the rabbit immediately and crouched beside the butterflies, reaching for them with slow, open hands.

Clair watched her for a moment and turned her attention toward the pasture.

Adam was in the lower pasture, maybe a quarter mile out, on horseback. He rode along the fence line at a walk, and even at that distance she could see the fence posts loaded across his saddle, three of them balanced lengthwise. The pasture spread out around him in every direction, the grass thick and green and standing tall against the horse's legs. The mountains rose behind him in dark, timbered ridges that climbed until the trees gave way to rock and the rock gave way to sky. He stopped at a section of fence and dismounted.

The scale of his work on this large ranch registered in her mind. One man. Hundreds of acres. Every fence post, every head of cattle, every repair and supply run, and every predawn chore—all of it carried on one set of shoulders.

"He does that alone every day," Lydia said.

Clair looked at her, and Lydia's expression carried concern.

"He hired seasonal help for the hay harvest last year, and he'll do the same this summer," Lydia said. "But the daily work is his and his alone. He doesn't ask for help because asking means admitting the load is more than he can carry, and he hasn't been willing to admit that."

Clair looked back at the pasture. Adam had set the first post and was digging the hole for the second, his body bending to the work with a rhythm that was steady and unbroken.

"Has he always worked the ranch by himself?" Clair asked.

"Since his father died, yes. Before that, the two of them managed it. His father, William, was a strong man and a steady worker, and between the two of them, the operation ran well. After we lost him, Adam simply absorbed his father's share of the labor on top of his own."

Clair turned back to the weeds and pulled three more before she spoke again.

"Lydia, may I ask you about Emma's mother?

Emma was twenty yards past the garden fence, crouched in the clover with butterflies rising and settling around her, entirely absorbed and entirely out of earshot.

"Yes," Lydia said. "You should know."

She looked out toward the pasture again, where her son was still working.

"Her name was Ruth. She was a girl from the Mc Elroy ranch, the next valley over," Lydia said. "Her family ran cattle, same as us. Adam knew her from Sunday gatherings and community suppers. She was small and dark-haired, and she laughed at everything, Clair. Not because everything was funny, but because she saw the joy in things, the rest of us walked past without noticing."

"How old were they when they married?"

"Eighteen, both of them. Young, I know. But being young and married is different out here compared to the city, I would imagine. Eighteen on a ranch meant you'd already been working for years. Adam had been building fences and driving cattle since he was twelve. Ruth had been managing a kitchen and a garden since she was fourteen. They were young, but they weren't children."

"Were they happy?"

"They were." Lydia paused. "Ruth moved into this house right after they married, and from the first week she was here, the house changed. She sang while she cooked. She rearranged the kitchen several times in the first month because she said the flour should be closer to the stove and the sugar closer to the window, and none of it made any practical sense, but it made her happy, and that made Adam happy, and I was glad enough to have another woman in the house that I'd have let her put the flour on the roof if she'd asked."

Clair smiled. "She sounds as if she brought a great deal of life with her."

"She did. My daughter, Adam's older sister, had married and moved to Washington that same year. I missed her fiercely. Having Ruth here eased that. Ruth and I became close very quickly. She called me Mama from the second month, and I let her because it felt true."

"How long were they married before Emma was born?"

"Not even a year," Lydia said. "Ruth carried the baby well. She was healthy and strong, and she worked right up to the day she went into labor. I remember her weeding this very garden with her belly so round she couldn't bend forward anymore, so she'd sit on an overturned bucket and reach sideways."

"Emma came in the night," she continued. "It was a hard birth. The midwife rode out from town, but by the time she arrived, Ruth was already in trouble. There was too much bleeding, and it wouldn't stop. The midwife did everything she knew. I did everything I knew. And Ruth held on long enough to hear her baby cry. She heard Emma's first sound in this world, and then she was gone."

Clair's hands had gone still in the soil. She sat with her fingers pressed against the warm earth and listened.

"Adam held his daughter for the first time while Ruth was still lying in the bed beside him," Lydia said. "He held this tiny, perfect girl that he and Ruth had made, and he was looking at her face and hearing her cry, and his wife was three feet away, and she was already gone. I was standing in the room, and I watched my son hold his daughter for the first time with joy and grief so tangled together that I don't think he's ever been able to separate one from the other."

"I'm sorry, Lydia," Clair said.

Lydia nodded. "I am too. Every day."

They said nothing for a few moments, the garden quiet around them except for the small sounds of Emma talking to the butterflies beyond the fence and the distant, rhythmic thud of a post driver carrying across the pasture.

"And Adam's father?" Clair asked eventually.

"That same year," Lydia said. "Not three months after Ruth died. My husband was out with the herd when a storm came up fast. He was trying to drive the cattle toward shelter, and a steer spooked and broke from the line. The animal struck him, and he fell, and the fall killed him. Adam was nineteen years old, Clair. In the space of one year, he lost his wife and his father and inherited a ranch, had a newborn daughter, and had a mother who was just beginning to notice the stiffness in her hands.”

“And his sister had already gone to Washington.”

“She was. Adam lost her too, in a manner of speaking. Not to death, but to distance. She’s alive and well and married with a family of her own, but she’s miles away, and we haven’t seen her in quite some time. And years before all of this, they lost another sister, my little Esmi, Adam’s other sibling. She died of scarlet fever when she was ten. Adam was only fifteen at the time, and he grieved her terribly. So by the time Ruth died and his father died, Adam had already learned what it cost to love someone and lose them.”

Clair pulled a weed from the soil as her mind was turning the information over. A boy who lost a sister at fifteen. A young husband who lost his wife at nineteen. A son who lost his father in the same year. A man who had been carrying the full sum of those losses for years.

“What happened to him after?” Clair asked.

“He became the man you see,” Lydia said. “He stopped talking about anything that wasn’t the ranch or Emma’s immediate needs. He stopped visiting the friends he’d had since boyhood. He goes into town for supplies, and he comes home. He attends worship because I expect it and because the habit is too deep to break, but he stands in the back of the room, and he leaves when the closing prayer is finished and waits for me in the wagon. I’m fairly certain he hasn’t had a close relationship with God in years, Clair. I know my son, and I know what a man’s faith looks like when it’s gone silent.”

"Does he ever speak about Ruth?"

"Very rarely, and when he does, it's because I might have brought her up specifically. Everything in this house that was hers is gone. Her clothes, her sewing, the little things she kept on the shelf in their room. I don't know where he put her things. He removed them within a week of her death and has never mentioned them since."

Clair looked at the house from the garden, imagining the bare walls and functional curtains inside. The shelves that held only what was necessary and nothing that was personal. The house was clean and maintained and stripped of every trace of the woman who had rearranged its kitchen several times in a month. Adam had edited Ruth out of the visible record of his life.

"He's a good father," Lydia said. "He provides everything Emma needs. He feeds her and clothes her and keeps her safe and teaches her about the land and the animals, and the work. But there is no joy in his life anymore, Clair. He works, and he does what needs doing, but he never seeks out anything for himself. He hasn't courted anyone. He doesn't visit people who used to be his good friends. He goes, and he does, and he comes home, and he does more, and the doing fills every hour so there isn't room left for the feeling, and I think that's the point."

"You think he fills the hours on purpose."

"I know he does. I've watched him do it for six years. And it breaks my heart because I remember the boy he was before his world crashed around him. He was a boy who laughed and sang hymns on Sunday mornings and talked to his father about the land the way other boys talked about girls. That boy had dreams. The man he's become has objectives."

A silence followed, and in it Clair could hear Emma's voice beyond the fence, high and clear, saying something to a butterfly about its wings.

"And Emma," Clair said. "Does she ask about her mother?"

"Not yet," Lydia said. "But she will someday. She knows her mother died when she was born. Adam told her that much, plainly and honestly, when she was old enough to ask. But she doesn't know what she's missing because she's never known anything different. She's a happy child. Bright, curious, and full of life. She is content with what she has." Lydia turned her gaze toward Emma, who was now lying on her stomach in the grass, her chin propped on her fists, watching something in the clover. "But that contentment has a ceiling. One day she'll visit a friend's house and see that friend's mother brush her hair. One day she'll hear another girl talk about what her mother made for supper, or what her mother said about a boy, or what her mother wore to church. And Emma will begin to understand the shape of what she doesn't have. And when that day comes, it will matter that someone was here who could help her carry it."

Clair listened, and she understood what Lydia was saying and what Lydia wasn't saying, and the distance between the two was where the real meaning lived.

"My mother died when I was sixteen," Clair said. "She was ill for several months before the end. I watched her lose her strength a little more each week, and I tried to hold the household steady around her the way you hold a cup level when the table shakes. I managed the meals and the house, and the servants, and I sat beside her bed in the evenings and read to her from the Psalms because those were the passages she loved most."

"The Psalms are faithful company in those hours," Lydia said.

"They were. She died on a Tuesday morning in March, and I remember that the light was coming through her bedroom window at an angle that made the quilt look like it was glowing, and she was looking at the window when she went, and I have always been grateful that the last thing she saw was light."

"After she died, my world fell apart in a way I didn't know a world could fall apart. I was sixteen, and I had lost the person who had taught me everything I knew about being a woman. How to run a household, how to cook, how to braid hair, and how to pray. My father was devastated, and he grieved her as deeply as any man could grieve, but he was also a practical man with a business to run, and he couldn't stop. So he didn't. And I didn't either. We kept going because stopping wasn't an option, and he became my whole world after that. He was my father and my teacher and my employer and my closest friend, and everything I did from that day forward I did alongside him."

"And then you lost him too," Lydia said.

"Four months ago," Clair said. "And losing him was different from losing my mother, because when I lost her, I still had him. We held each other up and continued on in life. After he passed, I was a grown woman who felt like an orphan."

Lydia reached over and placed her hand on Clair's forearm. Her fingers were warm and swollen, and they rested against Clair's skin gently.

"You have people now," Lydia said.

Clair looked at Lydia's hand on her arm, her curved fingers, and thick knuckles. She placed her hand over Lydia's and held it there.

"For a time I do, and I will enjoy every moment of the time I spend here with you and your family," Clair said.

From beyond the fence, Emma's voice rose in a burst of delighted frustration. "It got away! The rabbit came back, and I almost touched it, and it got away again!"

She ran toward them, breathless and grinning, her pinafore torn at the hem where it had caught on something. She climbed between the fence rails and crossed the garden in five strides and dropped to her knees between Clair and the potato row.

"It was so close," she said. "Its nose was twitching and its ears were going back and forth, and I was this far from it." She held her hands eight inches apart. "And then it jumped, and it was gone. Did you know rabbits can jump sideways? They don't just go forward. They go sideways."

"I didn't know that," Clair said.

"And there were butterflies everywhere in the clover. Orange ones and yellow ones and one that was almost white. I tried to catch the white one, but it went up too high." She pulled a weed and tossed it aside. "What were you and Grandma talking about?"

"Gardening," Clair said.

"Just gardening?"

"Mostly gardening."

Emma accepted this and turned her attention to the weeds, pulling them with small, busy fingers that worked steadily along the row.

Lydia rose from the fence rail, pressing both hands against the wood for leverage. She picked up her hoe and stood for a moment looking at Emma working beside Clair in the dirt, the two of them kneeling side by side, their hands in the same soil.

"She is such a precious child and deserves more than this world has given her so far in life," Lydia said, her voice quiet and even. "But I have faith that God has great plans for her."

She rested the hoe against her shoulder and walked toward the house.

Clair stayed in the garden and watched Emma beside her, pulling weeds with her small, dirt-streaked fingers, her braid still holding tight, her face close to the soil. She was absorbed in the work as though it were the most important task in the world.

Chapter 8

Adam came through the back door with the day still on him, the dirt ground into the seams of his shirt, and the grit packed under his nails where no amount of scrubbing ever reached on the first try. His shoulders carried the deep, settled ache of a man who had spent ten hours on horseback and on foot, resetting fence posts and checking stock. He had also ridden the upper pasture to count heads where the cattle had drifted toward the benchland grass. His hat went on the peg on the wall, and then he removed his boots. He crossed to the washstand on the back porch and poured water from the pitcher into the basin.

The water was cold, and it hit his face like a rebuke, sharp enough to strip the fog from the last two hours of riding when the work had gone from labor into endurance. He scrubbed his neck and forearms, working the cloth over his skin until the worst of the day's accumulation ran brown into the basin. Through the open back door he could hear the music of a household preparing supper: a pot being set on the trivet, the scrape of a spoon against cast iron, and Emma's voice rising and falling in a current of words that hadn't paused for breath since he'd come within earshot.

He dried his hands and his face, draped the cloth over the basin's edge, and went inside, where the table was set for four. Plates, cups, and flatware in their usual arrangement. Tonight it registered as fact rather than interruption, the way a gate registers as closed when you've already checked it twice and stopped expecting it to be open. He pulled his chair back and sat down.

Emma was at her place, her knees tucked under her, her elbows on the table despite two years of Lydia's corrections on the subject. Her face was flushed with color that came from a full day spent outdoors.

"Papa, we were in the garden for ages," she said. "Miss Whitmore pulled more weeds than Grandma and me put together, and she didn't even know which ones were weeds at first."

"Is that right?" Adam said.

"And there was a jackrabbit. It came right up to the fence, Papa. Right up to it. I went out to look at it, and I got this close." She said as she held her hands apart. "Did you know rabbits jump sideways?"

"I've seen it."

"And I found eleven tomato worms. Eleven. Grandma said they go to the chickens so the chickens had a good supper tonight. And I found a toad under the bean stakes. Grandma said Grandpa used to say a garden with a toad was a garden that didn't need watching."

"He did say that."

"Did you ever see the toad? When Grandpa was alive?"

Adam looked at his daughter. The question had come the way Emma's questions always came, without warning, carried on the same breath as tomato worms and jackrabbits.

"There was a toad in the garden every summer I can remember," he said. "Your grandfather was convinced it was the same one. Your grandmother told him toads don't live that long, and he told her she didn't know the particular toad he spoke of."

Emma grinned. "Was it the same one?"

"I expect it was a different one each year. But I never told him that."

"Miss Whitmore taught me three new letters after we came inside," Emma said. "I can write H now. I couldn't write it before because the two lines go up and down and the one in the middle goes across, and I kept making the middle one crooked. But she showed me how to do the up-and-down ones first and then put the middle one in after, and now it comes out straight."

"Can you show me after supper?"

Emma's face opened with the uncomplicated delight of a child who has been asked to demonstrate a skill she has only just acquired. "Yes. I'll get the primer and the slate, and I'll show you all three letters I can do now... H and K and R."

At the stove, Clair lifted the lid on a pot and stirred, then replaced it and wiped her hands on the cloth tucked into the waist of her apron. She had been moving between the stove and the table while Emma talked. She had set down a bowl of boiled potatoes, a plate of sliced ham fried in the skillet, and a dish of green beans from the garden cooked with salt pork. She set the last dish on the table and took her seat across from Adam.

"Shall we pray?" Lydia said.

"Lord, we come to the end of this day with full hands and grateful hearts. You have given us work that is honest and a table that doesn't go empty, and we are thankful. We thank You for the food before us, for the garden that grew it and the hands that prepared it, and we ask Your blessing on each person who sits here tonight. Watch over this house and the people under its roof. Give us rest that is true and strength enough for tomorrow. We ask it in the name of Your son. Amen."

Adam lifted his head and reached for the potatoes, spooned some onto his plate, and set the bowl close to Lydia's plate.

After he had filled his plate and begun to eat, Adam noticed the ham was good, crisped at the edges, and seasoned with pepper. The potatoes were cooked through but still firm enough to hold their shape on the fork. The green beans had the faint sweetness of produce that had been picked the same day it was cooked.

"Mr. Dawson," Clair said after a few minutes of eating had passed. "How many heads of cattle are on your ranch?"

He looked at her. "Eighty-two, as of this morning's count."

"And they graze where you were working today? In the lower pasture?"

"In summer they spread up onto the higher benchland. The grass cures on the lower ground first, so I push the herd to the upper range while the lower pastures recover. By fall, the cattle come back down to the valley floor for winter."

"So you rotate them," Clair said. "The way a field is rotated between crops."

"Same idea. The grass needs rest, the same as soil does. If cattle stay on one piece of ground too long, they eat it down past the roots, and it won't come back the same. The benchland above the creek gives me a couple of good months of summer graze, sometimes longer if the rain holds."

"How far does your property extend toward the mountains?"

"The deeded ground runs to the creek on the north and east. South, it extends past the hayfields. West, it runs to the wagon road. Beyond that, the cattle use open range, the same as every outfit in the valley. No one's fenced the upper country yet."

"And the hay," Clair said. "When does that come in?"

"Late July, if the weather cooperates. First week of August if it doesn't. Depends on the grass. The timothy needs to head out and cure on the stem before it's ready to cut, and you can't rush it. Cut too early, and the feed value is poor. Cut too late, and it goes to seed, and the cattle won't eat it."

"How long does the harvest take?"

"A couple of days usually. I'll hire a couple of hands this year, and then two other ranchers will come to help."

"And until then?"

"Until then, I'm getting ready for it. Checking the equipment, sharpening the sickle bar, and making sure the hay rake runs true. There's a lot of preparation before the first blade goes down." He cut a piece of ham and ate it. He had said more about the hay harvest in thirty seconds than he typically said about any subject that didn't involve Emma's immediate welfare, and the fact of it sat at the back of his awareness.

Clair set her fork down and folded her hands beside her plate. "I checked on the mare this afternoon. I stayed outside the stall, as you said. She didn't seem distressed, but she was shifting on her front feet quite a bit. Is she comfortable?"

Adam looked at her. "She's close to foaling," he said. "Could be tonight, could be another few days. When a mare shifts like that, it usually means the foal's settling lower. I'll check her after supper."

Clair nodded. She picked up her fork and returned to her food. The kitchen was quiet for a moment, the four of them eating, Emma swinging her feet beneath her chair in the restless rhythm of a child who had been sitting long enough.

"The creek that runs through your property," Clair said. "Where does it come from?"

"Comes down out of the Absarokas," Adam said. "Snowmelt and spring water. It starts above the timberline, and it runs year-round."

"Does the creek have a name?"

"Not an official one. My father called it Dawson Creek because he didn't see the point in waiting for someone else to name a thing that ran through his land. The maps, the ones that exist, call it a branch of Providence Creek, which feeds the Yellowstone River, eventually."

"Your father named a creek."

"He named the ranch, too. He wasn't a man who left things unnamed. He said, If you worked a piece of ground long enough to know where the water ran and where the frost settled and where the elk bedded in October, you'd earned the right to call it yours."

Across the table, Clair was watching him with a curious expression on her face. He turned his attention back to his dinner plate.

Lydia had not spoken during the exchange. She ate her supper and drank her coffee, and her gaze had moved between Adam and Clair as they spoke. Adam knew his mother well enough to know she was cataloging what she heard, filing it in the same careful order she filed everything, from canning schedules to Scripture references to observations about her son that she kept to herself until she decided otherwise.

"Papa," Emma said, "did you know that Miss Whitmore didn't know what a tomato worm looked like? She thought the first one she saw was a caterpillar."

"It is a caterpillar," Clair said.

"But it's a tomato caterpillar," Emma said. "That's different. Regular caterpillars turn into butterflies. Tomato worms just eat everything and get fat, and you have to feed them to the chickens."

"I stand corrected," Clair said.

"And she pulled up a bean sprout," Emma said, turning back to Adam. "Grandma said it wasn't the end of the world because there were plenty more, but Miss Whitmore's face went all pink, and she put the sprout back in the ground and pressed the dirt around it and said she was sorry to the plant."

Adam looked at Clair. She had pressed her lips together, but the corners of her mouth had turned up in spite of it, and for a moment the composure she wore at this table like a clean apron gave way to something less guarded: a woman caught between embarrassment and laughter by a child who reported events with the accuracy of a witness and the editorial instincts of a town gossip.

"The sprout is still alive," Clair said. "I checked."

"You went back to look at it?" Emma asked.

"I did."

"Why?"

"Because I wanted to be sure the patient survived."

Emma laughed. The sound was sudden and bright, and it filled the kitchen the way a bird fills a room it has flown into: with motion and color and the brief, undeniable proof of something alive. Adam watched his daughter laugh with her head tipped back, and the sight of it made him grin.

"The beans are doing well this year," Lydia said. "We should have more than enough for canning if the second planting takes. Clair, I'll need your hands for that."

"I wouldn't mind learning at all," Clair said.

"It's hot work and tedious, and enormously satisfying when you see the jars lined up on the shelves in the cellar at the end of it," Lydia said. "Ruth used to say canning was the only job on the ranch where you could count your accomplishments in a row and none of them tried to wander off."

The name landed on the table the way a stone lands in still water. His mother had spoken it without emphasis, folded into a sentence about canning jars. Adam's fork stopped for one beat and then resumed its path. He didn't look at his mother nor Clair. He looked at his plate; he chewed the bite he'd taken, and he let the moment pass.

Clair said nothing. She didn't react to the name, and she didn't ask who Ruth was. Her hands stayed steady on her fork and knife, and she ate her next bite of ham.

Adam noticed the absence of the question. A woman who didn't know the name would have asked. The fact that Clair didn't ask meant she already knew, and the fact that she already knew meant someone had told her, and that someone could only be his mother.

"Papa," Emma said. "Miss Whitmore said she would braid my hair again tomorrow morning. Can she?"

"If Miss Whitmore said she would, then she will," Adam said.

"She does it tighter than Grandma," Emma said. She reached back and touched her braid where it hung between her shoulder blades, running her fingers along its length. "See? It's still in. It didn't come out. Not even after the garden and the rabbit and my primer lesson. It stayed the whole day."

Adam looked at his daughter's face. She was watching him with the open, expectant expression she wore when she wanted him to see something she considered important. Her cheeks were still flushed from the day. Her eyes carried a brightness that came from a day filled with activity and attention. She was more animated tonight than she'd been at this table in a long time. Her words came faster, the stories ran longer, and the laughter arrived without prompting. She looked like a happy child.

Adam was aware, in the steady, cataloging way he was aware of everything that happened under his roof, that his daughter had attached herself to Clair Whitmore. The attachment had taken root within two days.

He stood and carried his plate to the dry sink.

"Emma, go find the primer and your slate. You said you'd show your father the letter H before bed," Clair said.

Adam stood at the dry sink with his back to the table and his hands on the edge of the counter and thought about what Clair's leaving in the future would cost Emma.

Chapter 9

Adam sat low in the porch chair with his legs stretched out as he enjoyed the view in front of him. The sun had slipped behind the mountains, and the sky above them had layered its colors from the peaks upward. A band of gold still burned where the sun had just been, giving way to a rose color above it, and the rose deepened into a violet that spread and climbed until it met the pale blue overhead. The colors shifted while he sat there, the gold thinning and the rose reaching higher, the entire sky rearranging itself slowly enough that a man could watch it happen and still not catch the exact moment one color became another.

Through the open window, he could hear the reading lesson going on inside. Emma's voice first, high and intent, working through the sounds of a word one letter at a time. Then Clair's voice, steady and unhurried, repeated the sound until Emma caught it. They'd been at it for ten minutes when Emma's voice came through clear and whole: "Cat." Not the individual letters strung in a row, the way she'd been practicing all week, but the word itself, spoken as a single piece, the sounds fused into meaning. Then his daughter's voice again, bright and fast: "I did it, Miss Whitmore. Did you hear? I said the whole word."

The reading lesson went on for a few more minutes, and then the sounds shifted. The primer closed. Small feet on the stairs, quick and certain, and Clair's steps behind them. The house was quiet above him for a few minutes, and then Clair came back down.

Lydia's voice from inside was low and brief. "Goodnight, Clair."

"Goodnight, Lydia. I hope you get some good rest tonight."

"I'll try. Don't stay up too late."

He heard the closing of his mother's bedroom door.

Moments later, the front door opened. Clair came out onto the porch and sat down on the top step.

"Chair's open," he said.

"I'm fine here," Clair said.

Neither of them spoke for a stretch. Adam watched as Clair looked out at the mountains, her profile still against the fading sky. He wondered what she'd had to look at in Helena. Buildings, he supposed. Storefronts and rooftops, and the narrow slice of sky between them. Nothing like this. Nothing a person could rest her eyes on and let her thoughts go wide. He wondered if the peace and quiet here suited her or if she missed the noise and constant movement of a city. What had it been like for her, growing up in a place where the mountains were something you saw between buildings instead of something you lived inside? She'd been here over a week now, and he still knew very little about her. That gap in his knowledge had begun to bother him in a way he couldn't set aside the way he set aside most things that didn't concern the ranch or Emma.

"I expect this is a fair sight different from Helena," Adam said.

Clair turned her head toward him, then back to the view. "It is," she said. "Helena is built into a gulch. The buildings crowd up against each other, and the streets are narrow. You can stand on the boardwalk in front of a mercantile and see rooftops and chimney stacks in every direction."

"What was it like growing up there?" he asked.

Clair was quiet for a moment before she answered. "It was a good life. My parents made it good. My father ran his business, and my mother ran the household, and between the two of them everything had its place and its purpose. We lived in a respectable house on a quiet street. My father left for work each morning and came home each evening, and my mother kept a home that was warm and orderly and full of small routines that made the days feel steady. Saturday mornings she walked to the market and knew every shopkeeper by name. On Sundays, we went to church as a family. Evenings after supper, my father would read, and my mother would sew."

"That sounds like a good childhood."

"It was. My mother had been the center of my world before her passing."

"What happened after?" he asked.

"My father," Clair said. "He became everything. After my mother passed, he could have sent me to live with relatives in St. Louis. My mother's sister offered to take me, and it would have been the expected thing. But he kept me with him. I think losing my mother made him hold tighter to what he had left, and what he had left was me. He ran a business in Helena, and after my mother died, he started bringing me along. At first, it was just so I wouldn't be alone in the house all day. But then he began teaching me the work. He'd sit me across from him at his desk and explain what he was doing and why, and he'd ask me what I thought, and he listened when I answered. He treated my mind as if it had value, and that was not a common thing for a father to do with a daughter."

"No, it isn't," Adam said.

"By the time I was eighteen, I was managing his correspondence and keeping some of his books balanced. He handled the men and the operations, and I handled most of the paperwork and some planning, and between the two of us and a secretary, the business ran well." She looked down at her hands resting on the step. "At home we enjoyed our time together, but it was different after Mother passed away . We ate supper together every evening, and he read from the Scriptures after the dishes were cleared. On Sundays we walked to church together, and on the way home he would ask me what I thought of the sermon, and we would discuss it for the rest of the walk. Those walks were my favorite part of the week."

"I can only imagine what it must have been like," Clair continued, "growing up in a place like this. All of this land, and the mountains, and the sky. You must have felt as if you had the whole world to explore as a boy."

Adam looked out at the dark where the pasture met the foothills. He hadn't talked about his boyhood in a long time. The memories were there, solid and clear, but they lived in a part of his mind he kept shut the way.

"I had a good childhood," he said. "My father had me on a horse before I could read. He'd take me with him when he rode the property, and I'd sit in front of him in the saddle, and he'd tell me the names of things as we passed them. Every ridge, every stand of timber, every bend in the creek. He wanted me to know the land the way he knew it, like it was a member of the family."

"That's a lovely way to teach a child."

"He wasn't a man who sat you down and gave lessons. He taught by doing. If he wanted me to learn how to judge when the grass was ready for cutting, he'd ride me out to the hayfield and pull a stem and hand it to me and ask me what I saw. He'd wait until I answered before he told me whether I was right. Sometimes he'd wait a good long while."

"A patient man."

"Patient with the land. Patient with livestock. Less patient with people who didn't pull their share, but he didn't encounter many of those because he didn't keep company with people who didn't work." Adam paused. "He built most of what you see here. The house, the barn, and the corrals. He and my mother came to this valley with a wagon and not much else, and he put this ranch together one board at a time. By the time I was old enough to help, the hardest work was already done. I just had to maintain what he'd built."

"That's no small thing," Clair said. "Maintaining something well takes as much care as building it. Perhaps more, because the building has the excitement of creation, and the maintaining is just faithfulness, day after day."

Adam looked at her. "Had you ever been outside a city before coming here?" he asked.

"No. The farthest I'd been from Helena were Sunday drives along the valley road with my father and visits to the mining camps in the area that we worked with."

"What surprised you most about this place?"

"The quiet," she said. "In Helena, there was always sound. Wagons on the street, the mills running day and night, voices from the houses on either side of ours, and church bells marking the hours. Here, the first night I lay in the dark and heard nothing but silence mostly, and the silence was so complete it kept me awake."

"It kept you awake."

"That it did. I kept listening for something... anything that sounded familiar. But those sounds never came, and the waiting for them was louder than the noise in Helena ever was."

"And now?"

"Now I listen for the creek the way I used to listen for the church bells. It tells me where I am. I now hear birds chirping, the wind rustling the leaves in the trees, and the sounds of animals stirring and calling out to one another. Those are things I'm not used to at all, but I'm finding I quite enjoy them."

"How is Emma's reading and learning coming along?" he asked.

"She's a bright child and a quick learner," Clair said. "She wants to read whole sentences before she's finished learning all the letters, and she grows frustrated when the sounds don't match what she expects. But she's making real progress. She learned three new letters this week, and she can sound out short words now if I give her enough time and don't rush her. Earlier this evening she sounded out the word 'cat,' and when the word came together, she was so proud of herself." Clair turned slightly on the step. "She learns differently than I expected. Most children her age sound out each letter and then try to assemble the word from the pieces. Emma does better when she hears the whole word spoken first and then finds it on the page. She recognizes patterns before she recognizes the parts. It's the mark of a mind that sees how things fit together rather than taking them apart one at a time."

"She's a good child and smart as a whip. I appreciate your helping with her learning. Has the stove given you any more trouble?" he asked.

"The stove and I have come to terms," Clair said. "Your mother was right that it has opinions. The back left plate runs hotter than the front, so I move the coffeepot there when I want it to hold heat through the morning. And I've learned to rotate the biscuit tin halfway through baking because the oven heats unevenly on the left side. If I leave the tin in one position, the biscuits on the near edge brown before the ones on the far edge have finished rising."

Adam realized he had spent more time in conversation tonight with someone other than his mother and daughter.

"I'll be on the south fence line in the morning," he said. "Several posts need resetting where the bank shifted. Then in the afternoon I'll be out checking on the herd."

"I'll have coffee on early," Clair said. "I also intend to try the biscuits with a little less lard tomorrow. I think the ratio is close, but not quite right."

She stood from the step and brushed her skirt with one hand. She stood for a moment facing the valley, and the darkness made her outline simple against the sky, a woman standing on a porch with the mountains behind her and the quiet of the ranch settling around her.

"Goodnight, Mr. Dawson."

"Goodnight."

She went inside. The door closed behind her, and then her steps moved through the kitchen, careful and sure, and then the low click of the bedroom door.

Adam sat in his chair. The mountains were black against the sky, and the stars were thick above the ridgeline. The peaceful evening was his again, the way it had been his every evening for years, and he sat in the quiet she'd left behind and listened to the creek.

Chapter 10

Clair sliced the beef roast against the grain, the knife drawing through the cold meat in long, even strokes that separated each piece at the thickness Lydia had shown her. The roast had come from last night's supper, wrapped in cloth and set on the shelf in the root cellar, where the air stayed cool enough to keep meat through a summer day. She laid the slices across the bottom of the pail in overlapping rows, then covered them with a clean cloth and set the biscuits on top.

The hard-boiled eggs sat in a bowl of cold water on the counter. She lifted them out one at a time and dried them, and nested them beside the biscuits. The sugar snap peas she'd picked from the garden before breakfast went in next.

Through the window above the washbasin, she could see Adam.

He was near the barn, bent over a piece of equipment that sat on the ground. The machine was low and angular, with a long wooden beam extending from its front and a flat, toothed bar running along one side close to the ground. Even from the kitchen window, Clair could see that the equipment was built for a specific purpose, its parts fitted to one another with the economy of a tool designed to do one thing and do it well.

She had grown accustomed to the pattern of his mornings. He rose early, drank his coffee, and ate breakfast. She sometimes packed his midday meal when he intended to be gone for the better part of the day and left it wrapped on the counter near the door. He took it with him when he headed out for the day's work. At the end of the day's work, he came home to dinner on the table or close to it.

This morning Adam had told her he wouldn't be taking a midday meal with him as he would be working close to the house. He had asked her to simply have the meal ready around noon, and he'd come eat on the front porch so as not to interrupt the normal routines she, Lydia, and Emma had established.

Clair glanced out the window again. Adam had moved to the other side of the machine and was testing a set of bolts along the toothed bar, turning each one with a wrench and checking the play in the mechanism.

"Why don't you take his lunch out to him?" Lydia said from where she sat at the table, reading her Bible. "And take Emma along. The child has been bent over that slate since breakfast, and she's been fidgeting for the last half hour. She needs to move, and the morning's too fine to spend it indoors."

Clair turned and watched as Emma concentrated, her pencil moving in slow, deliberate strokes as she traced the letters of her name.

"In fact, pack more food in the pail, and you both go join Adam for lunch. Go enjoy eating outside and enjoy the fresh air and sunshine," Lydia said. "It will do you both good."

"What about you?" Clair asked. "You could come with us."

"I want to lie down for a spell. My achy body kept me up through the small hours last night, and I didn't get the rest I should have."

Clair had heard Lydia shifting on the bed during the night. Twice Clair had woken to the sound of Lydia sitting upright, adjusting her pillow, shifting around, or simply standing up and walking around the room trying to loosen her joints.

"Emma," Clair said as she placed more food inside the pail. "Would you like to bring your father his dinner outside?"

Emma looked up from her slate. "Can we eat out there too?"

"Of course."

Emma set the pencil down and slid from her chair. "Can I carry something?"

Clair looked at the pail, then at the jar of preserves she hadn't yet placed inside. She held it out. "Carry this with both hands and don't tip it."

Emma took the jar and held it against her chest. "I won't tip it."

Clair covered the pail with a cloth, tucking the edges around the contents, and then turned to look at Lydia.

"Rest well," she said.

"I intend to." Lydia was already rising from her chair, one hand braced on the table. "Tell Adam I said not to bolt his food standing up the way he does when he thinks no one is watching."

Clair carried the pail through the front door and down the porch steps with Emma beside her, the jar of preserves held in both hands against the front of her dress. The yard between the house and the barn was hard-packed earth where the daily traffic of boots and hooves had worn the grass away. Beyond its edges, the pasture grass stood tall and thick in the full green of mid-July.

"Miss Whitmore," Emma said as they crossed the yard. "Did you have a garden in Helena?"

"No," Clair said. "We didn't have a garden. We had a small yard behind our house with rosebushes my mother planted the year I was born. When my mother was still alive and they bloomed, she would cut one stem every morning and put it in a cup of water on the kitchen table."

"Do you miss it?"

"Yes, I miss the roses," Clair said. "But I'm enjoying your grandma's garden because it grows things you can eat. Rosebushes never fed anyone supper."

"But roses are prettier than beans."

"They are, but beans are more useful."

"Grandma says useful things are beautiful in their own way."

"Your grandmother is quite correct."

Emma nodded, satisfied, and adjusted her grip on the jar.

Adam was on one knee beside the machine, his sleeves pushed past his elbows, his forearms smudged with grease. He had removed a section of the toothed bar and laid it across a piece of canvas on the ground. The individual blades of the machine were visible, each one triangular and sharp-edged, and fitted into the bar like teeth in a jaw.

Adam looked up when they were ten paces away.

"Your mother wanted to rest," Clair said. "She suggested we bring dinner to you and we all eat together and enjoy the sunshine. She also said to tell you not to bolt your food standing up."

The corner of his mouth moved a fraction. "She said that."

"Her words."

He wiped his hands on a rag, working the grease from between his fingers. He stood and tucked the rag back through his belt and looked at Emma, who was holding the preserves jar with both hands.

"What have you got there?" he asked.

"Blackberry preserves," Emma said. "I carried it the whole way, and I didn't tip it."

"Good work."

They settled on the grass near the tool shed, where the barn threw a wedge of shade across the ground. Clair spread one of the cloths flat and laid out the food: the roast beef slices arranged on their wrapping, the biscuits set to one side, the eggs, and the snap peas in a loose pile between them. She opened the preserves jar and set it where Emma could reach it.

Adam sat on the grass with his legs crossed and ate steadily. Emma sat cross-legged beside him and ate her egg in small bites, and told him about the letters she had been practicing all morning.

"I can write my whole name now," she said. "All four letters. E-M-M-A. Miss Whitmore showed me how the two M's go next to each other. I practiced until they looked the same size. Can I show you after supper?"

"I'd like that," Adam said.

"The A is the hardest because you have to make both sides even, or it tips over. Miss Whitmore says the trick is to start at the top and pull down both sides at the same time, but I can't do both sides at the same time because I only have one hand that holds the pencil."

"You'll sort it out," Adam said.

Emma spread preserves on a biscuit with her fingers and ate it with pleasure. When she finished, she licked the preserves from her fingers and stood, her attention already migrating to the grass beyond the shade where a cluster of wildflowers grew.

"Can I pick some?" she asked, pointing toward them.

"Stay where I can see you," Adam said.

Emma walked to the edge of the grass and crouched beside the flowers, selecting them one at a time.

As Clair continued eating a biscuit, she noticed Adam's hands were large and square-palmed, the tendons visible, and there were thick calluses along the base of each finger.

She looked at the mowing machine behind him. The wooden beam drew her eye again. Its surface was different from the iron frame it connected to, lighter in color, and the wood was close-grained and dense. Near the base where the beam joined the machine's frame, a set of letters had been carved into the wood, small and square, cut with the precision of a chisel rather than a knife.

"The beam on the front of the machine," she said. "The wood is different from the rest of it."

Adam turned and looked at the mowing machine. "The tongue," he said. "That's what connects the cutter to the horse team. My father built it."

"He built it from scratch?"

"The original broke during one of the hay harvests. It snapped clean at the pivot during the first pass through the timothy field.

He couldn't wait for a replacement from Livingston. The hay was ready and waiting; a week meant losing half the crop to weather or seed. He went down to the creek bottom that same afternoon and cut a piece of ash. He shaped it with a drawknife on the barn floor, fitted it to the machine in two days, and finished the harvest on schedule."

"That must have been hard work."

"It was. Every other part of that cutter has been replaced or repaired at least once. The sickle bar, the gears, and the wheel assembly. All of it has broken and been fixed or swapped for new. That tongue is the original piece my father cut, and it runs truer than any factory timber I could order."

Clair looked at the letters carved near the base. From this angle, she could make out the initials. W.D. for William Dawson.

Emma returned with a fistful of wildflowers, their stems crushed where her grip had held them. She sat beside Clair and collected three snap pea pods from the remains of the meal and arranged them in a row on the cloth, sorted by length, the longest on the left and the shortest on the right.

"These go from biggest to smallest," she said, pointing at the pods. "Miss Whitmore is teaching me about putting things in order. You can order letters, you can order numbers, and you can order pea pods."

"Can you?" Adam said.

"You can order anything if you know which rule to use. Miss Whitmore says the rule is the most important part, because without a rule, you're just making a pile."

Adam looked at Clair.

"It applies to more than pea pods," Clair said.

He held her gaze for a few seconds and smiled. Then he stood and brushed the grass off his trousers.

"I need to check on the mare," he said.

Emma was on her feet before the sentence finished. "Can I come?"

Adam nodded, and the three of them walked to the barn.

The barn's interior was cooler, offering a bit of relief from the heat of the day.

Adam opened the stall door and stepped inside. The mare stood with her head lowered, her belly enormous and round, her legs slightly apart in a wide stance. She turned her head when Adam entered and watched him approach.

He moved along her side and placed his hand flat against her barrel, then ran it slowly down her flank, his palm pressing into the curve where the foal's position could be read through the wall of muscle and skin. He spoke to her while he worked, a low, continuous murmur.

Emma stood beside Clair at the stall door, her hands resting on the rail.

"You're getting so big," Emma told the mare. "Your belly is almost touching the straw."

The mare's ear flicked toward Emma's voice and then forward again.

Clair watched Adam's hands move along the mare's side, steady and sure. The foal had settled lower since the last time she had looked in on the mare; the shape of her belly carrying further down and forward, and the mare's stance had widened to accommodate the shift.

"What is her name?" Clair asked. "I've been looking in on her for days, and I never thought to ask."

"Mercy," Adam said.

"Grandma named her," Emma said.

Adam confirmed it with a nod, his hand still resting on the mare's flank. "My mother said a mare that would carry foals needed a name that meant something."

Mercy. A name chosen by a woman whose faith lived in the ordinary language of her household, who named a horse the way she prayed, with conviction and without apology.

Emma's attention moved to the far end of the barn, where the tack hung from wooden pegs along the wall, the bridles, halters, and lead ropes arranged in a row. She walked toward them and began counting the pegs under her breath.

Adam ran his hand once more along the mare's barrel and then stepped back. Mercy shifted and lowered her head to the hay, and the sound of her pulling at the dried grass filled the stall with a rhythmic, tearing sound.

He came out through the stall door and stood beside Clair, the space between them no wider than a hand's breadth. Somewhere above them in the hayloft, a barn swallow called once and fell silent.

Adam turned his head and looked at Clair. His eyes were dark and steady, and in them Clair found something she had not seen before: a tenderness that made her aware of exactly how close he stood beside her.

"Papa, can I climb the ladder and play in the loft?" Emma called from across the barn.

Adam turned. "No, Emma, not today. I need to get back to work."

He turned and walked toward Emma, and Clair followed.

Emma reached for Clair's hand as they exited the barn.

"When the foal comes, will it be a boy or a girl?" Emma asked.

"We won't know until it arrives," Clair said.

"I want it to be a girl. If it's a girl, can we name her? Grandma could help; she's good at names. She named the barn cat Solomon because he sits in the sun all day and doesn't do any work, and she said that sounded like a king to her."

Clair let Emma's voice carry her across the yard, answering when an answer was needed and listening when it wasn't.

At the edge of the yard, where the packed earth gave way to the porch steps, Clair stopped and looked back toward the barn.

Adam had returned to the mowing machine. He was bent over the ash tongue, his hands on the wood his father had cut and shaped, his attention folded into the equipment with the same absorption she had seen through the kitchen window that morning.

"Miss Whitmore," Emma said from the porch steps. "Are you coming inside?"

"Yes," Clair said. "I'm coming."

Chapter 11

Emma pointed to a line of rock on the eastern ridge where the timber broke and the bare slope above it ran upward to a jagged crest. "That's where Papa saw the bear," she said. "It was eating berries, and Papa said it was big enough to block the whole trail."

"How big?" Clair asked.

"He said if it stood up on its back legs, it could look over the barn roof."

Clair smiled and adjusted her hold on the side of the wagon bed as the wheels dipped through a rut. The morning opened around them in every direction as the road carried them away from the ranch and toward town.

She hadn't expected the valley to be this expansive and beautiful. In her memory, this country existed only as darkness, wind, and rain, a landscape reduced to what lightning permitted in half-second flashes. She had walked through this same ground soaking wet, her world contracted to a few yards in front of her. Now, in the clear mid-July daylight, the land revealed itself as though pulling back a curtain she hadn't known was hanging.

The valley floor stretched on for miles, carpeted in bunchgrass that was shimmering green and stood waist-high. Sagebrush grew in patches among the grass, its gray-green leaves giving off a sharp, medicinal scent when the wagon wheels crushed the plants growing close to the road's edge. The road itself was packed earth, dry and rutted from wagon traffic, and it ran through the grass like a line drawn by someone who had measured the most direct course between two points and then followed it without apology.

To the east, the Absaroka Mountain Range filled half the sky. The mountains rose from the valley floor with vertical authority. Timbered slopes climbed thousands of feet above the valley, lodgepole pine and fir standing so dense the individual trees blurred into a single mass of color. Above the timber, the rock began, gray and rust-colored, broken into ridgelines and cliff faces that climbed to peaks.

To the west, the Gallatin Mountain Range rose in a long, dark wall of timbered ridges running north to south. Less dramatic than the Absarokas but completing the sense of enclosure so thoroughly that the valley felt like a room with the ceiling removed.

The wagon rolled through the creek, water barely reaching the iron rims, and climbed the opposite bank with a lurch that pressed Clair's shoulder against the sideboards. She steadied herself and smoothed the skirt of her dress over her knees.

The dress she wore was her own. The one she'd arrived in, cleaned of its mud and pressed with Lydia's flatiron yesterday. She had debated the choice that morning in the gray light before dawn, standing in Lydia's room with the dress held at arm's length, examining the seams and the fabric. The tailored waist and the covered buttons running from collar to bodice. The fabric itself, a dark blue, too fine for ranch country. Everything about the dress announced the life she'd come from, and everything about it would be read by the people she was about to meet. Lydia had a Sunday dress she'd offered, but Clair had chosen her own. If the community was going to assess her, she preferred they assess what was true.

From the bench seat at the front of the wagon, Lydia turned her head partway and spoke over her shoulder. "I'll introduce you, most likely after the church service. Today you'll meet Reverend Webb and Eunice Hale. As well as Leora Hanscombe, who owns the boardinghouse, and Amos and Margaret Pemberton from the mercantile."

"How will you introduce me?" Clair asked.

"As a young woman who has been helping with the household and with Emma's education." Lydia said. "That is the truth, and it's enough."

"Thank you, Lydia," she said.

"Don't thank me yet," Lydia said. "Small towns have long memories and sharp eyes. You'll do fine if you remember that the people here are kind, but they are also curious, and curiosity in a town this size is a working tool, not an idle one."

Adam said nothing. His attention stayed on the road and the team, his hands steady on the reins, his hat set low against the sun. He wore a clean shirt, dark trousers, and a vest Clair hadn't seen before, and his boots had been brushed.

Clair straightened her collar and folded her hands in her lap as the road curved east around a low rise, and the Yellowstone River came into view.

The river ran wide and fast across the valley floor, its current visible in the broken surface where water piled against submerged rocks and slid over gravel bars. The bridge was new, its timbers still pale and ungrayed, spanning the river on heavy pilings that stood in the current without trembling. The wagon's wheels changed their sound when they crossed from packed earth to planking, the hollow drumming of wood beneath iron rims marking the transition from ranch country to the town's domain.

Clair watched the river pass beneath them through the gaps between the bridge planks. The water was fast and clear, and the sound of it filled the wagon bed with a low, constant rush that vibrated in her chest.

On the far side of the bridge, the road followed a gentle curve southward, and Providence Ridge began to assemble itself ahead of them like an inventory coming into count. First a fence line, then a shed, then a corral with two horses standing hip-shot in the shade of a lean-to. A quarter mile on, the first proper buildings appeared on either side of the road, small frame houses set back from the wagon ruts with kitchen gardens visible behind them and woodpiles stacked along their sides. Then the road widened and straightened, and the town's center came into full view.

Main Street was a wide dirt road flanked by buildings on both sides. Wooden boardwalks connected the storefronts, raised on timber frames above the road surface. Hitching rails ran along the boardwalk edges at intervals, and a few wagons sat alongside the road. To the east, Clair could see the false front of the mercantile, a two-story building with a squared face and a wide porch. Directly across the road stood the boardinghouse, also two stories, timber-framed, with a broad front porch and benches on either side of the entrance.

The town was smaller than she had imagined. Lydia's description in the kitchen that first week had prepared her for modest, but "modest" in Helena terms and modest in Providence Ridge terms occupied different categories entirely. Helena had brick and gas lamps and streets that could hold four wagons abreast. Providence Ridge had one road, a handful of buildings, and the mountains.

Fresh-cut lumber showed pale against older, grayed siding on several buildings. A fence along the south end of the road stood half-finished, its posts set but its rails not yet hung. The boardwalks were solid and level, but they ended abruptly past the last storefront, giving way to bare ground and foot-worn paths. Every surface told her that this town was still in the act of becoming, still adding boards and driving nails, still assembling itself into something it hadn't fully decided to be.

And yet, the smallness registered as something other than a lack. Clair looked at the single street, the handful of buildings, and the mountains standing on every horizon, and she felt a loosening in her chest. This wasn't a place where powerful men came looking. The very quality that made Providence Ridge small also made it invisible, and invisibility was the only thing Clair cared for at this point.

Adam pulled the wagon to the boardinghouse and set the brake. The team stood quietly, their ears tipped toward the open door of the building where voices carried out into the street.

He climbed down from the bench seat and came around to Lydia's side. He offered his arm, and his mother lowered herself from the wagon seat. Adam held steady until she was standing steadily, then released her arm and turned toward the back of the wagon.

Emma was already on her feet and standing at the back of the wagon bed, arms extended toward him. He lifted her out and set her on the ground, and she smoothed her dress.

Adam looked at Clair and extended his hand toward her without speaking, his palm open and turned upward.

His hand closed around hers with a firm grip, his fingers rough with calluses.

"Thank you, Mr. Dawson," she said.

He nodded and turned to check the team's ties.

Clair smoothed her skirt and followed Lydia and Emma into the boardinghouse.

The dining room had been rearranged for worship. The long tables that normally served boarders and travelers had been pushed against the walls, and chairs were set in rows facing the far end of the room, where a small table held an open Bible and a water pitcher. The arrangement was practical and unadorned, a room repurposed for a function it had not been designed to serve, and the practicality of it struck Clair. In Helena, First Presbyterian had stained glass, an organ, and polished pews.

People were filing in, greeting each other with the ease of a community where every face was known and every absence noted. Clair counted over thirty people already seated or standing along the walls, with more coming through the door behind her.

Lydia led Clair and Emma to chairs near the front, three seats together on the left side of the makeshift aisle. Emma sat between Clair and Lydia, and before she was fully settled, she laced her small fingers through Clair's.

Along the far wall, a side table held several covered dishes and plates brought by community members. Beside them, a large coffeepot sat on a trivet. Lydia had mentioned there would be fellowship after the service.

Clair glanced over her shoulder and found Adam standing against the back wall with his hat in his hands.

She turned back to the front as a man stepped to the front of the room, and the conversation around her settled into quiet. Reverend Webb Hale was lean with a weathered face. His beard was white and kept short, close to his jaw. His hands were large, the knuckles scarred, and his fingers were thick. He wore dark trousers, a clean white shirt, and a vest.

"Good morning," he said, and his voice carried across the room without strain.

The congregation responded, their voices overlapping in a warm, uncoordinated murmur.

"We'll begin with a hymn," Webb said. "Page forty-three for those who have a hymnal."

He began to sing the first line alone, setting the pitch and the tempo for the congregation to follow. "Abide with me; fast falls the eventide."

There was no organ, no piano, nor pitched pipe to hold the melody true.

Clair sang the words and enjoyed the surrounding voices, imperfect and earnest and present.

After the hymn ended, Webb opened the Bible on the table before him. "The Lord is my shepherd," he read. "I shall not want. He maketh me to lie down in green pastures; he leadeth me beside the still waters. He restoreth my soul: he leadeth me in the paths of righteousness for his name's sake."

"Yea, though I walk through the valley of the shadow of death, I will fear no evil: for thou art with me; thy rod and thy staff they comfort me."

Clair had walked through a valley. In darkness, in rain, in the kind of fear that strips everything from a person except the next step.

"Thou preparest a table before me in the presence of mine enemies: thou anointest my head with oil; my cup runneth over. Surely goodness and mercy shall follow me all the days of my life, and I will dwell in the house of the Lord forever."

Webb closed the Bible and rested his hands on the table's edge and looked out at the people in the room..

"Every shepherd knows," he said, "that a sheep will choose its own pasture if given the chance. It will find the grass that looks greenest and the water that runs closest, and it will stay there until the grass is gone and the water has turned to mud, because a sheep's judgment about what it needs and what the shepherd knows it needs are rarely the same thing."

He let the sentence rest for a moment.

"The psalm doesn't say the Lord is my advisor. It doesn't say the Lord is my suggestion. It says the Lord is my shepherd, and a shepherd doesn't ask the sheep where it would like to go. A shepherd leads. And the sheep's only task is to follow. To lie down in the pasture, the shepherd has chosen, not the one the sheep would have picked for itself. To walk beside the waters, the shepherd has found, not the ones the sheep stumbled across on its own."

He spoke without notes, his scarred hands resting on the table, his voice carrying across the room. There was no performance in it. No flourish, no rise to a dramatic pitch, no moment designed to produce tears or conviction by volume. He spoke the way a neighbor spoke across a fence about the condition of the hay or the likelihood of rain, and the plainness of his delivery gave the words a credibility that polish would have stolen.

"As a young man, I spent time choosing my own pasture," Webb said. "I spent a fair portion of that time wondering why the grass kept running out. It took me longer than I care to admit that the running out was the lesson. God doesn't redirect us with a voice from the clouds. He redirects us by letting the pasture we chose go dry so that we're thirsty enough to follow when He leads us to the water He had in mind all along."

"Let us pray."

Heads bowed throughout the room, and Webb's prayer was brief and plain, asking for provision and guidance and the grace to trust what was provided even when it arrived in forms the recipient hadn't ordered. The prayer ended with a collective amen that moved through the room in a wave of quiet voices.

The room shifted as people rose from their chairs and began speaking to one another. Several women moved toward the side table where the covered dishes waited, removing cloths and arranging plates and cups. A woman standing near the coffeepot began pouring cups of coffee. She was sturdy and direct in her bearing, with iron-gray hair pinned with a severity that matched the set of her jaw, and her apron was spotless.

Lydia rose from her chair and touched Clair's elbow. "Come," she said.

Lydia walked toward Reverend Hale and Clair, and Emma followed.

"Lydia," Webb said. "Good to see you this morning."

"Lovely sermon, Reverend," Lydia said as she turned and gestured toward Clair. "This is Clair Whitmore, a young woman who has been helping with our household and with Emma's education."

Webb extended his hand to Clair. "Miss Whitmore, welcome to Providence Ridge. I hope the valley has been treating you kindly."

"It has, Reverend Hale. Very much so."

A woman stepped forward. She was shorter than Webb, round-faced, and bright-eyed.

"I'm Eunice, Webb's wife. Where are you from, dear? How are you finding the valley? It must be quite different from what you're accustomed to. I can tell from your dress that you're not from ranch country, and I mean that as a compliment because the fabric is lovely, and I haven't seen covered buttons like those since my sister sent a catalog from Chicago a year ago."

"I'm from Helena," Clair said. "And the valley is quite different from what I'm accustomed to, but I've found it very welcoming."

"Helena! Well, that explains it. My cousin's husband works for the railroad up there, and he says you can hardly walk down the street without bumping into someone important or someone who thinks they're important, which he says amounts to the same thing."

"Eunice," Webb said.

"I'm being friendly, Webb." She turned back to Claire. "You must come visit us sometime. We stay here at the boarding house for a few days when Webb preaches. Our daughter and son-in-law live here, just past the livery on the south side of the road, in the house with the blue shutters. I'm there quite a bit when we're in town, and my daughter always has coffee on and usually has a cake or some fritters baked. Do you bake? I imagine Lydia has you baking."

"I've been learning to bake a few things from Lydia," Clair said. "She's a patient teacher."

"She is. She has the patience of Job and the standards of a bishop." Eunice patted Clair's arm. "I'm glad you're here, dear. The Dawson home has needed another pair of hands for such a long time."

Lydia excused themselves and steered Clair toward the side table.

"Leora," Lydia said. "This is Clair Whitmore. She's helping us in our home and providing Emma with an education while she's here."

Leora Hanscombe's gaze moved over Clair.

"Miss Whitmore, how do you do? I'm Leora Ridgway, owner of this fine establishment," Leora said as she held out a cup. "Coffee?"

"Thank you, Ms. Hanscombe."

"Leora will do." She poured a second cup and handed it to Lydia, then looked at Emma. "There's a plate of your favorite sugar cookies on the far end of the table, Emma. Your grandmother will say whether you may have one."

Emma looked up at Lydia.

"One," Lydia said. "We mustn't spoil your dinner."

Emma released Clair's hand and moved toward the cookie plate, and Leora watched her go, then turned back to Clair. "Where are you from, dear?"

"Helena."

"Long way from home."

"It is."

Leora held her gaze for a beat. "Well. Lydia doesn't bring just anyone into her home. If she's decided you belong at her table, that tells me what I need to know for now." She picked up a cloth and wiped the rim of the coffeepot. "If you need anything while you're settling in, don't be afraid to come find me."

"Thank you, Leora. I appreciate that."

Lydia moved on, and Clair followed. They had crossed half the room when a man stepped into their path, medium in height, with thinning hair combed carefully over his crown and eyes that held attentiveness.

"Lydia, good morning," he said. "I see you've brought company."

"Amos Pemberton, it's good to see you. This is Clair Whitmore. She's been helping with our household and with Emma's schooling."

Amos took Clair's hand briefly. "Miss Whitmore. Welcome to Providence Ridge. If you need supplies, the mercantile is across the road, and I keep a fair account."

"Thank you, Mr. Pemberton."

"Reverend Hale mentioned you're from Helena."

"That's correct. Word spreads fast, I see."

He nodded and grinned. "That it does. Good supply lines come out of Helena. Are you related to the Whitmores that own the freight business there, by any chance?"

The question startled Clair. "Yes. My father owned it. He passed away some months ago."

"I'm sorry to hear it. I never had business dealings with your father, but sat with him in a few territory meetings over the past several years," Amos said. "If you find yourself in need of anything at all, come see us. Margaret dear, come say hello."

A woman stood nearby, shorter and rounder, with a face that carried open warmth and the practiced smile of someone who had spent years greeting every person who walked through a mercantile door. She took Clair's hand in both of hers.

"I'm Margaret, Amos's better half. What a pleasure to meet you," Margaret said. "You must come into the mercantile when you get a chance. I'll show you everything we carry, and if there's something we don't have, Amos can order it from Livingston. It takes a week or two, but everything arrives eventually. How are you finding things at the ranch? Are you comfortable? Is there anything you need?"

"I'm quite comfortable, thank you. The Dawson family has been very generous."

"Lydia is a generous soul. And that little Emma is a treasure. She's grown an inch since spring, I promise you she has." Margaret leaned closer. "And between you and me, I think it does Lydia a world of good having another woman in the house. She's been managing that place alone for far too long, and I don't know how she's done it for as long as she has."

Clair accepted this with a nod, without encouraging further discussion.

Emma returned from the cookie table and reclaimed her position at Clair's side, pressing close against her arm with a sugar cookie in her hand.

Lydia continued to speak with Margaret, and Clair moved to the side table with Emma. The fellowship continued around them, voices rising and falling. Through the front windows she could see the street and the mercantile across the road and the mountains beyond.

She looked toward the back of the room and noticed that Adam was gone. She hadn't seen him leave and assumed he had slipped out the way Lydia said he did, after the closing prayer and before the fellowship began.

The fellowship continued for another half hour before Lydia returned and collected them. They walked out into the bright midday, crossed the porch, and descended the steps to the street. Adam sat on the bench seat of the wagon with his forearms resting on his knees, his hat pushed back on his head.

He climbed down when he saw them and came around to Lydia's side first and offered his arm, steadying her as she climbed up to the bench. Then he walked to the back of the wagon.

Emma raised her arms, and he lifted her over the tailgate and set her on the folded blanket. She settled immediately and pulled her knees up.

Adam turned to Clair and offered his hand again. She swung her leg over the tailgate into the bed of the wagon and sat beside Emma.

"Did you enjoy the service, Miss Whitmore?"

"I did," Clair said. "Very much. Reverend Hale's message was one of the finest I've heard in quite some time."

Adam held her gaze for a moment. "Webb's services are enjoyable."

He nodded and walked to the front of the wagon. He climbed up to the bench seat, gathered the reins, and released the brake. The wagon lurched forward, and the team pulled them north along Main Street.

Clair sat in the wagon bed with Emma leaning against her shoulder and watched Providence Ridge grow smaller behind them.

Eventually, Emma's breathing slowed; the business of the day had brought a drowsiness that would have the child asleep before they reached the bridge. Clair rested her chin against the top of Emma's head and looked east, where the Absarokas stood in the full blaze of noon. Their peaks sharp and clear against a sky so wide it could hold everything she was afraid of and still have room for the things she was beginning to hope for.

Chapter 12

Adam braced his boot against the base of the fence post and leaned into the come-along, pulling the wire taut between the anchor post and the corner where the fence line turned south along the hayfield. He released the come-along and tested the wire with his gloved hand. It sang back at him, tight and true, and he let the line go and stepped back to check the spacing from the post below.

The boundary between the hayfield and the grazing pasture had to hold before the harvest started. Once the mowing began and the cut hay lay in windrows drying in the sun, cows pushing through a weak fence could devour a day's work flat in a matter of hours.

He pulled his gloves off and hung them over the top rail, then crouched beside the post to check the base. The ground here was dry and packed from a week without rain; the grass around the post's footing cropped short where the cattle had grazed along the fence line.

He stood and looked across the field. The timothy stood waist-high and thick; the seed heads formed and had begun to lean under their fullness. A good stand. Better than last year's, which had come in thin after a dry June. This year the rain had held through the first week of July, and the crop had been given what it needed at the right time.

He looked toward the house and saw Lydia, Clair, and Emma cross the yard toward the barn. Emma was between them, holding Clair's hand, and even from this distance he could see the bounce in his daughter's step. He watched them disappear through the barn's open doors and then turned back to his work.

The next post needed resetting because it was leaning a few inches off plumb, enough to slacken the wire on both sides. He dug around the footing with the posthole bar, working the iron point into the packed earth and levering out clods that broke apart dry and pale in his hands.

He was tamping the reset post with the flat end of the bar when he looked up and saw Clair in front of the barn.

She had both arms raised above her head, waving them in wide, crossing arcs, and her voice carried across the distance in fragments that the breeze tore apart before they reached him whole. He dropped the bar and started toward her at a run.

The ground between the fence line and the barn was uneven, tufted with bunchgrass and pocked with gopher holes, and he covered it at a pace that made his boot heels strike hard enough to jar his knees. Clair stood where she was, her arms down now, watching him.

He reached her, breathing hard, and stopped. "What is it?"

"Something's wrong with Mercy," Clair said.

Adam was past her and through the barn doors before she finished the sentence.

He moved down the center aisle of the barn to the stall, where Mercy lay on her side in the deep straw. Lydia stood just outside the stall door with Emma pressed against her hip, one hand resting on the child's shoulder.

"She went down moments ago," Lydia said. "She'd been pacing the stall when we came in, circling and pawing at the straw. Then she went down hard on her left side, and she's been there since. Her water's broken, Adam."

He looked at the mare. Mercy's barrel rose and fell in deep, uneven draws, her chest expanding and contracting with an effort that was visible from ten feet away. Her neck was extended, her nostrils flared wide, and the muscles along her flank rippled in contractions that moved in waves from her hindquarters forward.

He stepped into the stall and crouched beside the mare's hindquarters. The foal's presentation was visible, but Mercy was fighting it. As he watched, she groaned and lurched, throwing her front legs forward in an attempt to stand. She got her chest off the straw, and her front hooves scrabbled against the packed earth beneath. Then the contraction hit again, and she went back down with a heavy, shuddering drop that sent straw scattering against the stall walls.

"Easy," Adam said. He put his hand on her hip and held it there, firm and flat, letting her feel his presence without startling her. "Easy, girl."

He looked back toward the stall door where his mother stood with Emma and Clair, watching.

"If she stands and goes back down again during a contraction, she could injure the foal. I need someone to hold her head and keep her down on her side," Adam said.

Lydia looked at her hands and flexed them once, and the slow, careful movement told Adam everything her voice didn't. She couldn't hold a thrashing mare's head steady. The arthritis had taken that from her the same way it had taken the bread kneading, the heavy pot lifting, and a dozen other tasks, one by one.

"Clair," Lydia said. "Stay here with Adam."

"I've never done anything like this," she said.

"Makes no difference. Listen to Adam and do as he says," Lydia said as she took Emma's hand and turned toward the barn doors. "Come along, Emma. You and I are going to take a short walk, and then we'll start on supper."

"But Grandma, I want to see the foal."

"You'll see it when it's here. Right now Mercy needs quiet, and I need to stretch my legs."

Their footsteps crossed the barn floor and faded through the open doors, and then the barn was quiet except for the mare's labored breathing and the rustle of straw as her legs moved against it.

Clair stood at the stall door with her hands at her sides, and Adam could see the tremor in her fingers.

"Come in here," he said. "Come around to her head."

Clair entered and knelt in the straw near Mercy's head and looked at Adam.

"Put her head across your lap," he said. "Both hands on her neck. When she tries to get up, lean your weight into her shoulder and talk to her. Keep your voice low and steady. Don't let her stand."

"What do I say to her?"

"It doesn't matter what you say. She'll listen to the sound, not the words. Just keep talking."

Clair gathered her skirt beneath her knees and settled lower in the straw, then slid both hands under the mare's jaw and lifted Mercy's heavy head onto her thighs. The mare's eye rolled toward her, the white showing at the rim, and a tremor ran through the long muscles of her neck. Clair placed one hand flat against the side of Mercy's face and held the other against her neck, her fingers spread wide, and she began to speak.

"You're all right," she said. "You're all right, Mercy. I know this is hard, and you're tired, but you're doing so well. Just stay here with me. Stay right here."

The next contraction was building in the muscles along Mercy's flank, the ripple starting deep and rolling forward like a wave crossing a pond. When it hit, the mare groaned and threw her head.

"Steady," Clair said. "Steady, girl. Stay down. I've got you."

The mare's legs churned in the straw, but she didn't rise. Clair held her, and Adam watched the foal's hooves extend another inch with the contraction before the effort eased and the mare's body settled.

"Good," he said. "Just like that. Keep her there."

He positioned himself behind the mare and waited for the next contraction. When it came, the hooves pushed forward, and the muzzle cleared, and he could see the foal's face pressed between its front legs, the thin membrane of the birth sac stretched across its features. The contraction faded, and the progress stopped.

Mercy threw her head again, and from the other end of the stall, Clair's voice continued, unbroken, the cadence of it carrying a quality Adam registered in the back of his mind while his hands worked. She sounded nurturing and loving, like a woman who had comforted a child waking from a bad dream.

"I need to help with the shoulders," he said. "They're caught. When the next contraction comes, I'm going to pull. She'll fight it. Hold her."

"I have her," Clair said.

The contraction built. Adam gripped the foal's forelegs above the fetlocks, his hands slick, and when the wave of muscle crested, he pulled downward and toward Mercy's hocks in a steady, firm draw that worked with the mare's effort rather than against it. The foal's shoulders resisted, held, and then gave, one shoulder sliding free and then the other in a sudden release that sent the rest of the foal onto the straw in a rush.

Mercy's head came up from Clair's lap, and the mare's whole body shuddered, a deep, rolling tremor that traveled from her hindquarters to her ears. Adam sat back on his heels and looked at the foal lying on the straw.

It lay still for two seconds. Then a foreleg moved, straightening against the straw, and the foal's ribcage expanded with its first breath, a hitching, stuttering intake that lifted its thin sides and held them for a beat before releasing in a soft exhale. The foal blinked, its eyes dark and unfocused, seeing light for the first time.

"She did it," Clair said.

Adam watched the foal's second breath come easier than the first, the rhythm already finding its pace. The foal was small and dark, its coat slicked flat against its body, its legs folded beneath it at angles that looked impossible. He leaned forward and cleared the remaining membrane from around its nostrils and mouth, working with his fingers until the airway was fully open. The foal sneezed once and shook its head with a motion so sudden and indignant that it startled itself.

Mercy lifted her head and turned to look behind her. Clair moved out of the way as the mare adjusted herself to reach the foal and began to clean it .

Adam stood and stepped back to the stall wall to give the mare room to work. His shirt was soaked through with sweat, and straw clung to his knees, his boots, and the front of his trousers. His hands ached from the grip he'd held during the pull.

Clair was still kneeling near where the mare's head had lain. Her skirt was covered in straw. A strand of hair had come loose from its pins and hung along the side of her face. She was watching the mare clean the foal with an expression Adam had never seen on her in the two weeks she'd been at the ranch. Every layer of composure she carried, every careful arrangement of her features, had come undone. She looked at the mare and the foal with her lips parted and her eyes bright with moisture, and her face held nothing back.

The foal moved beneath its mother's attention, its legs unfolding from the angles they'd been pressed into. One front leg extended, then the other, and the foal pushed against the straw with its hindquarters. Its first attempt to stand was pure ambition and no coordination; the front end rising while the back end stayed where it was, the whole effort collapsing sideways into the straw after seconds of concentrated striving.

Clair made a small sound, a breath caught between laughter and something else.

The foal tried again. This time both front legs went forward, and the hind legs gathered underneath. For one trembling second, the foal stood, its legs splayed wide, its head bobbing, the entirety of its body vibrating with the effort of holding itself upright against a force it had never encountered before. Then a hind leg buckled, and the foal went down in a heap, its legs folding beneath it like fence posts rotted at the base.

"Come on," Clair said, her words barely above speaking volume.

The foal shook its head and tried a third time. Front legs, hind legs, the lurch upward, the wobble, the full-body tremor of muscles finding the work they were made for. It stood. It swayed. Its head dropped and rose and dropped again, searching, and then its legs carried it in three lurching, unsteady steps toward Mercy's flank, where it pushed its muzzle against the mare's side and began to nurse.

Clair pressed her hand over her mouth, and tears ran down her face as she watched the foal nurse for the first time.

Adam stood against the stall wall with his arms at his sides, his breathing still settling from the work. The barn was quiet around them, except for the small, rhythmic sounds of the foal nursing and the mare's deep, contented breathing.

Clair stood and wiped her face with the back of her hand, and the gesture smeared a line of dirt across her cheek. She turned to Adam, and her face was open and unguarded and wet with tears. She stepped forward and put her arms around him and pressed her face against his chest, and held on.

Adam's body locked. His arms stayed at his sides, his hands open, his fingers rigid against the seams of his trousers. The contact registered in him the way a sound registers in a house that has been empty for a long time, loud and foreign and echoing through rooms that had forgotten what occupancy felt like. Her arms were tight around him, and her forehead rested against the hollow of his collarbone. The specific, physical fact of another person holding him voluntarily sent a shock through his chest that had nothing to do with surprise and everything to do with the six years of nothingness that preceded it.

He didn't move. He stood in the straw with his dirty shirt and his aching hands and let himself be held. The seconds passed, three of them, four, each one landing in a place inside him that he had bricked over and mortared shut and considered permanently closed.

Clair released him and stepped back, and as she did, her composure returned in visible stages, the way a gate swings closed after the wind that opened it dies. She wiped her face again and pressed her hands flat against the front of her skirt and straightened her shoulders.

"I'm sorry, Mr. Dawson. I don't know what came over me. I shouldn't have done that."

He looked at her. The streak of dirt on her cheek. The strand of hair was still loose at her temple. The straw caught in the fabric of her sleeve. Her eyes, reddened from the tears she hadn't tried to hide, met his with the steadiness of a woman who was embarrassed and refused to look away from it.

"Don't apologize," he said. "This ranch hasn't had that kind of joy in it for a long time. It needed some."

Clair held his gaze for a moment and then turned to stand beside him as she watched Mercy.

They stood side by side in the stall, close enough that Adam could feel the warmth of her near him. The foal nursed with its eyes closed, its legs braced wide, its dark coat beginning to dry in patches that showed the lighter color underneath. Mercy's breathing was slow and deep; the crisis of the last hour already passing into the ordinary rhythm of a mother tending what she'd brought into the world.

Adam could still feel the specific pressure where Clair's head had rested, the exact spot below his collarbone where the contact had landed. The tingly sensation didn't fade the way a touch was supposed to fade when it was over.

The foal turned its head toward them, its eyes open and curious, seeing the world in its first hour with the blank, astonished attention of a creature for whom everything was new.

Chapter 13

The colt's legs were planted in the straw, his small hooves braced at angles that looked improvised but kept him upright while his dark eyes tracked Emma's fingers along the bottom rail of the stall. Two days ago those same legs had buckled after the trembling effort of trying to stand for the first time.

"She's watching me," Emma said. "See? Every time I move my hand, she looks."

"He, Emma... it's a colt," Clair said.

"He's watching me."

"He is. You're the most interesting thing in this barn."

The colt tracked them, his ears pricked forward, his muzzle bobbing in small investigative jerks toward the rail before Mercy swung her head around and nudged him back, the broad flat of her nose pressing the colt sideways until he gave up his expedition and returned to nursing.

"Will he always have to stay with his mama?" Emma asked.

"For a while," Clair said. "He's too young to be on his own. He needs Mercy's milk, and he needs to learn from her."

"Learn what?"

"How to be a horse, I expect. How to eat grass and drink from a trough and walk without falling over."

"He falls over a lot."

"He does, but he'll soon be steadier."

Emma pulled her chin from the rail and looked up at Clair. "Does he have a name?"

"I don't think so," Clair said.

"Who gets to name him?"

"I imagine that's your father's decision."

"I want to name him." Emma said. "Grandma named Mercy and Solomon. I'm old enough to name something."

"You may well be," Clair said. "But you'll need to ask your father."

Emma returned her attention to the stall, pressing her face between the rails to watch the colt nurse. The foal's tail moved in small, contented flicks.

Clair leaned her shoulder against the post beside the stall door and let the quiet of the barn settle over her. She'd come here with Emma after the midday dishes were washed and put away, partly because Emma had been asking about the foal since breakfast and partly because Clair wanted to see him herself.

"Papa!" Emma said as she turned. "He's standing, and he's only fallen down once so far."

"He's still getting used to his legs," Adam said.

"It was barely a fall; it was more like sitting down . He just sort of went down on his back legs, and then he stood right back up again."

Adam set his hat on the hook beside the stall and stepped beside Clair to look over the rail.

He studied the colt for a long moment.

"He's getting stronger," Adam said. "His barrel's filling out, and he's got better purchase on those hind legs. Another week and he'll be ready for the paddock if the weather stays fair."

"Papa," Emma said. "Can I name him?"

Adam looked down at his daughter.

"Grandma named Mercy and Solomon. I haven't named anything yet. I'm six... isn't that old enough to name an animal?"

He looked at the colt, then back at Emma. "All right. What's his name?"

Emma turned to the stall and studied the foal with a concentration that drew her brows together and made her press her lips into a line Clair had seen before during difficult letter-tracing.

"Sunrise," Emma said. "Because he's that color. The color the mountains are when the sun comes up and the tops go all orange and red before the rest of the mountain wakes up."

Adam looked at the colt. The lighter chestnut of his coat did hold something of the warm, reddish cast that the Absaroka peaks caught at first light.

"Sunrise," Adam said. "That'll do."

Emma's face broke open with a smile. "Sunrise," she told the colt. "That's your name now. Sunrise."

Adam opened the stall door and went in. Clair watched him run his hand along Mercy's barrel and down her flank. He then crouched and ran both hands along the colt's front legs, pressing lightly at the joints and watching the animal's response. Sunrise shifted under the attention but didn't startle, and Adam moved to the hind legs and repeated the check.

"Legs are straight," he said. "No heat in the joints. He's nursing strongly, and Mercy's producing well." He stood and wiped his hands on his trousers. "Give it four or five more days, and we can turn them out into the small paddock in the mornings when it's cool."

"Can I be there when he goes outside for the first time?" Emma asked.

"If you stay by the fence and do what I tell you."

"I will."

Adam came out of the stall and closed the door behind him.

"The other day," Adam said as he moved to stand beside Clair. "When you were holding Mercy's head and talking her through the contractions."

"Yes."

"You spoke to her the way a person speaks to a child who's frightened. Calm and steady. You have natural mothering instincts."

Clair looked at Mercy. "I spent time at the orphanage in Helena," she said. "Saint Anne's on the west end of town. Many Saturdays I went and stayed through the day to help where I could, and sometimes through the night when they needed me. They were often short of help."

Adam turned his head toward her. "An orphanage?"

"It was something I could do that felt useful in a way the business didn't always feel useful. Ledgers are honest work, but they don't cry at two in the morning or need their forehead cooled or someone to sit beside them and read until they fall asleep. My time spent with those children filled me with great joy."

Adam was quiet for a moment.

"That explains a great deal," he said. "You're very good with Emma, and when you were holding Mercy down and talking her through the worst of it, it was the steadiest I've seen anyone handle an animal they'd never worked with. That kind of calm doesn't come from nowhere. Your soothing voice really helped her, I believe."

"Thank you, Mr. Dawson."

Emma sat on a hay bale near the stall, her legs swinging, her attention still fixed on the colt.

"I'd like to know more about your life in Helena," Adam said. "If you're willing to tell me. You've been here more than two weeks now, and I know you helped your father with his business and you lost your mother at a young age. Beyond that, I don't know much."

"What would you like to know?"

"What you did. What your work was like. I've been watching you run my home like a quartermaster's depot and ask about cattle counts the way a man asks about his bank balance, and I've been curious where it came from."

Clair let the question sit for a moment, measuring what information to give him.

"My father's business, Whitmore Freight and Supply," she said. "It was a mining supply and freight operation. We supplied mining camps throughout the territory with the things they needed to operate. Tools, blasting powder, timber supports for the mine shafts, food staples, dry goods, equipment. We ran freight wagons to camps that were too remote for the regular supply lines to reach."

"How many wagons?"

"At our peak, nineteen. Some of them ran routes that took four days each direction, depending on the roads, the weather, and the condition of the mountain passes. My father built the operation from one wagon and a contract with a single mine foreman when I was a very young child. By the time I was old enough to help, our company supplied many camps and employed several men: drivers, loaders, and a warehouse clerk."

"And you kept the books."

"I tracked shipments against invoices," Clair said. "Over time, I also managed the correspondence with suppliers. I read shipping manifests and compared them against what was received, and when the figures didn't reconcile, I found where the error was. Sometimes it was an honest error, a miscount, or a transposed number. As of most recently, it wasn't."

"And you could tell the difference."

"Arithmetic doesn't have opinions, Mr. Dawson. A column of figures either balances or it doesn't. If it doesn't, there's a reason, and the reason is always in the numbers if you're willing to follow them far enough."

Adam watched her while she spoke, and his attention had the quality of a man listening to something he was fitting into a picture he'd been assembling from separate pieces.

"Was it work you enjoyed?" he asked.

"I loved it," Clair said. "I loved the precision of it. The way a well-kept ledger tells the truth even when the people around it are being careless or dishonest. I loved the order of it, the way every transaction has a place and every figure answers to the figure before it and the one after. My father trusted me with the majority of his business books, and he trusted me with the correspondence, and he trusted me with details that most men in his position wouldn't have trusted a daughter with. I was his assistant in everything but title."

"That's a considerable thing for a young woman in this territory," Adam said.

"It was a considerable thing for any woman anywhere," Clair said. "My father didn't see it that way. He saw a person who was good with numbers and letters, and who noticed when things were out of order, and he put that person to work."

The barn was quiet around them. Mercy pulled hay into her mouth in long, slow tears. Sunrise had finished nursing and stood beside his mother with his head drooping in the drowsy surrender of an animal whose stomach was full. Emma had a piece of straw and was threading it through her fingers, weaving it under and over in a pattern Clair had taught her two days ago.

"Is it something you hope to go back to someday?" Adam asked.

Clair looked at the ground. The question opened a door she kept latched, and behind it was a room she hadn't organized yet.

Adam noticed the change in her demeanor right away.

"I'm sorry," he said. "I shouldn't have asked that."

She looked up. "It's a fair question. It's just a hard one to answer." She watched Emma threading the straw, the child's fingers moving in careful loops, and chose her words the way she chose figures for a final tally, one at a time, each one tested before it was set down. "I believe I will have to go back to Helena, eventually. There are things to settle with my father's business and other matters I'm not ready to speak of. But that answer doesn't feel complete anymore, like it once would have."

"What do you mean?"

"These past two weeks," Clair said. "Being here has really made an impression on me. I've spent my entire life in Helena, Mr. Dawson. My entire life. The city was everything I knew, and the business was everything I did, and the routine of it was so familiar that I never thought to question whether it was the only life available to me. I never stopped to consider that a quieter life existed or that I might want it."

She turned toward the open barn door, where the view stretched past the yard and the fence line to the benchlands rising toward the Absarokas, the grass tall and various in shade. The mountains held their blue-gray distance against a sky that went on longer than any sky she'd seen from Helena's streets.

"I'd rarely left the city, and when I did, it was only to visit the outskirts of Helena... the mining camps, a bit of the countryside," she said. "I'd read about the broader Montana territory in the newspapers and in my father's correspondence. But I'd never seen any of it. I didn't know the mountains looked and felt like this... without all the noise and smog. I didn't know the air could feel like this. I didn't know a person could stand on a porch in the evening and watch the light change on a ridgeline for half an hour and not need anything else."

She stopped and gathered her thoughts for a moment.

"Being here has made me question what I want for myself," she said. "I hadn't allowed myself that question before. There wasn't room for it. But there's room here, and I find I quite enjoy it."

Adam was quiet for a long moment. "I understand that," he said. "From the other direction. This ranch and this valley are all I've ever known, and they're all I've ever wanted. When I go to Livingston for supplies, I go and I come back as fast as the team can manage. The noise of that town sets my teeth on edge. The trains, the wagons, the people on every corner talking at a volume that doesn't make sense when you've spent a lifetime hearing nothing louder than a creek and a horse. I load the wagon, and I start home as fast as I can, and I've been known to sleep under the wagon on the road rather than spend a night in town."

"You've never wanted to live somewhere else?"

"Not once. Everything I need is here. I couldn't tell you what's on the far side of those mountains, and I've never felt the lack of knowing."

Emma had finished her straw weaving and was watching Sunrise sleep standing up beside his mother, the colt's head bobbing in a slow rhythm.

"What happened after your father died, Clair?" Adam asked.

She'd been Miss Whitmore for over two weeks now, and the sound of her Christian name spoken in his voice struck her immediately.

"I've known since the day I found you in this barn that something terrible happened to send you here," he continued. "A woman doesn't travel for days through open country alone and sleep in a stranger's hayloft unless she's running from something worse than what she's running toward. I haven't pushed because it wasn't my place to push. But I'd like to know if you're willing to tell me. And if there's anything I can do to help, I will."

Clair looked at Emma on the hay bale, the child's legs swinging, her attention on the colt, her ears within range of every word spoken.

"After my father died, I grieved deeply. I stayed home and didn't tend to the business as I should have. I couldn't bring myself to go to work, and I trusted our employees to keep everything running. Our secretary and a few others would check in with me at home during the week and keep me updated," Clair said. "Eventually, I forced myself to go. I went through my father's records and office deeply. That is what an heir does. I needed to understand the state of the business and our personal affairs, which accounts were current, which debts were outstanding, which contracts needed to be honored or renegotiated, and so on."

"And you found something."

"I found discrepancies," she said. "Numbers that didn't reconcile. Transactions recorded in ledgers that didn't match what I could verify against the few receipts I was able to locate. Patterns in the figures that made no sense unless you assumed that someone had been altering them."

"And you suspect someone inside the business... not being honest?"

"Yes, I reviewed the records carefully, and I was thorough. I visited the bank and sat down with an official and combed through all the accounts. When I was certain of what I was looking at, I brought it to this man's attention that I suspected."

"And he didn't welcome the attention."

"He did not." Clair paused. She tilted her head toward Emma, a slight motion, the angle of it as precise as the notch in a surveyor's mark. Adam's eyes followed the gesture and then came back to hers, and the understanding that passed between them required no words.

"He made it clear that my observations were unwelcome," Clair said. "And a few other things besides. That is when I decided to leave, and now that I'm gone, I'm not sure what to do. Please, let's not speak on this any further for now, if you'll allow me to."

Adam nodded. "When we can talk more and you're ready to share, I'll listen."

"Very well. Thank you. Now... the hay harvest," she said. "When does the cutting start?"

"Two days from now, if the weather holds. The timothy's headed out, and the stems are curing. Another day of sun, and it'll be ready."

"How many men are coming?"

"Four. Two of them are day laborers I hired after church on Sunday. The other two are neighbors. Cal Stackhouse runs a place north of here in the valley, about three miles past the creek crossing. Jesse Mayhew has a smaller operation south, near the foothills. They come help me cut, and when their hay's ready, I go help them. That's how it works in this valley."

"Your mother mentioned the family whose ranch is being hayed feeds the crew. She said it was too much for her to manage alone last year."

"It was." He rubbed his thumb along the rail beside him. "The cooking for several men and bringing cold water to the fields was hard on her. It took her several days to recover."

"That won't happen this year," Clair said.

"I know it won't, and I'm grateful you're here to manage it."

"What will the men want to eat?"

"Whatever you make, make plenty. Cold meat, biscuits, beans if you've got the time. The men will eat what's put in front of them and be glad of it."

"Is there anything you'd like specifically?"

Adam thought about it. "Coffee," he said. "After the midday meal, if you can manage it. Strong coffee. My father used to say the second half of a haying day runs on coffee more than food, and I've found he was right about that the way he was right about most things."

"Very well. I'll speak with your mother this evening," Clair said. "We'll need to plan the meals and check the stores. If there's anything we're short of, may I use the wagon to go into town?"

"You may; the wagon is yours any time you need it."

Clair turned to Emma. "Emma, come along. We need to get back to the house and see to your father's supper."

Emma slid from the hay bale and took one last look at the colt through the stall rails. "Goodbye, Sunrise," she said. "I'll come see you tomorrow."

The colt slept against his mother's side now, and Emma crossed to Clair and took her hand.

Adam watched them from the stall and spoke before they reached the barn door.

"Clair."

She stopped and turned.

"My mother is calmer since you came," he said. "She doesn't worry the way she used to worry about the house, about Emma, and about whether things are being tended to the way they ought to be tended. She laughs more. I hear her laughing with you in the kitchen some days when I come in from work, and it's a sound I haven't heard from her in a long time." He paused. "The house runs the way it used to run before her health started failing. You did that. I want you to know I see it, and I appreciate you."

"I'm the one who should be grateful, Mr. Dawson," she said. "Your family took me in when I had nowhere to go and no claim to anyone's kindness. If it weren't for your mother and Emma and you, I don't know where I'd be right now." A chill passed through her at the thought, brief and involuntary. "You gave me a place to lay my head and peace in my heart while I consider the next steps for my life. I won't forget that."

Adam nodded.

"Come, Emma," Clair said.

***

Adam stood in the barn doorway and watched them cross the yard.

Clair walked with Emma's hand in hers. Emma's voice carried back to him in fragments, bright and ceaseless, and he watched Clair tilt her head toward his child and answer.

The sight of them made him smile.

Lord, he thought. I'm not sure why you brought this woman to our home or what your plans may be, but she's making a difference in our lives, and for that I thank you.

He watched as Clair and Emma disappeared inside his home, and he tried to see it the way it had looked a month ago. Before a woman with light-brown hair and city manners and blisters on her feet had appeared in his barn. He couldn't envision the old picture as much. The new one had been written over it.

He shook his head and pushed off the doorframe and went back into the barn to check the harness for the mowing machine. The hay cutting was coming in two days, and there was work to do.

Chapter 14

The sickle bar chattered through the timothy in a rapid, percussive rhythm. Adam held the reins steady in both hands and kept the team at a walk, the two draft horses leaning into their collars. Behind him the grass fell in long, even rows, the cut stems collapsing against one another. Cal Stackhouse followed two passes back on the hay rake. Cal was built solid, and he handled the rake with the unhurried ease of someone who had turned hay on his ground for a dozen seasons and didn't need instruction from anyone else. Jesse Mayhew and the two hired men worked the field edges. Jesse was lean and quiet, a man who kept his hat pulled low and his opinions lower. He swung his scythe with a rhythm that never varied, the blade whispering through the grass in long, curving arcs that left clean stubble behind. Tom Fergus and Dale Wilson worked the opposite edge, both of them young and strong enough to keep pace.

When the sun reached its midday height, Adam pulled the team to a stop at the end of the row and checked the sickle bar, running his gloved hand along the toothed edge to feel for nicks or bent sections. The blades were holding. He'd spent the better part of a day sharpening them before the harvest, filing each triangular tooth until the edge was clean and true. He wiped his forehead with his sleeve and looked across the field at what they'd done. A third of the timothy lay in windrows, the cut grass already beginning to pale as the sun drew the moisture from the stems.

Cal brought the rake alongside and stopped his team. "Drying fast," he said, looking at the nearest windrow. "If this sun keeps up, you'll have good hay."

"Ground's been dry enough to help," Adam said. "The stems aren't holding water the way they did last year."

"Last year was a poor cut all around. Mine came in thin, and half of it rained on before I could stack it. This is better grass. You'll get more tonnage per acre than you've seen in three seasons."

Adam nodded. He could see it in the density of the windrows, the way the cut timothy lay thick and close against the stubble. Good hay. Enough to carry eighty-two head through a Montana winter and still have a reserve against a bad March.

Jesse walked in from the far edge of the field, his scythe resting across his shoulder, and Tom and Dale followed, their sleeves rolled and their faces flushed from the morning's work. The five of them gathered near the cottonwoods where Adam had set up a makeshift table that morning: two sawhorses with planks laid across.

Adam looked up and watched as his small wagon came down the track from the yard, a single horse pulling it at a steady pace. Clair held the lines, and beside her sat Lydia with Emma between them, the child's legs swinging above the footboard.

Clair brought the wagon to a stop near the makeshift table and wrapped the lines around the brake handle. She climbed down and turned to help Lydia, offering her arm for the step down from the seat. The morning's kitchen work had brought color to her face, a flush across her cheekbones that the breeze at the field's edge did nothing to cool, and a strand of light brown hair had come loose from its pins and lay against the side of her neck. She tucked it behind her ear with her free hand while she steadied Lydia with the other.

"Papa!" Emma called as she ran toward him. When she reached him, she wrapped both arms around his leg, pressing her face against his trouser leg.

"You're all dirty," she said as she pulled back.

"I am," Adam said.

"Your face, too. There's grass in your hair."

He reached up and found the chaff tangled above his ear and brushed it away.

Clair had already begun setting out what she'd brought. She moved between the wagon bed and the table, setting each item in its place. Lydia stood nearby and supervised the arrangement.

"That's a spread," Cal said. "Looks like we'll be eatin' good today."

"I believe we will," Adam said as they began walking to the table.

"Gentlemen," Lydia said. "There's plenty, so eat your fill and don't be shy about seconds."

Cal nodded to her. "Mrs. Dawson, we appreciate the hospitality. Those beans smell as if they've been given serious attention."

"They have," Lydia said. "Since before dawn." She glanced at Clair, who was setting the last of the cups along the table's edge.

"Though I can't take full credit for them. Most of what you see here came from this young woman's hard work."

Clair looked up from the cups and acknowledged the men with a nod. "Please help yourselves," she said.

Cal extended his hand. "Cal Stackhouse, ma'am. I run the place north of here. Adam and I have been trading labor since his father's time."

Clair took his hand. "Clair Whitmore. It's a pleasure to meet you, Mr. Stackhouse."

Jesse stepped forward and removed his hat, holding it against his chest. "Jesse Mayhew, ma'am."

"Before we eat, let's bless the food," Cal said.

Cal bowed his head, and the others followed. "Lord, we thank You for this food and the hands that prepared it. We thank You for fair weather and good grass and the strength to bring it in. Bless this meal and this household, and keep us safe through the afternoon's work. Amen."

"Amen."

The men ate steadily after a morning of physical labor, their conversation coming in the pauses between bites. Emma sat on the grass near Lydia's feet with a plate balanced on her knees and a biscuit in one hand, and talked to anyone who would listen.

"That's the mowing machine," she told Cal, pointing across the field to where the machine sat at the end of its last row, the ash tongue angled toward the uncut grass. "My grandpa built part of it."

"Did he now?" Cal said.

"Yes, sir, my papa told me."

"Your grandpa was a fine craftsman," Cal said. "He built half the fence line between our two places, and every post he set is still standing."

"Papa says he built things to hold," Emma said.

Cal glanced at Adam over the rim of his cup. "He did."

Clair carried the coffeepot between the men as they ate beneath the cottonwoods, filling the cups that needed filling. She poured for Cal first, and then Jesse, and then Tom, and when she reached Dale, she said something to him that Adam couldn't hear, and Dale grinned and nodded and held his cup steady while she filled it. Adam watched her walk back toward the table and set the coffeepot down. She glanced his way as she straightened and smiled at him.

The meal wound down the way working meals do, the men eating until their plates were clean and their conversation slowing with their forks. Clair moved between them and collected the empty plates, carrying them in a stack back to the makeshift table. The men settled back against the cottonwood trunks with their coffee, hats tipped against the sun and boots stretched into the grass. Cal lay flat on his back. Jesse sat against a tree with his legs crossed. Tom and Dale talked between themselves in low voices. Lydia sat in the shade with Emma beside her, the child leaning against her grandmother's arm.

Adam stood and walked to where Clair was at the table. She was scraping the leavings from the plates into a scrap pail and stacking them, organizing the remaining food back into the containers she'd brought it in. The bean pot was nearly empty. The biscuit bowl held two. The beef platter had three slices left. The hand pies were gone.

"Thank you, Clair. The men and I appreciate your hard work," he said.

Clair set a plate into the stack. "I made more than I expected to need, and I still underestimated how much five men could eat."

"There was plenty, and it was all good."

Adam noticed that her face was flushed pink from the heat of the day.

"I don't want you fussing over supper tonight," he said. "Something simple is fine. Bread and cold meat, whatever's easy. You've done enough today."

Clair looked up from the plates. "I don't mind, Mr. Dawson."

"I know you don't mind. That's not what I'm saying." He looked at the field behind her. "I'm saying you've earned a quiet afternoon. Take the rest of the day. You and my mother and Emma, take the afternoon for yourselves. Read, rest, sit in the shade. Whatever you like. The work will keep."

"That's kind of you," she said.

"It's not kindness. It's sense. A person can't work from dawn to dusk every day without it catching up. I watch you work, Clair, and I see someone who gives this household everything she has. I'd like to make sure she keeps some of it for herself."

"All right," she said. "I'll keep supper simple."

Adam nodded.

She turned to look at the field behind him, the windrows stretching in long parallel lines across the stubble, and the breeze caught the loose strand of hair again and laid it across her cheek. She pushed it back without looking away from the field.

They stood for a moment without speaking, the sounds of the field around them, the horses shifting in their harness near the mowing machine, the low murmur of Tom and Dale's conversation, the dry rustle of the cottonwood leaves above them.

"Clair," he said.

"Yes?"

"I've been thinking about the evening we talked on the porch. The conversation about Emma's reading and the stove. It was the first evening in a long time that I sat out there and enjoyed having company. I was hoping you might sit with me again tonight. After Emma's down. If you're willing."

"I'd like that very much, Mr. Dawson," Clair said.

"There's something else," he said. "I'd like you to call me Adam. Please can we do away with the formalities?"

Clair smiled. It was the kind of smile he'd seen from her only three or four times since she'd come to the ranch, unguarded and full and warm enough that it changed the whole shape of her face. The composed, careful expression she wore like an apron fell away, and what replaced it was the face of a woman who was genuinely happy.

"I'd like that very much as well, Adam," she said.

He picked up the bean pot and carried it to the wagon bed, settling it against the folded blanket so it wouldn't shift on the ride back. Clair handed him the stacked plates and the scrap pail and the bundled silverware, and he arranged each piece in the spaces between the heavier items.

After cleaning up, Clair climbed onto the wagon seat and unwrapped the lines from the brake handle. Lydia was already seated beside her with Emma on her lap. His mother looked down at him from the seat, and he saw her glance move from his face to Clair's and back again, and the corner of her mouth curved.

"I'll bring fresh coffee and cold water after a while," Clair said. "Is there anything else?"

"No," Adam said. "That's enough."

She held his gaze for a moment and smiled again before she snapped the reins lightly to nudge the horse forward.

Cal stepped up beside him. "Miss Whitmore's a ray of sunshine on an already beautiful day, Adam."

"That she is," he said.

Behind him, Jesse had already reclaimed his scythe, and Tom and Dale were on their feet and rolling their sleeves.

Adam walked back toward the mowing machine. He stepped up onto the iron platform and gathered the lines in his hands. He spoke to the horses, and they leaned into their collars, and the sickle bar found its rhythm, and the timothy began to fall again.

But his mind stayed at the table under the cottonwoods, where a woman had said his name for the first time and smiled as if the saying of it was a gift.

Chapter 15

Clair set the last cup on the shelf beside the others and straightened the row until the handles all faced the same direction. The kitchen was clean. The dishes from the field lunch had been washed, dried, and returned to their places, and the counters held nothing but the butter dish and the breadboard with half a loaf covered in cloth.

In the sitting room, Lydia had settled into her chair by the window with a book open across her lap. Emma lay on the settee with her rag doll tucked beneath her chin, her bare feet drawn up, and her breathing was slow and heavy as she slept.

Clair couldn't remember the last time she'd stood in a kitchen, or anywhere else for that matter, with nothing ahead of her to fill her day. The ranch had given her days a structure she hadn't realized she'd been starving for since she'd left Helena; every hour accounted for by some task that needed doing, and the rhythm had suited her. Adam had asked her to rest, and the absence of an obligation felt odd.

She turned to Lydia and said, "Care to join me for a cup of coffee?"

"I'd like that very much," Lydia said.

Clair moved to the stove, where the coffeepot sat on the back plate, keeping warm. She poured two cups and carried them to the table as Lydia sat down.

"I was thinking about supper," Lydia said. "Adam said to keep it simple, and I'm inclined to agree with him. A good skillet hash with eggs on top would fill him up without either of us standing over the stove for an hour."

"That sounds fine," Clair said.

"Good. That's settled then." Lydia lifted her cup with both hands and drank. She set it down and looked at Clair with the unhurried regard of a woman who had something on her mind and intended to arrive at it in her own time. "It was rather nice of Adam to suggest we take the afternoon to rest. I don't think I've ever heard my son say something like that. Telling us to read, or sit in the shade, or do whatever we please."

Clair turned her cup on the table, her fingertips against the warm ceramic. "I think he noticed how much work went into feeding the crew. He wanted to make sure you and I rested."

"I think he noticed you and wanted you to know he'd noticed, and telling you to rest was the only way he could think of to say it."

Clair kept her eyes on her cup.

"Have you not noticed that my son seems to be showing some interest in you, Clair?" Lydia asked.

The warmth climbed Clair's neck, rising from beneath her collar and spreading across her cheekbones in a flush she could feel as plainly as she could feel the cup beneath her fingers.

"I have noticed," she said.

Lydia was quiet for a moment. "I'm glad you have. I'd have worried about your eyesight otherwise."

Clair looked up, and the corner of Lydia's mouth was curved in a way that meant she was enjoying herself.

"How does his attention sit with you?" Lydia asked.

Clair considered the question. She owed Lydia honesty. This woman had opened her home, shared her room, taught her to manage a kitchen and a garden and a cookstove with opinions. She had done all of it with a generosity that asked nothing in return except that Clair be present and truthful. A partial truth wouldn't serve here.

"It sits well," she said. "That's what makes it difficult."

Lydia waited.

"My experience with courtship is limited," Clair said. "I was courted once, back in Helena. A young man who was kind and respectable and everything a courtship ought to be on paper. It didn't come to anything. My father died, and grief changed my circumstances. I ended things because I couldn't in good conscience keep accepting his attention when I had nothing steady to offer him in return."

"Was it a hard decision?"

"It should have been," Clair said. "The fact that it wasn't told me something about what I'd been feeling, and what I'd been feeling wasn't enough. He deserved more than a woman who was settling for sufficiency, and I deserved more than settling. I didn't understand that until the courtship was over and I could see it from outside."

"That's a hard thing to learn about yourself at any age," Lydia said. "And a brave one."

"It didn't feel brave. It felt lonely." Clair ran her thumb along the edge of her cup. "And since then, there hasn't been anyone. The months between breaking the courtship and leaving Helena were consumed by grief, my father's affairs, and by circumstances I'm not yet able to fully explain. I haven't thought about courtship. I haven't had the luxury of thinking about it."

"And now?" Lydia asked.

"And now I'm sitting in a kitchen miles from everything I knew, in a household that took me in out of kindness, doing work I was never trained for and loving every minute of it, and the son of the woman who is helping me is looking at me in a way that no one has ever looked at me before, and I don't know what to do with it, Lydia, because my situation is not simple."

"I didn't suppose it was," Lydia said.

"You and Adam brought me into this house in exchange for my help. I understood the arrangement from the first day, and I've tried to honor it. Help with the household, help with Emma's education, earn my keep, and when the time comes, move on. The arrangement was never meant to be permanent. I know that."

"Clair."

"I don't have a plan for what comes next," Clair continued. "I don't know where I stand with the situation I left behind, and I don't know where I stand with whatever is happening between Adam and me. I came here accidentally, Lydia. I walked out of a storm and into your barn, and everything that has followed has been so far beyond what I expected or deserved that I sometimes lie awake at night wondering when my bill will come due."

Lydia set her cup down. "You think you owe us something."

"I think I've been given something I haven't earned. A place at your table, a child who trusts me, and a home that feels more like a home than the one I left. I'm afraid that wanting more than I've already been given is greedy, or foolish, or both."

"Let me tell you something about this household," Lydia said. She leaned forward slightly, her forearms resting on the table. "Before you came, this house was running on a string and a prayer. I won't pretend it wasn't. Adam kept the ranch, and I kept the household the best I could, and Emma was fed and clothed and loved. But it ran the way a clock runs when the spring is wound too tight. Everything worked, and nothing breathed. My son came in from the field and ate his supper and went to the porch in the evenings and sat alone. My granddaughter ran around with a braid that was coming undone because my fingers couldn't hold a comb properly, and moreover, she craved to learn, and I did the best I could, and I prayed for help and guidance."

She paused and leaned back in her chair.

"Three weeks ago, you walked into our barn soaked to the bone, half-starved, and carrying a carpetbag and nothing else. And within a week, my granddaughter was reading words she'd never read before. My kitchen was running better than it had in quite some time, and my son was beginning to show signs of living again. You didn't do that accidentally, Clair. And you didn't earn it by scrubbing my pots."

"Lydia, I'm grateful beyond measure for everything you've done for me. I hope you know that."

"I do know it." Lydia reached across the table and laid her hand over Clair's. "The Lord doesn't bring people into our lives by accident, Clair. He brings them on purpose. And if you're wondering whether you've earned the right to be here, I'd like to suggest that you stopped needing to earn it some time ago."

Clair looked at Lydia's hand on hers, the swollen knuckles and the bent fingers and the steady, deliberate pressure of a woman whose grip cost her something and who offered it anyway.

She didn't trust her voice to answer, so she turned her hand beneath Lydia's and held it.

Chapter 16

Clair's voice carried from the sitting room in a low, steady cadence that rose and fell with the rhythms of the story she was reading to Emma, and Adam sat at the kitchen table with his coffee and listened.

She was reading The Swiss Family Robinson, the old cloth-bound edition his mother had kept on the sitting room shelf since he was a child. Emma was curled against Clair's side on the settee, her bare feet tucked beneath her nightgown.

Lydia sat in her chair by the window with her Bible open across her lap, her reading spectacles low on her nose.

Clair turned the page. "And with that," she read, "Fritz declared that the shelter they had built among the roots of the great tree was the finest house he had ever known, finer even than the one they had left behind, because this one they had built together, with their own hands, from what the island had given them."

Emma's eyes were barely open. Her breathing had begun to slow into the deep, even rhythm that meant she was minutes from sleep.

"I think our explorer has had enough for tonight," Clair said, and she closed the book and set it on the cushion beside her.

"One more page," Emma said, but her voice was thick and distant.

"Tomorrow night," Clair said. "Fritz and his brothers will still be on their island in the morning."

Adam pushed his chair back from the table and crossed into the sitting room. He gathered her up and settled her against his shoulder.

He carried her up the stairs and into her room, where the quilt was already turned down. He lowered her onto the mattress and drew the quilt up to her chin, tucking the edges around her shoulders the way she liked.

"Papa," she said.

"What is it, sweetheart?"

"Is Miss Clair going to read to me every night?"

Adam smoothed her hair back from her forehead, his calloused fingers careful against her temple. "We'll talk about it tomorrow."

"I hope so. She does the voices better than anyone."

Adam stood beside her bed for a moment. Her breathing deepened, and her grip on the rag doll loosened, and the room was still.

He went back downstairs. Clair was on the settee where he'd left her. Lydia had set her Bible on the small table beside her chair and was saying something about the garden.

"The squash vines are running over the fence again," Lydia said. "And the beans need picking before they go tough on the vine. I was thinking tomorrow morning, before the heat comes up, might be the best time."

"I'll pick the beans first thing," Clair said. "And I can train the squash vines back along the fence if you show me how you'd like them redirected."

"Tie them to the lower rail with strips of cloth. They'll grow where you point them if you catch them early enough." Lydia pressed her knuckles against her thigh and flexed her fingers slowly. "The tomatoes could use checking, too. A few of them were starting to turn color yesterday."

"Ma," Adam said. "Clair and I are going to sit on the porch for a while. Would you like to join us?"

Lydia looked at him.

"No," she said as she stood. "I'm tired, and I think I'll go lie down." She paused and looked at them both, her gaze moving between Adam and Clair.

"Have a good evening," she said. "Both of you."

"Goodnight, Lydia," Clair said. "Rest well."

"Goodnight, Ma."

Lydia crossed toward her bedroom door, and Adam took the kerosene lamp from the sideboard and carried it through the kitchen. He held the front door open with his shoulder, and Clair passed through ahead of him, her skirt brushing the doorframe as she stepped onto the porch. He followed her out and set the lamp on the porch rail, turning the wick low until the flame settled into a steady, small glow that would give them enough light to see each other without drawing every moth in the valley.

The air had cooled from the day's heat, and a breeze moved through the yard from the direction of the creek. Clair settled into one of the porch chairs, and Adam took the one beside her.

"The breeze tonight feels wonderful," Clair said. "It was an extremely hot day today."

"July is the worst for heat," Adam said.

"Is it always this warm here?"

"Some years are worse than others. My father used to say you could judge a Montana summer by how many times the creek dropped below the top of the boulders. If you could see the waterline on the rocks, the summer was winning."

Clair smiled. "And this summer?"

"The waterline's been showing for a week."

They sat for a moment, enjoying the breeze. A bat crossed the yard in a darting, irregular line, chasing something too small to see, and disappeared beyond the barn roof.

"Emma was fighting sleep this evening while you read to her," Adam said.

"She held on longer than I expected," Clair said. "She was fighting it from the second page, but she didn't want to miss the part where they built the treehouse. She told me before supper that she's been wanting you to build her one in the cottonwood by the garden."

"She's mentioned it to me at least four times. I keep telling her the branches aren't spaced right for it."

"She told me that too. She said you always say the branches are wrong, and she doesn't believe you because she's seen squirrels live in them perfectly well."

Adam let out a chuckle. "A squirrel's got different requirements."

The lamp on the rail flickered as the breeze shifted, and the small flame steadied and held. From beyond the barn, the horses moved in the corral, and their hooves made soft, irregular sounds against the packed earth.

"You told me about the orphanage," Adam said. "In the barn that day with Mercy and the colt. You said those children filled you with great joy. I've been thinking about it since." He turned his coffee cup between his hands. "I'd like to hear more about that, if you're willing."

Clair looked at him. "You remember that."

"I remember most things you tell me."

She was quiet for a moment, and he watched the way her expression changed in the low light, the careful precision softening into something more open.

"There was a boy named Daniel," she said. "He came to Saint Anne's after losing both his parents to fever. His mother first, and his father three weeks later. He was seven years old, and he had stopped speaking. He wouldn't say a word to anyone. Three months passed, and Daniel hadn't spoken a single syllable. The sisters tried everything they could think of. Games, treats, gentle coaxing, firm encouragement. Nothing reached him."

She folded her hands in her lap and looked out past the rail toward the dark line of the mountains.

"I started sitting beside him every Saturday morning and reading aloud. I didn't ask him to respond, or to follow along, or to do anything at all. I just read to him. I read adventure stories and fairy tales and a book about the animals of Africa that he seemed to like. Saturday after Saturday, week after week. I read to him for nearly two months before anything changed."

"What happened?"

"I was reading a passage about a lion, and I paused at the end of a sentence. And Daniel finished it. His voice was small and rough from all those months of silence, like a hinge that hadn't been worked in so long it had nearly rusted shut," she paused. "I cried, Adam. Right there in the reading room with six other children staring at me, I cried like a fool, and Daniel looked at me as if I'd lost my mind entirely. And then he smiled, and that was the first smile anyone had seen from him since he'd arrived at Saint Anne's."

"There was another child," she continued. "A girl named Rose. She was four, and she was terrified of the dark. Every night at bedtime she would wail until someone sat beside her cot and held her hand. On the Saturdays I stayed late, I'd sit with her and sing quietly until her grip loosened and her breathing slowed, and I knew she was truly asleep. Some nights it took an hour. Some nights it took two."

"Emma's lucky to have you," he said. "I watch her with you every day, and I see a little girl who's happier than she's been in a very long time. You gave her something I couldn't give her on my own, and I'm grateful for it."

Clair turned her head toward him. "You gave her everything, Adam. She's a wonderful and happy child, and that's because of you. You have raised her well."

The breeze shifted again, and the lamp flame leaned sideways on the wick and righted itself. A coyote called from somewhere beyond the south pasture, distant and thin, and another answered from farther off, and then the valley was quiet again.

"So, tell me something about yourself," Clair said. "When the day's work is finished, and the stock is tended, what do you do for yourself, Adam?"

He considered the question with the honest attention it deserved, and the honest answer sat hollow in his chest. "Not much," he said. "This porch in the evenings, when the weather's right. That's about the extent of it, beyond sitting in the saddle and letting my mind wander a bit while I'm out with the cattle."

"You don't read?"

"My mother's the reader. I never sat still long enough for books to take hold."

"What did you do as a boy? Before the ranch was yours?"

He rubbed his thumb along the arm of his chair, tracing the grain of the wood. "My father used to take me to the creek, and we'd fish," he said. "There's a deep pool about a quarter mile downstream where the creek bends around a stand of cottonwoods. The cutthroat trout hold behind the boulders there, and when the light comes through the water at the right angle, you can see the red-orange slashes along their jaws, bright as paint. We'd sit on the bank with our lines in the water, and those were some of the best times I spent with him."

"That sounds like a fine way to spend an afternoon."

"It was. He wasn't a man who had much to say under most circumstances, but he didn't need to say anything out there. The creek and the fish and the quiet between us did the talking."

"Do you still fish there?"

Adam was quiet. The coyotes had gone silent, and the breeze carried the sound of the creek itself, faint and steady beyond the barn, the same sound he'd listened to from this porch for his entire life.

"The last time I fished that pool was with my father," he said. "It was a few months after Ruth passed. My mother insisted that we go. She said we both needed to get out of the house and spend some time together, and that she'd take care of Emma. So we went. We sat on the bank the way we always had, and my father didn't push me to talk, but after a while I did." He set his cup on the rail beside the lamp. "I told him I didn't know how to do it. Raise a daughter alone and help run the ranch. He listened the way he always listened, which was to say he didn't move or interrupt or try to fix what I was telling him. And when I finished, he said the truest thing anyone has ever said to me."

He looked out past the rail at the dark shapes of the mountains against the stars.

"He said, 'You don't carry it alone, son. You carry it with God, and you carry it with your family, and you let the rest fall where it falls.'" Adam paused. "It was one of the most important conversations I ever had with him."

"The next morning he rode out to move the herd ahead of a storm that was brewing," Adam continued. "A steer spooked and broke from the line and struck him. By the time I found him, he was already gone. Just like that. My father was gone. I haven't been back to that spot on the creek to fish since. Every time I think about going, I think about that last afternoon with him, and I can't make myself walk down there."

"Would you take me sometime?"

Adam turned his head toward her. Whatever he'd expected her to say, it wasn't that.

"Do you want to go fishing?"

She smiled. "I've never been fishing in my life. Not once. I wouldn't know which end of the line to hold. But you could teach me, and then you'd have another memory of that place. One that isn't the last one with your father."

He opened his mouth and closed it, and then he shook his head, and the sound that came out of him was close to a laugh.

"I never imagined you as the fishing type, Clair."

"I never imagined myself weeding a garden or milking a cow or gathering eggs from a chicken coop, either," she said. "And yet here I am."

He looked at her for a long moment, and what he saw in her face wasn't pity nor sympathy. It was the simple, warm offer of a woman who wanted to share something with him.

"I'd like that," he said. "I'd like that very much. I took Ruth fishing once, not long after we were married. She said the water was too cold, and the fish were too clever, and she sat on the bank and talked so much that the trout didn't come within fifty yards of us." He smiled and shook his head. "She tried to convince me that the fish could hear her, and that if she spoke quietly enough, they might come closer. She couldn't speak quietly if someone had paid her."

Clair laughed, and the sound of it moved through the evening air, brief and warm.

"May I ask you something else?" Clair said. "You mentioned your mornings start before dawn and your days don't end until the light goes. In all of that, is there anything you've wanted to build here that you haven't had the time or the hands for?"

He considered it. "A proper bridge across the creek at the east crossing. The ford works when the water's low, but every spring runoff I lose three or four days waiting for it to drop enough to move the cattle across. My father talked about bridging it. Never got to it."

"What would it take?"

"Good timber. Cut logs, squared on two sides. Stone footings sunk deep enough that the spring melt can't shift them. Two men, maybe three, working a solid week."

"That sounds like a project worth doing."

"It's on the list. The list is long."

"Lists usually are," she said. "But the things worth doing tend to stay on them until someone decides they've waited long enough."

He looked at her sideways. "You sound like my mother."

"Your mother is a wise woman. I'll take that as high praise."

The lamp had burned low on the rail, the flame no larger than a fingertip. The stars above the ridgeline were sharp and distinct now, the kind of night sky that made a man feel small.

Adam rubbed his thumb along the chair arm again. He looked out at the dark because looking at her while he asked this was more than he could manage.

"Clair, I hope you'll forgive me if this is too forward," he said. "But there's something I'd like to know. Was there anyone in Helena who was important to you? Someone who was courting you, or someone you had an understanding with?"

"There was a man named Theodore," Clair said. "A clerk at one of the banks in Helena. He was introduced to my father through a business connection, and my father thought well of him. He called at the house on Sundays, and we walked together in the afternoons. The courtship lasted several months."

"What happened?"

"I ended it. He was a good man, and I liked him well enough. But I came to realize that 'well enough' was the best I could say about him, and I didn't think that was fair to either of us. There ought to be more to it than pleasant and reliable. I didn't know what that 'more' looked like at the time, but I knew its absence, and I couldn't keep pretending I didn't."

Adam sat and thought about what she'd said. The honest clarity of it sat well with him, because it told him she was a woman who didn't build on ground she knew was unsound.

"And is there anyone now?" he asked. "If you were to go back to Helena tomorrow, is there someone waiting for you?"

Clair looked at him. "No. There's no one waiting for me in Helena."

Her chin lifted a fraction after she said it, and the careful composure she carried through most of her days eased at the jaw and softened around her eyes. What remained on her face was open and unhurried and entirely present. She held his gaze for a few more moments and let the quiet between them carry what the words had left unsaid.

Eventually, Clair looked away. "I should turn in. It's been a long day, and tomorrow the beans won't pick themselves."

She rose from her chair, and as she turned toward the door, she paused and faced him. The lamplight caught the line of her jaw and the pale blue of her eyes, and she stood there for a moment studying him with the quiet, unhurried attention of a woman who knew exactly what she wanted.

"Goodnight, Adam," she said.

"Goodnight, Clair."

She smiled and went inside. The door closed behind her, and her footsteps moved through the kitchen, steady and sure, and then came the low click of Lydia's bedroom door.

Adam reached over and turned the wick down until the flame died. He sat back in his chair. The stars were thick above the ridge; the valley dark and still.

He had talked more tonight than he'd talked in a single evening in years, and the talking hadn't cost him anything.

Chapter 17

"Sunrise kicked the bucket clean across the paddock this morning," Adam said, "and the milk went everywhere. He stood there looking at me like I was the one who'd done something wrong."

Lydia shook her head and said, "He has your stubbornness."

Clair passed the bowl of green beans across the table to Adam. The fried chicken had come out well; the pieces were golden and crisp. Lydia had shown her the trick of soaking the meat in buttermilk before dredging it in flour, which made the coating hold better and the meat stay tender. The potatoes she'd roasted with salt and dried rosemary from the garden sat in a crock at the center of the table beside a plate of sliced tomatoes.

"I love Sunrise... he's my favorite horse ever. He's going to be big and strong when he grows up," Emma said.

Clair watched Emma as the child talked. The girl's plate was nearly untouched. She'd eaten half a drumstick and two bites of potato, and now she was pushing a piece of tomato from one side of her plate to the other with her fork. Clair had noticed her picking at supper from the start, but the conversation had been lively enough to explain a distracted appetite in a six-year-old who would rather talk than eat.

Emma rested her chin in her hand.

"Emma, are you feeling all right?" Clair asked.

"I'm tired," Emma said. "My head feels fuzzy."

Clair reached across the table and touched Emma's forehead with the back of her fingers. Warm.

"She's had a full day today," Lydia said. "She was out with Sunrise for the better part of the afternoon, running that poor animal back and forth across the paddock until I thought one or both of them would drop."

Adam looked at Emma across the table.

"Can I go lie down? I don't want any more supper," Emma said. She set her fork down and pushed her plate toward the center of the table.

Adam glanced at Clair, then at his mother. "All right," he said, and he started to push his chair back from the table.

"Papa," Emma said. "Can Miss Clair take me up?"

Adam's hands stilled on the chair arms. "Of course," he said.

Clair rose from her chair and came around the table, and Emma slid from her seat and reached for Clair's hand. Her fingers were warm and slightly damp.

"Come on, sweetheart," Clair said. "Let's get you tucked in."

They crossed the kitchen to the stairs, and as they reached the first step, Emma raised both arms the way she did when Adam carried her, and Clair bent and lifted her. Emma's arms wound around Clair's neck, and her face pressed against Clair's shoulder.

Clair held her close and climbed the stairs carefully, one hand on the rail.

Clair lowered her onto the mattress, drawing the thin summer blanket up to her shoulders.

"Will you tell me a story?" Emma asked. Her eyes were heavy, and she pulled her rag doll against her chest and curled onto her side.

Clair sat on the edge of the bed and smoothed Emma's hair back from her forehead. "What kind of story would you like?"

"One you make up. Not from a book."

Clair thought for a moment, her fingers still moving gently through Emma's hair. "Once, a very long time ago, in a valley between two great mountain ranges, there lived a little girl named Rosemary who had a horse that could understand every word she said."

Emma's eyes brightened a fraction. "Like Sunrise."

"Very much like Sunrise, except this horse was the color of new snow, and her name was Starlight, and every evening when the work was done, Rosemary would climb onto Starlight's back, and they would ride together along the creek that ran through her family's land. One evening they rode farther than they'd ever gone before, past the cottonwood bend and past the beaver dam and past the place where the water ran over flat stones and made a sound like someone tapping on a windowpane. And there, in a clearing where the grass grew thick and soft, they found a garden."

"What was growing in it?" Emma asked.

"Everything. Tomatoes on their vines and beans climbing their stakes and squash with leaves so broad that a rabbit could shelter beneath a single one. And in the very center of the garden, a sunflower taller than Starlight's head, with a face turned toward the mountains as if it were watching for someone to come home."

"Who planted it?" Emma asked, her voice already thickening.

"Rosemary didn't know. She asked Starlight, and Starlight tossed her mane, which was her way of saying she didn't know either, but she thought they should stay and find out. So Rosemary slid down from Starlight's back and walked into the garden, and the first thing she noticed was that every plant was exactly what her family needed most. The beans were the kind her mother used for winter stew. The tomatoes were the variety her father liked best on bread with salt. And the sunflower, when Rosemary looked at it closely, had seeds arranged in a perfect spiral, and each seed, when she held it to her ear, hummed a note of her favorite hymn."

Emma smiled against her pillow, her eyes closed now. "That's a good garden," she murmured.

"It was the best garden anyone had ever found," Clair said. "And Rosemary sat down in the soft grass beside Starlight and decided she would come back every evening to tend it, because a garden that gives you exactly what you need deserves someone who will care for it in return."

Emma's breathing had deepened, her grip on the rag doll loosening. Clair tucked the blanket around Emma's shoulders and rose from the bed. She stood for a moment looking down at the sleeping child, at her slightly flushed cheeks, and at her small fingers curled around the rag doll's worn fabric. A tenderness so fierce it startled her moved through her chest like a hand closing around her heart.

She went downstairs. Adam was at the dry sink with his sleeves pushed past his elbows, washing the supper dishes while Lydia dried them and set them on the shelf.

"She fell asleep quickly," Clair said. "Her forehead still felt warm to me."

Lydia set a plate on the shelf and turned. "How warm?"

"Warm enough that I noticed it, but she wasn't distressed. She was talking and settled easily. The story put her right to sleep."

Adam dried his hands on the cloth draped over his shoulder. "Could be nothing. She's been in the sun today, and she didn't eat much at supper."

"Children get fevers," Lydia said. "They come on fast, and half the time they're gone by morning without ever explaining themselves. She may wake up perfectly fine and wanting two breakfasts to make up for the supper she missed." Lydia hung the drying cloth on its hook and flexed her fingers slowly, pressing her knuckles against her thigh. "We'll check on her before we turn in."

Clair nodded. The assurance was sensible and delivered with the calm authority of a woman who had raised children through fevers and teething and all the small crises that came with a body still learning how to be in the world.

***

Emma's cry brought Clair upright on the pallet before she was fully awake.

The sound that came from above was high and thin with the unmistakable pitch of a child who was frightened. The words didn't connect to each other; fragments of sentences tangled with crying, and the sound of it went through Clair like a needle.

"Something seems wrong," Lydia said from across the room.

Above them, footsteps moved fast across the upstairs hallway. Muffled sounds followed: Emma crying harder and Adam's voice beneath it, low and steady, the words indistinct.

Clair looked at Lydia across the dark room. Moonlight came through the two windows and laid pale squares on the floor between the pallet and the bed, and in the half-light, Lydia's face was drawn in alert sharpness.

"Should I go up?" Clair asked.

Lydia listened. Above them, Emma's crying had shifted from the wild, directionless wailing to something smaller and more desperate, the sound of a child who had found her father and was clinging to him.

"She wasn't right when she went to bed," Lydia said. "Go up the stairs and listen. If it sounds like Adam needs help, go to them."

Clair pushed the quilt aside and stood. Her nightgown fell around her bare feet, and she paused and turned to Lydia. "Do you have a wrapper I could put on?"

"In the wardrobe, on the top shelf," Lydia said.

Clair opened the wardrobe and felt along the top shelf until her fingers found soft fabric. She pulled the wrapper down and slipped her arms into it, wrapping the front closed and tying the sash at her waist.

She opened Lydia's bedroom door and crossed the kitchen toward the stairs on the far side of the room. As she reached them, she saw the warm glow of lamplight coming from the open door of Emma's room at the top of the staircase.

She climbed the stairs quietly, her bare feet on the wooden treads, and as she neared the top, the sounds sharpened and separated. Emma's crying had subsided into ragged, hitching breaths, the kind that came after a child had spent the worst of her tears and was left with the ache beneath them. Adam's voice was low, a steady murmur.

Clair reached the top of the stairs and looked through Emma's open doorway.

Adam sat on the edge of the bed. She could see that Emma's nightgown was damp, and her cheeks were flushed a deep, vivid pink. Her rag doll had fallen to the floor.

"Tell me where it hurts, sweetheart. Does your head hurt? Your stomach? Show Papa where."

"Everywhere," Emma said, her voice small and cracked. "Papa, I don't feel good. I'm so hot. Papa, please."

"I know," Adam said. "I know you're hot. We're going to fix that. Can you tell me if your throat hurts? Does it hurt to swallow?"

Emma swallowed and shook her head. "Just hot. And my head is fuzzy, and it hurts."

Clair stepped into the room, and Adam looked up. His face in the lamplight was composed, his jaw set, and the eyes steady.

She went to the opposite side of Emma's bed and sat on the mattress. Emma came to her immediately, her small arms wrapping around Clair's neck, and the heat of Emma's body was startling.

"We're here, sweetheart," Clair said, keeping her voice steady and calm. "Your papa and I are right here. We're going to cool you down, and you're going to feel better."

She looked at Adam across the bed. "I need cool water and clean cloths. A basin. Can you bring them up?"

"I'll get them," he said, and he was on his feet and moving toward the door before the sentence was finished. His footsteps went down the stairs quickly, and Clair heard him cross the kitchen floor.

Clair rocked Emma gently, smoothing her damp hair with long, steady strokes. Emma's face was pressed into the hollow of Clair's shoulder, and her breathing came in the shallow, rapid rhythm of a body working to cool itself and failing.

"Miss Clair," Emma said. "Why am I so hot?"

"Your body is fighting something," Clair said. "That's what fevers do. They fight the things that make us feel poorly, and when the fight is over, the fever goes away and you feel like yourself again."

"I don't like it."

"I know you don't. Nobody likes fevers. But you are very strong, and your body knows exactly what to do."

Adam's footsteps came back up the stairs, and he appeared in the doorway.

"I'm going to carry her downstairs to Ma's room," he said.

Clair nodded and eased Emma away from her chest as Adam bent over and slid his arms beneath his daughter. Emma's head dropped against his shoulder, her face turned into his neck, and her legs hung limp against his side.

Clair followed Adam out of the room and down the stairs.

Emma curled onto her side after Adam placed her on his mother's bed. Lydia touched the child's forehead with the back of her wrist.

"She's burning up," Lydia said.

Adam went out of the room and came back with a chair in each hand.

"I'll go and prepare some willow bark tea," Lydia said. "It needs to cool before she can drink it, but I want it ready."

Clair went to the washstand and poured water from the ceramic pitcher into the basin. She dipped a cloth into the water and wrung it until it stopped dripping, then crossed to the bed and sat in one of the chairs Adam had carried in.

Adam stood at the foot of the bed with his arms at his sides, his gaze fixed on his daughter.

"What brought this on?" he said. "She was fine this morning. She was running in the paddock all afternoon. Children don't go from running to this in a few hours."

"They do, sometimes," Clair said. She laid the cloth across Emma's forehead, and the child flinched at the coolness and then settled, her eyes closing. "Children's fevers climb fast. It doesn't mean it's serious. It means her body found something to fight and went to work on it with everything it had."

"What can I do?"

"Refill the pitcher with cool water from the well. We'll keep the cloths on her forehead and her wrists, and when your mother brings the tea, we'll see if we can get her to drink some."

Adam nodded and picked up the pitcher from the washstand and left the room.

She turned back to Emma and spoke in the small, steady cadence she'd learned at Saint Anne's. "There we go. That's better, isn't it? Nice and cool. You're doing so well, Emma."

Emma's hand crept across the quilt and found Clair's where it rested on the mattress. Her small fingers closed around Clair's thumb and held on.

Adam returned with the pitcher and set it on the washstand.

Eventually Lydia came back into the room carrying a cup of willow bark tea, the steam still rising from its surface. "Let it cool a few minutes," she said as she set it on the bedside table. She lowered herself into the chair beside Clair, and she began to hum, soft and low, a melody Clair recognized as "Rock of Ages."

The hours folded into each other. Clair lost count of how many times she dipped the cloth and wrung it and laid it gently across Emma's skin, across her forehead and her wrists and the back of her neck where the fever concentrated. Emma drifted in and out of sleep, sometimes restless and murmuring fragments. Sometimes lying still and heavy against the pillow.

They managed two sips of the willow bark tea when Emma surfaced long enough to swallow, Lydia lifting Emma's head and Clair holding the cup steady against her lip, and the child grimaced at the bitterness but drank it.

When the quiet of the room became too much for Clair to take a moment longer, she began to sing. Her voice rose from a place in her that answered fear with the only language she trusted when all other words fell short.

Abide with me; fast falls the eventide. The darkness deepens; Lord, with me abide.

She sang the second verse and the third, and when she reached the end, she prayed.

Lord, please. This child. Not this child. You cannot take this child from this family. They have buried enough. Please. I am asking You with everything I have. Watch over her. Hold her through this night. Bring her through.

At some point in the deep hours of the night, when the moonlight through Lydia's windows had shifted from one wall to the other, Lydia's chin settled against her chest, and her breathing deepened into the uneven rhythm of a body that had given everything it could and had finally surrendered to exhaustion. Her hand still rested on the quilt near Emma's shoulder, her swollen fingers curled loosely against the fabric.

Clair rose to refresh the cloths and looked toward the doorway.

Adam sat on the kitchen floor just outside the open door, his back against the wall. His forearms rested on his drawn-up knees, and his head was bowed. He had been there for hours, close enough to hear everything that happened in the room and far enough to leave the bedside to the women who knew what to do.

Clair set the cloth in the basin and went to him. She crouched beside him on the kitchen floor, the boards cool beneath her bare feet, and put her hand on his forearm. The muscle beneath her fingers was rigid with tension.

"She's sleeping peacefully," Clair said. "The fever hasn't broken, but it hasn't climbed, either. She's resting, Adam; she's fine."

Adam lifted his head. His eyes were red-rimmed with tiredness.

"You don't know that she's fine," he said. "Things change fast. Ruth was fine in the afternoon and gone by morning."

Clair lowered herself to sit beside him on the floor, her back against the wall, her shoulder close enough to his that she could feel his warmth. "Emma will be fine," she said. "You have to believe that. Sitting here and carrying the worst possibility alone won't help her, and it won't help you. Take your worries to God, Adam."

He was quiet for a long moment.

"I can't lay worries down that easily," he said. "Worrying is how I'm built now. It's what's left when you've lost the people you thought you'd have forever." He rubbed one hand across his face and let it drop to his knee. "I've been sitting out here listening to her breathing. Every time there's a pause between one and the next, the fear in me clutches harder."

Adam drew a slow breath and got to his feet, and Clair rose with him. He followed her through the doorway into Lydia's room and stood for a moment looking at his daughter in the bed. He sat down in the chair beside his sleeping mother and watched Emma's chest rise and fall.

Clair went to Lydia and touched her shoulder gently. "Lydia," she said. "Go lie down on the pallet. You need to rest properly. Adam and I will sit with her."

Lydia surfaced slowly, blinking in the lamplight. She looked at Emma, then at Adam in the chair beside her, then at Clair standing over her with one hand still resting on her shoulder. She nodded without argument and rose from her chair with the careful, staged motion of a body that had stiffened while it slept, and Clair steadied her elbow as she crossed the room to the pallet along the wall. Lydia lowered herself onto it and was asleep again within minutes.

Clair sat in the chair beside Adam. He was leaning forward with his elbows on his knees, watching Emma sleep. The lamplight caught the sharp line of his jaw and the dark circles under his eyes.

"She was colicky as an infant," he said. "Three months old, and she'd scream from sundown to midnight, every night, like someone was sticking her with a pin. My mother would walk her through the house, and I'd walk her around outside, and between the two of us, we kept her moving because movement was the only thing that settled her."

"Your mother told me Emma was a strong baby," Clair said. "She said she was healthy from the start."

"She was. Healthy and loud. She had opinions about everything before she had words for any of it. The first time she got truly sick, she was cutting her first teeth. Nine months old. The fever came on at mid-morning and climbed all afternoon; she was limp in my arms, and her eyes were glassy, and I was certain I was going to lose her. I didn't know what to do. I refused to let Ma help me; I was too afraid to set Emma down. I remember standing in this kitchen, holding her and staring at the door like the answer was going to walk through it."

"What happened?"

"Ma had been outside for most of the day handling my chores and tending the garden because I refused to let her help me. Ma came through the door, took one look at my face, and took Emma out of my arms and said, 'Adam, heat water for a lukewarm bath, and stop looking like the world is ending. She's teething, and teething fevers are as normal as a child learning to crawl. Now get ahold of yourself,'" he smiled. "She bathed Emma in the basin on the kitchen table, and by morning the fever had broken, and Emma was chewing a hard biscuit my ma had made her and grinning at me like nothing had happened."

"Lydia has seen her family through a great deal," Clair said.

"More than any one woman should have to see through," Adam said. "I don't know where she keeps the strength. I've been carrying this ranch for six years, and I'm worn to the bone most days. She's been carrying so much for years, and she still gets up every morning and makes coffee and reads her Bible and thanks God for the day," he looked at his hands. "I haven't thanked God properly for a day in a long time."

Clair rose and crossed the room to where her carpetbag sat on the floor beside the pallet. She opened it and lifted out her Bible, the leather worn soft at the spine. She brought it back to her chair and sat down beside Adam and placed her hand on his forearm.

"I'm going to read for a bit," she said. "How about I read aloud so we can both enjoy the words? It would be a comfort to me, and perhaps to you as well."

Adam nodded.

"Is there a book or a passage you'd like to hear?"

He was quiet, and she waited. His gaze stayed on Emma, and when he spoke, his voice was rough at the edges. "Psalm ninety-one," he said. "My mother would read it to me when I was small, and bad storms would come through and rattle the house. She'd sit on my bed and read it until I fell asleep."

Clair opened her Bible and turned the thin pages until she found the Psalms and began to read, her voice low and steady.

"He that dwelleth in the secret place of the most High shall abide under the shadow of the Almighty. I will say of the Lord, He is my refuge and my fortress: my God; in him will I trust."

Chapter 18

Clair opened her eyes to see the lamp on Lydia's bedside table had burned low, its flame a thin thread barely holding against the wick. She was on the pallet along the far wall; the quilt twisted around her legs where she'd turned in her sleep, and her neck ached from the angle of the folded blanket she'd used as a pillow.

Lydia sat in a chair at Emma's bedside with her hand resting on Emma's arm. In the other chair, Adam had folded forward with his head on his arms at the edge of the mattress. His breathing was deep and slow, his shoulders rising and falling in the even rhythm of sleep.

Lydia turned her head and looked at Clair. She spoke quietly, her voice pitched just enough for Clair to hear her. "He just fell asleep a few minutes ago. He fought it as long as he could."

Clair sat up and pushed the quilt aside and stood. "I apologize if I slept too long."

"Nonsense. We all need our rest so we don't lose our strength. We're no good to this child if we've worn ourselves down to nothing."

Clair reached the bed and laid her hand across Emma's forehead. The skin beneath her palm was warm, still carrying the remnants of the fever that had climbed through the night, but the burning quality had eased. Emma's lips were parted and dry, but no longer pressed together against discomfort. The deep pink flush that had colored her cheeks in the small hours had faded to something softer, and her breathing moved in and out with steadiness.

"She took a little water about an hour ago," Lydia said. "That's a good sign."

Clair nodded and withdrew her hand.

"I'll start the coffee and get some biscuits in the oven," Clair said.

Lydia nodded. "Before you do, go down to the root cellar and bring up a package of the deer bones from the back shelf and a few root vegetables. Carrots, a turnip, an onion if there's one left. I want you to put the bones in the big pot with water and set it on the stove to boil. A good bone broth is what this child needs."

Adam lifted his head from his arms. He blinked and turned immediately to look at Emma. Then he straightened in his chair and looked at Lydia and Clair.

"I'll get the things from the cellar," he said. "It's still dark out. I don't want you going outside alone."

He rose from the chair stiffly, his hand bracing against the chair back as his legs took his full height, and Clair followed him out of the bedroom into the kitchen. Adam sat on the bench beside the front door and pulled on his boots. He stood and crossed into the sitting room, where a kerosene lantern sat on the mantel above the fireplace. He struck a match, and the flame caught and steadied, throwing a circle of warm light across his face. He adjusted the wick, lifted the lantern by its bail, and went out through the back door.

Clair opened the stove's firebox and cleaned the ash from the grate. Then she built a fire from the kindling stacked in the box beside the stove, laying the splits of dry pine in a lattice and touching the match to the shavings beneath. The fire caught and began to draw, and she added two thicker pieces of wood and adjusted the damper until the draft pulled evenly. She filled the coffeepot from the water pitcher on the counter, measured the grounds into the basket, and set the pot on the stove.

Adam returned a few minutes later and laid the package on the counter beside the stove, then placed the vegetables beside it: three carrots with their greens still attached, a turnip the size of his fist, and a yellow onion whose papery skin had dried and cracked in the cool air of the cellar.

"That should be enough," he said.

"Thank you," Clair said. She unwrapped the cloth and found the deer bones inside, pale and dense, with shreds of dried meat still clinging to the joints. She lifted the big pot from its hook on the wall and set it on the stovetop, filled it with water from the pitcher, and lowered the bones into the water one at a time. Then she took a knife from the shelf and began on the vegetables, peeling the carrots in long strokes and cutting them into thick rounds, quartering the turnip, and slicing the onion into wedges. She added them to the pot and pushed it to the center of the stove, where the fire burned hottest.

The biscuit dough came next. Flour, lard, a pinch of salt, and buttermilk from the crock on the shelf. She worked the dough with her hands in the bowl until it held together, then turned it out onto the floured board and patted it flat and cut rounds with the rim of a cup. She laid them on the baking tin and slid the tin into the oven.

Adam sat at the kitchen table. He had not spoken since setting the vegetables on the counter, and when Clair glanced at him, she saw a man sitting very still with his forearms resting on the table and his gaze fixed.

The coffeepot began to rattle on the backplate. Clair took a cup from the shelf and poured, and the coffee was strong and dark from the fresh grounds and the stove's climbing temperature. She carried the cup to the table and set it in front of him.

"What chores need doing on the ranch today?" She asked as she pulled out a chair and sat across from him. "Tell me what needs tending, and I'll help where I can."

Adam wrapped his hand around the cup and held it without drinking. "I'll do what needs done. Some things can wait. The horses need feed and fresh water, and I'll see to that later this morning." He lifted the cup and took a slow sip of the coffee. "The cattle can graze. They don't need me today."

"I can help with the horses," Clair said.

"I'd rather you stayed inside with Ma when I step out. In case Emma needs something." He set the cup down. "Between you and Ma, she's in good hands. That's where I need you."

"Adam, you need to rest," she said.

He shook his head. "I'm fine."

"You slept for a few minutes. That's not enough. You won't do Emma any good if you can't think straight. Go lie down on the pallet for a while."

He looked through the open doorway toward Lydia's room. His jaw worked once, and Clair could see the resistance in his expression.

Then he nodded as he pushed back from the table and stood, and he carried his coffee cup with him through the doorway into Lydia's room.

Clair stood, returned to the stove, and tended the broth. Small bubbles rose along the sides of the pot and broke at the surface, and she adjusted the damper to hold the fire at a steady simmer. The biscuits in the oven had risen and turned golden across their tops, and she pulled the tin out and set it on the counter to cool.

Through the window above the dry sink, the sky had begun to lighten along the tops of the mountains.

She thought about the night before and the sound of Emma crying from her upstairs bedroom, the way the sound had gone through like a hand reaching in and closing around something vital. The hours of cool cloths and willow bark tea and the hymn she'd sung. She thought about Adam sitting on the kitchen floor with his head bowed and his forearms braced against his knees.

She understood his fear. A father afraid for his child needed no explanation, and the fear itself was as natural as breathing. But she wished he wouldn't carry it so far into himself, where no one could reach it and no comfort could touch it.

Her own mother had told her that once, sitting at the kitchen table in the Helena house with a cup of tea, listening while Clair described the sick children she'd tended that Saturday at Saint

Anne's. Clair had been upset, her voice tight with the worry of a young woman who had spent the day pressing cool cloths to small foreheads and singing lullabies. Her mother had set her teacup down and looked at her with a calm, level expression and said, 'Every child weathers at least one fever that terrifies the household. And then they bounce back as if nothing happened, and the household is left standing there wondering what all the fuss was about.' Clair smiled at the memory and the sound of her mother's voice as it lived in her mind.

Clair stood stirring broth at the stove, and she realized that she was more at home and at peace than she'd felt since her father had passed. She felt blessed. Even with Emma sick and Adam worn thin, she felt a calm that had no explanation beyond the one she trusted most: that God had placed her here, in this house, beside these people, and the placement was provision.

***

The broth had simmered for the better part of three hours by the time Clair ladled a cupful into a ceramic mug and carried it into Lydia's room.

Lydia was sitting forward in her chair, adjusting the pillows behind Emma's back. She had propped the child up against two pillows stacked together, supporting Emma's shoulders at an angle that would allow her to swallow easily. Adam stood leaning against the wall with a cup of coffee in his hand.

Emma's eyes were open. They were glassy and tired, the lids heavy, but they tracked Clair as she entered the room and sat on the edge of the mattress. The child's face had lost the deep, angry flush of the night's worst hours and settled into a milder pink, the kind of color that suggested warmth without alarm. Her hair was tangled against the pillows, damp at the temples where the fever had worked through the night, and her rag doll was tucked into the crook of her arm where Clair had placed it hours ago.

"Hello, sweetheart," Clair said. She held the mug steady in one hand and dipped a spoon into the broth with the other, bringing it to Emma's lips. "I made you something yummy. It will help you feel stronger."

Emma took the first sip and made a face, her nose wrinkling and her lips pressing together. "It tastes like the garden," she said.

"That's because it has carrots and turnips in it," Lydia said. She smoothed Emma's hair back from her forehead with the back of her wrist and held it there, reading the child's temperature. "It will make you strong. Take another sip."

Emma looked at Lydia, then at the spoon Clair held near her mouth, and took another sip. She swallowed and let her head settle back against the pillows.

Clair brought the spoon up again, and Emma accepted it. The rhythm was slow and patient, one spoonful at a time, with pauses between each one while Emma gathered herself for the next. The child managed seven spoonfuls before she turned her face away and closed her eyes. Clair set the mug on the bedside table and wiped Emma's chin with the corner of a cloth.

"Should I ride to town and fetch Dr. Porter?" Adam asked.

"I don't think we need to," Lydia said. "She's taking broth with no issues. Her fever is coming down. If it climbs again, we'll send you. But I think she's going to be just fine."

Clair turned and looked at him. His face was perfectly still, every line and angle held in place with composure. Then a tremor started in the muscle along his jaw and traveled upward, and his mouth tightened and his brow drew in, and the careful architecture of his expression shifted. He took a deep breath, then turned and left the room. Clair heard his boots cross the kitchen floor and heard the front door open and close.

She looked at Lydia. "Do you think he's all right? Should I go after him?"

Lydia held her gaze. "Yes. Go to him. He holds such fear every time Emma, or I have fallen ill. Every fever, every cough, and his mind goes straight to the worst place, which for him is the night Ruth died. And he bears it alone because he thinks that's what strength looks like." She paused. "He needs someone, Clair. Go."

Clair crossed through the bedroom doorway into the kitchen, sat on the bench beside the front door, and pulled on her boots. She laced them quickly, opened the front door, and stepped onto the porch.

Adam wasn't there. She looked toward the barn and saw that the door was open. She stepped off the porch and crossed the yard.

The ground was dry beneath her boots, the packed earth of the path worn smooth by years of traffic.

She reached the barn and stopped in the open doorway.

Adam was near Mercy's stall, in the aisle between the stalls and the stacked hay. He was on his knees. His head was bowed, and his hands were resting on his thighs, and his shoulders were curved forward.

His voice reached her in fragments, rough and quiet, broken at the edges the way a voice breaks when the words are being pulled from a place that has been sealed shut for a long time.

"...thank You for not taking her..." The words came unevenly, pulled apart by the breath between them. "...I couldn't have survived it... please give me strength as we get through this and ease my worries..." A pause. His shoulders moved, and when his voice came again, it was lower and rougher than before. "...I can't lose anyone else, Lord. I can't do it again."

Mercy shifted in her stall, and the straw rustled beneath her hooves. Sunrise's small shape was visible through the rails, pressed close against his mother's side.

Clair watched Adam kneeling in the aisle, and what she saw was not a man brought low by his fear. What she saw was a man who had been carrying the terror of loss for six years, through every cough Emma ever had; through every bad morning when Lydia's fingers wouldn't close around her coffee cup; and through every stumble and every silence. Every moment when someone he loved didn't seem right.

Adam lifted his head when he finished, and he saw her.

For a moment, neither of them moved. Then he looked away, wiped his face with the back of his hand, and got to his feet. His shoulders squared and his jaw set, and she watched his composure begin to rebuild itself.

Clair walked toward him. "Don't."

He looked at her.

"Don't hold it all in. Not with me. You don't have to."

Adam stood still. His hands hung at his sides, and the knees of his trousers were dusty from the barn floor where he'd knelt.

"You can talk to me, Adam. Get this off your chest. Tell me your fears."

He spoke slowly, the words arriving one at a time, as if each one had to be located in a room he'd kept dark for years.

"When Emma was born," he said, "Ruth was tired, and the labor had been long, but she looked at me, and I thought she was all right. Then Emma came, and Ruth heard her first cry. Ruth took a deep breath and was gone." He lifted his hand and snapped his fingers; the sound was sharp and sudden in the still barn. "Like that. One breath. The midwife couldn't stop the bleeding. There was nothing anyone could do. I watched my daughter come into the world, and in the next moment I watched my wife leave it."

"My father died a few months later. Two people I thought would always be there, gone in the space of months, and both times I couldn't do a thing to stop it." He looked at his hands. "Life is so fragile. It can be gone between one breath and the next. Ever since Ruth's passing, anytime Ma's joints are worse than usual, anytime Emma pushes her plate away at supper, anytime either one of them so much as sneezes, this fear seizes me. I can't stop and I can't set aside. It sits right here." He pressed his fist against his chest, below his collarbone. "And it tells me this is the beginning of the next loss. Every time. I know it isn't rational, but I've never been able to make it stop."

Clair nodded in understanding.

"I watched my mother die slowly over the course of months," she said. "She was ill for a long time, and I sat beside her bed toward the end when she was getting worse by the day and read the Psalms to her because those were the passages she loved. The Psalms of lament, the Psalms of comfort, whichever ones she asked for. And every night I prayed that tomorrow she'd be stronger," she paused. "She never was."

Adam's gaze was steady on her face.

"After she was gone, I carried the same fear you carry. Every time my father coughed or looked tired or rubbed his chest, I thought, this is how I lose him too. Faith doesn't make the fear go away, Adam. I wish it did. But I prayed all night for Emma, and the fear was there the whole time, and I prayed anyway. That's what faith is. Not the absence of fear. Just the refusal to let fear pray louder than you do."

"What you did for Emma last night," Adam said. "It was comforting to know that I didn't just have Ma tending to Emma, but I had you there as well. I won't ever forget that. Not ever."

He looked at her, and his face had been stripped of its usual architecture, and what remained was a look of gratitude.

"When you sang to her," he said. "I was sitting in the kitchen, and I could hear you through the doorway. I hadn't heard that hymn sung like that since my mother used to sing it when I was younger." He swallowed. "I needed to hear those words."

Clair took a step closer.

"Adam," she said. "You've been carrying so many things alone for six years. This fear in you that you carry is deep, and it hurts, I know. Every worry over this ranch. Every fear and worry about your mother. You don't have to carry it alone anymore. That's what I'm trying to tell you."

He was quiet for a long time, and then he nodded and looked away.

"Do you want to come back inside with me?" Clair asked.

"You go ahead," he said. "I'll take care of the horses first. They need feed and water."

"Would you like my help?"

He shook his head. "I just need a little time alone."

Clair understood. She nodded, then turned and walked out of the barn.

Chapter 19

Emma had her grandmother's quilt pulled to her waist and a book open in her lap. She was propped against Lydia's side on the settee. The color had returned to her cheeks over the past few days in slow, uneven increments. She still got tired easily. Her appetite came and went. But the glassy, frightened look that had lived behind her eyes through the worst of the fever was gone, and in its place was the restless impatience of a child who had been kept inside long enough.

Adam sat in the chair along the back wall, his ankle resting on his knee, watching the two of them. Lydia's arm lay across the back of the settee behind Emma's shoulders, her swollen fingers resting against the cushion, and she was listening while Emma chattered on.

"This one is a dog," Emma said, pressing her finger to the page. "But it doesn't look like any dog I've ever seen. His ears are too small. Dogs in the valley have big ears."

"Not all dogs look like the ones you know," Lydia said. "The man who drew that picture may have lived somewhere that dogs look different."

"Where would a dog look different?"

"Boston, perhaps. Or Philadelphia. Cities have different dogs than ranches."

Emma considered this. "Do they have different cats too?"

"I expect they have all manner of cats."

"I think Solomon would be the best cat in Philadelphia," Emma said.

Adam grinned. Solomon, the barn cat, had survived three Montana winters and a run-in with a porcupine that had left him missing half his left ear. Adam doubted the old tomcat would last a week in any city east of the Mississippi. But Emma's loyalty to the animal was absolute and not subject to debate.

"Grandma," Emma said, tipping her head back against Lydia's arm. "When can I go outside? I've been inside for days and days."

"You've been inside for a few days, Emma Louise."

"It feels like a hundred."

"It does not feel like a hundred. It feels like a few, which is precisely how long the Lord has given your body to mend, and your body is not finished yet," Lydia said as she smoothed Emma's hair. "You fell asleep this morning before you'd finished half your breakfast. And I saw you nodding off on this very settee not an hour before the noon meal."

"I was resting my eyes."

"You were sleeping, child."

"My eyes were very tired. Can I at least go sit on the porch?" Emma asked.

"Not today," Lydia said. "How about this.. suppose you and I pick out a story and I read it to you, and afterward we'll play a round of the button game? Would that suit you?"

Emma's expression shifted from complaint to negotiation. "Two rounds of the button game."

"One round, and I'll let you pick the story."

"Two rounds, and you pick the story."

Lydia looked at Adam over Emma's head, and the expression on his mother's face carried the blend of amusement and admiration that she reserved for moments when Emma's stubbornness revealed itself as a perfect inheritance from her father.

"Two rounds," Lydia said. "But only if you drink the rest of the broth Clair left for you."

Emma wrinkled her nose. "The broth tastes like garden."

"The broth tastes like getting well. Drink it, and you'll have your two rounds."

Emma sighed. "Fine."

Lydia patted Emma's knee and rose from the settee. Adam watched her cross the room toward the kitchen, her gait measured, her posture carrying the slight forward lean she'd developed over the past year. She took her coffee cup from the sideboard and refilled it from the pot on the stove. Then she came back through to the sitting room and lowered herself onto the settee beside Emma.

Adam studied her. His mother had not slept through a full night in nearly a week, between the fever vigil and the days of broth-making and sponge-bathing and the endless small adjustments a sick child required. She looked tired; the lines around her eyes were deep.

"What's on your mind?" Lydia asked, looking at him over the rim of her cup.

"Nothing much," he said. "Just watching the two of you."

"Watching us do what?"

"Be yourselves."

Lydia's eyes stayed on him for a beat, and the small line between her brows smoothed. "Well," she said. "We're quite accomplished at that."

Adam shifted in his chair and looked out the window, where the garden fence posts were visible beyond the glass and the August sky stretched above the ridgeline. Clair was hanging the laundry she'd washed earlier.

"Ma," he said. "I'd like to take Clair down to the creek for a couple of hours, if you're all right sitting with Emma... maybe the two of you could nap some."

"The creek?" Emma said. "What for, Papa?"

"I think today would be a good day to go fishing."

Emma sat up straight, the quilt sliding to her waist. "I want to go. Can I go? I've never been fishing before."

Adam looked at his daughter. She was right. She had never held a fishing pole, never sat on a bank with her feet in the grass and a line drifting in the current. She didn't know what a cane pole felt like in her hands, or how the line looked when it settled on the water, or what it sounded like when a trout broke the surface after a fly. All she knew of fishing was what she'd heard in stories.

"Not today, sweetheart," he said. "But I promise I'll take you soon."

"But I feel fine."

Lydia spoke gently. "Emma Louise, your fever only left you a few days ago. You are better, and I thank the Lord for it, but you are not back to yourself yet. The creek will still be there when you're fully well."

"But what if the fish leave?"

"The fish have been in that creek since before your grandfather built this house," Lydia said. "They are not going anywhere."

Adam rose from his chair and crouched beside the settee. He rested his forearm on the cushion near Emma's knee and looked at her. "When you're stronger, I'll take you. That's a promise. But today you stay here with your grandma, and you rest, and you let Miss Clair and me go see if we can catch some dinner."

Emma considered this with her brow creased and her lips pressed together.

"Can I name a fish if you catch one?" she asked.

"If we catch one, you can name it."

"Even if we're going to eat it?"

"Even then."

Emma settled back against Lydia's side and pulled the quilt to her chin, satisfied enough to stop negotiating. "I'll think of a good name while you're gone."

Adam stood and crossed the sitting room to the back door, where his boots sat on the floor. He pulled them on, working his feet into the leather and tugging the tops into place. He opened the back door and stepped out onto the narrow back porch, where the afternoon met him with the dry, steady warmth of an August day.

He stepped off the porch and walked along the side of the garden fence. The clothesline ran from an iron hook set into the corner post of the house to a cedar pole sunk into the ground twenty feet out, and Clair stood midway along it with the wicker basket at her feet and a bedsheet pinned at one end, her hand reaching up to clip the other corner. Her sleeves were still rolled up , and the breeze that came down off the foothills moved the loose strands of hair along her temple. When she heard his boots on the packed earth, she turned her head and smiled.

"I have something to show you," Adam said, "if you can spare the afternoon."

Clair pinned the corner of the sheet and reached for the next piece in the basket, one of Emma's cotton nightgowns. "Show me what?"

"I believe I owe you a fishing lesson."

Her hands stilled on the clothespin. She turned to face him fully, and the expression that crossed her face was bright and open and pleased in a way that changed the entire shape of her features.

"You're serious," she said.

"I am. The creek's running clear, and the trout should be holding in the deep pool this time of day."

"I've never held a fishing pole in my life, so you'll need to be patient with me."

"I'm patient with livestock. I expect I can manage."

She laughed, and the sound of it traveled through him the way a hymn traveled through a quiet room, reaching places that had gone unused for so long he'd forgotten they were there.

"Give me a moment to finish these last few pieces," she said.

Adam picked up one of Emma's stockings from the basket and handed it to her, and they worked the rest of the line together. He held the fabric while she pinned, and when the basket was empty, he carried it to the back porch and set it beside the door. Then he came back to where she stood at the end of the clothesline.

He offered her his elbow. And her fingers settled against the inside of his forearm, light and warm through the cotton of his sleeve, and they walked together along the path that led from the house to the barn.

Adam led Clair through the wide doorway and into the aisle. Mercy lifted her head over the stall rail and whickered softly, and beside her, Sunrise pressed his muzzle through the lower gap in the boards to investigate.

"Give me a minute," Adam said and released Clair's arm.

He walked to the back wall, past the stalls and the stacked hay, to where two cane poles hung from wooden pegs. They'd been there since his father's time. Simple poles, cut from the creek-side cane that grew along the lower banks, each about eight feet long, with a length of linen line tied to the tip and a small iron hook at the end.

He checked the line on each one, running the linen through his fingers from tip to hook.

"Those are fishing poles?" Clair asked. She'd come closer and was watching, her head tilted, studying the cane.

"Cane poles," Adam said. "Nothing fancy. You don't need fancy for creek trout. The line is linen, and the hook does the rest. My father cut these from the cane bank below the south bend when I was nine or ten."

"And they've lasted all this time?"

"Cane is like a good fence cedar. Keep it dry and off the ground, and it'll outlast the man who cut it." He picked up a bait tin from the shelf beside the tack wall, a small round tin with a fitted lid, and shook it once. "Worms," he said.

"So, you've been planning this outing today?"

"Not for this day specifically, but after we talked about fishing, I started gathering worms because I knew you were keen to learn to fish."

"Well, I'm impressed, Mr. Dawson," she said.

Adam tucked the bait tin into his back pocket and lifted both cane poles, resting them over his right shoulder with the tips angled behind him and the lines coiled loosely around the shafts. He offered Clair his free arm, and she took it again, and they walked out of the barn and into the afternoon.

The pasture stretched wide on both sides, the grass thick and gold-tipped in the August sun, the stalks bending in the breeze that came down off the mountains. Grasshoppers launched ahead of them in short, clicking arcs, and in the distance a red-tailed hawk circled above. The cottonwoods along the creek were visible a quarter mile ahead, their crowns full and heavy with summer leaves, the green of them darker than the surrounding grass and swaying in a rhythm that was visible even at this distance.

"How far is it?" Clair asked.

"A quarter mile, give or take. The deep pool is just past the south bend, where the bank drops off and the current slows. That's where the trout hold."

"And that is where you used to fish with your father?"

"Every chance we got, from the time I was old enough to hold a pole and keep still long enough not to scare the fish." He adjusted the cane poles on his shoulder. "My father wasn't a talker, but he'd sit on that bank for hours and not say twenty words, and the quiet between us was good. It was the one place where not talking didn't feel like something was missing. It felt like the whole point."

The creek announced itself before they reached it, a low, constant murmur that grew as the cottonwoods closed around them and the grass gave way to the soft, sandy soil of the bank. Adam ducked beneath a low-hanging branch and held it for Clair, and they stepped through the tree line and onto the bank above the deep pool.

The creek was ten feet across at this point; the water running clear over a bed of smooth stones that caught and scattered the light in a shifting mosaic. Upstream, the current moved fast through a narrow riffle, the water breaking white around the tops of the rocks, and then it slowed and deepened as the bed dropped away into the pool. The pool itself was dark blue and still at its center, the current circling at its edges in lazy, curving lines. Adam could see the shadows of trout holding in the quiet water, their tails working just enough to hold position against the drift.

"This is the spot," he said as he set the bait tin on a flat rock near the bank's edge and lowered the cane poles from his shoulder, leaning them against a cottonwood trunk.

Clair stood beside him and looked at the water.

"It's beautiful," she said.

"It's a good stretch of water. The pool holds fish year-round because the boulders break the current and give them a place to rest. In spring, when the runoff's high, the pool fills up past the bank, and you can hear it from the house. In August it drops down and clears, and that's when the fishing is best."

He picked up one of the cane poles and the bait tin. "Come here," he said, "and I'll show you how this works."

He opened the tin and pulled out a worm, a thick, dark earthworm that curled against his fingers. He held up the hook and showed her how to thread it, pushing the point through the worm's body about a third of the way down and then running the shank through again near the end so the worm held in a curve along the hook's bend.

"You want it threaded, so it stays on when the line hits the water," he said. "If you just stick the point through once, the fish pulls it off before you know he's there."

Clair studied the way his fingers worked the worm onto the hook. "Let me try."

He handed her the tin and a fresh hook. She pulled a worm from the dark soil inside and held it at arm's length, her nose wrinkling, her mouth pressed into a line that was half concentration and half displeasure. Her first attempt pushed the hook through too close to the end, and the worm curled free and dropped into the grass. She picked it up and tried again, threading the point through the thicker middle section and pulling the shank through a second time the way Adam had shown her.

"There," she said, holding up the baited hook. "My father would be astonished if he could see me right now."

"That'll do."

He handed her a cane pole and showed her how to swing the line out over the water. The motion was simple with a cane pole: just the lift of the tip and a smooth swing that let the weighted line carry the bait out toward the deeper water. He stood close to guide her arm, his hand settling over hers on the cane shaft. His fingers covered hers, rough against smooth, and he lifted their joined hands to show her the angle of the swing.

"Smooth," he said. "Like swinging a gate open. Not like throwing a rock."

Her shoulder pressed against his chest for a moment as she leaned into the motion, and the warmth of her registered against him through the layer of his cotton shirt. She stepped forward and swung the line out.

The bait landed three feet from the bank, the hook and worm dropping into the shallow water with a small, defeated splash. Clair looked at the spot where it had landed and then looked at Adam.

"That was terrible," she said.

"That was your first try. Pull it back and go again. More arm this time, and let the pole do the work."

She pulled the line in and swung again. The bait sailed sideways and caught in a willow branch that hung over the water's edge, the line wrapping once around a thin green shoot. Adam waded into the shallow water, leaned out, and freed the hook from the branches.

"Try again," he said.

Clair squared her shoulders and swung the pole a third time. The bait sailed out over the shallows and dropped at the edge of the deep pool with a clean, quiet plop. She turned to him, and the look on her face was pure triumph.

"Don't celebrate yet," he said. "The fish haven't agreed to cooperate."

He swung his own line out with the ease of a motion he'd performed a thousand times, the bait landing near the far bank where the current ran along the boulders. Then he sat down on the grassy bank and stretched his legs toward the water, and Clair settled beside him with her pole braced against her knee.

The afternoon was warm and still around them, and Adam realized that he was happy. He was sitting on the bank of his father's creek with a cane pole in his hand and Clair beside him, and he simply felt happy being here.

"Tell me about the trout," Clair said as she watched the water where her line disappeared into the pool.

"Cutthroat trout," Adam said. "Native to this drainage. You can tell them by the red-orange slash beneath their jaw, right here." He touched the underside of his jaw with two fingers. "It looks like someone drew a line with a paint-soaked brush. They're not as big as the trout in some of the larger rivers, but they're strong for their size, and they fight harder than you'd expect."

"Do they taste good?"

"Best fish you'll eat in Montana. Fried in butter with a little salt, they're better than anything that comes out of a can or a mercantile."

"And they live behind those rocks?"

"Behind the rocks, in the slack water where the current breaks. A trout won't hold in a fast current if it can help it. Too much energy spent staying in one place. They find a spot where the water slows down and the food drifts past, and they wait."

"That sounds like a sensible arrangement."

"Fish are practical. More practical than most people I know."

Clair smiled. The breeze moved through the cottonwoods above them, and the leaves turned and flashed their pale undersides. The sound they made was a dry, papery rustle that mixed with the creek's voice and the occasional call of a bird from somewhere upstream.

"Why do the cottonwood leaves do that?" Clair asked. "Turn silver before a storm?"

"The leaves are flat on top and lighter underneath. When the wind shifts ahead of a storm, it catches them from below and flips them. Old ranchers used to say if the cottonwoods show you their bellies, get the stock in. My father said it, and his father before him, and it's never been wrong as far as I've seen."

"Your father taught you a great deal about this land."

"He taught me everything about this land. Most of what I know about everything else, too."

Adam's line drifted in the slow current near the far bank, and Clair's line hung in the deeper water near the pool's center, and the afternoon moved around them at the pace the creek set.

"Has Solomon ever caught a fish?" Clair asked.

Adam looked at her. "I wouldn't put it past him. That cat catches everything else on this property. I've seen him drag a ground squirrel through the barn door that was half his size."

"Emma told me last week that Solomon sleeps on the hay bales in the barn and refuses to sleep anywhere else."

"She's right. I made the mistake of bringing him inside the house one winter when the cold was bad, and he sat by the door and yowled until I let him back out. He walked straight to the barn, and when he reached the door, he looked back at me like I'd insulted him."

Clair laughed.

"I should tell you about the time Emma tried to catch a chicken," he said.

"Please do."

"She was four. Maybe four and a half. She'd decided she wanted to hold one of the hens. So she went into the coop by herself while I was mending the gate latch, and before I realized she had left my side, she was in there chasing this old red hen around. Ten minutes, Clair. Ten minutes of circles, feathers everywhere, Emma talking to the chicken the entire time like she could reason with it." He shook his head. "The hen finally stopped, pecked a couple of times on her shoe, then walked right between Emma's legs, calm as you please, and strolled to her nest and looked at Emma through the doorway like the whole thing had been beneath her."

"What did Emma do?"

"She sat down in the dirt and folded her arms, and said, 'That chicken is rude.'"

Clair's laughter came open and full, and Adam's joined it. The sound of both of them laughing together on the bank of this creek startled a kingfisher from a branch downstream, and the bird streaked low over the water in a flash of blue-gray and disappeared around the bend. Adam couldn't remember the last time he'd heard his own laughter sound like that, unplanned and real and carrying no effort behind it.

"Oh, let me tell you a humbling story of when I learned to ride sidesaddle," Clair said. "I was thirteen, and my father had arranged for lessons with a woman who taught riding in Helena. The horse was a perfectly gentle mare named Clover, and the sidesaddle was a fine English leather saddle that my instructor said was worth more than most men's monthly wages."

"And?"

"And I fell off twice before the horse took ten steps. The first time the mare shifted, I slid sideways and landed in the mounting yard. The second time, Clover took three steps forward, and I somehow went backward and landed in the water trough."

"In the trough?"

"In the trough. In my riding habit. In front of my instructor and two other students and a stable hand who was trying very hard not to laugh." Clair held her pole steady and shook her head. "My father picked me up from lessons that afternoon and asked how it went, and I told him I had formed a meaningful bond with the water trough. He laughed so hard he had to stop the buggy."

Adam grinned. He could picture it, a thirteen-year-old Clair sitting in a water trough with her dignity soaked and her chin still up, and the image was so vivid and so perfectly suited to the woman beside him that it felt less like a story and more like a memory he'd been given.

Clair's line tugged. The motion was small but sharp; the tip of her cane pole bending toward the water. Clair startled and nearly dropped the pole, her hands scrambling for a grip on the smooth cane.

"Steady," Adam said. "Keep the tip up. Let the fish tire himself."

Clair gripped the pole and lifted the tip, and the line went taut, and the pole bent in a deep curve. Beneath the surface something moved, a flash of shadow in the dark water, and Clair's eyes went wide.

"He's pulling," she said.

"He is. That's what they do. Hold the pole high and let him run against the line. When he stops pulling, you lift."

She held. The line went sideways across the pool, the trout driving toward the boulders, and the cane pole flexed and trembled in her grip. Clair leaned back and held the tip high, and for a moment the contest was even, the fish pulling and the line holding. Clair's arms locked and her jaw set with the same focused resolve she brought to everything she did.

Then she pulled too hard, and the line snapped taut and then went slack, and the pole straightened. Clair stared at the water where the trout had been and then turned to Adam with genuine dismay on her face.

"Don't you dare laugh at me, Adam Dawson. That fish was mine, and I had him."

"You had him, and then you didn't. That's fishing."

"That's robbery. I want another chance."

He opened the bait tin and threaded a fresh worm onto her hook. Clair watched with the focused irritation of a woman who had no intention of losing a second time. She swung the line out, and the cast was better this time, the bait landing clean near the far bank where the current ran along the boulders' edge.

"Better," Adam said.

"I'm learning."

"You are."

They settled back onto the bank, and the afternoon continued around them.

Eventually, Adam's pole bent. The motion was strong and decisive; the tip pulling down toward the water. He lifted the pole and set the hook with a sharp upward pull, and the line went taut, and the fight began.

The trout ran upstream toward the riffle, and Adam angled the pole to turn it, keeping the tip high and the pressure steady. The fish came around and ran toward the boulders, and Adam let it take line by lowering the pole tip and then lifted again as the run slowed and the trout began to tire.

He brought it to the bank slowly, working the pole in patient arcs, and when the trout turned on its side in the shallows, he reached down and lifted it from the water by the line. It was a fine fish, broad through the body and heavy in the hand, the scales dark green along its back and silver along its belly, and the red-orange slash beneath its jaw as vivid as paint. Adam held it up for Clair to see.

"I'd like to catch one more before we head back in," he said. "A fish this size will almost feed us all, but almost isn't quite."

He re-baited his hook and cast the line back into the pool. The trout lay on the grass beside him, its gills working slowly, and Clair sat beside him.

"Thank you for bringing me here," Clair said. "I know what this place means to you."

Adam looked at her and smiled. "It means something different now."

Chapter 20

The potato mounds had flattened since the last rain, and Clair worked her way down the garden row on her knees, pulling the soil back up around the stems with both hands and pressing it firm. The earth was loose and dark between her fingers, warm from the morning and still holding the moisture of the storm that had rolled through two nights ago.

Emma knelt beside her, pulling weeds. She had recovered from the fever fully, her appetite restored, and her energy returned in full measure.

"I dreamed about Sunrise last night," Emma said, depositing a fistful of weeds into her pail. "I was teaching him to count. He could do it up to four, but he kept getting confused after that because horses only have four legs, and he didn't understand what comes next."

"That's a very logical problem for a horse," Clair said. She pressed the soil around the base of a stem and moved to the next mound.

"I told him five comes next, but he just stamped his foot. So I said, 'Sunrise, stamping is not counting,' and he stamped again, and I think that meant he disagreed."

"Horses can be stubborn about arithmetic."

"Miss Clair, do potatoes know they're underground?"

Clair sat back on her heels and looked at Emma, whose face was streaked with dirt from her chin to her left eyebrow. "I don't think they do," Clair said. "But if they did, I imagine they'd be quite content. It's cool and dark and quiet down there, and nobody bothers them until they're ready."

Emma considered this and seemed satisfied. She pulled another weed and held it up for inspection before adding it to her pail. "I can spell 'garden,'" she said. "G-A-R-D-E-N. And I can spell 'horse.' H-O-R-S-E. I can almost spell 'butterfly,' but the middle part is tricky. There are too many letters, and they don't go where I think they should."

"We'll work on it this afternoon during your lesson," Clair said. "The middle part is easier once you hear it broken into pieces."

"Into pieces like what?"

"But-ter-fly. Three pieces. You already know 'but' and 'fly.' It's only the 'ter' in the middle that's new."

Emma's eyes widened. "But-ter-fly," she repeated. "That's only one new part."

"That's only one new part."

Emma grinned and plunged both hands back into the weeds with renewed purpose, and Clair turned back to her mounding. A meadowlark called from the fence post at the garden's eastern corner, two bright notes, and then a tumbling phrase that carried across the yard.

The sound of hooves drew Clair's attention, and she looked up to see Adam riding past on his bay gelding, heading toward the tool shed beside the barn. He sat easily in the saddle, his hat low against the brightness of the day, one hand holding the reins and the other resting on his thigh. As he passed the garden, he touched the brim of his hat and lifted it an inch.

His gaze held hers, and the warmth of it traveled through her chest and settled there.

"Morning, Papa!" Emma called, waving a fistful of weeds.

Adam raised his hand toward her and kept riding. Clair watched him go and turned back to the soil and pressed her palms against the mound she'd been shaping.

Emma returned to her weeding and her commentary. She told Clair that Solomon, the barn cat, had been sitting on the porch rail that morning watching a butterfly, and that she'd told Solomon he wasn't allowed to catch it because butterflies were too pretty to eat. She also informed Clair that her grandma had promised to teach her how to make biscuits as soon as she could reach the counter without standing on a stool.

Then Emma stopped talking, and she pointed with a dirt-streaked finger.

"Miss Clair, who's that man up there?"

Clair followed Emma's hand. The ridge was a quarter mile above them, the tree line a dark, uneven edge where the pasture grass ended and the pines began. A man sat on horseback, perfectly still, at the timber's margin, facing the ranch.

A chill pressed against the base of Clair's spine and climbed. Clair wrapped her arm around Emma and drew the child to her side. Emma looked up with surprise on her face, her weed pail tipping sideways.

"Do you know him?" Emma asked.

"I'm not sure, sweetheart." Clair kept her voice even and light. Her pulse beat fast against her collar, but her hand on Emma's shoulder was firm and still.

The rider sat for a few more seconds, his silhouette sharp against the timber behind him. Then he turned his horse and moved into the trees, and the ridge was empty.

Clair held Emma for another moment and then released her. "Stay right here."

She rose from her knees and brushed the soil from her skirt, and she walked to the split-rail fence and placed her hands on the top rail, and called across the yard. "Adam."

Her voice carried clean and steady across the distance between the garden and the tool shed. Adam stepped through the doorway with a coil of rope in one hand and looked toward her.

He crossed the yard and reached the garden fence. She kept her voice low, pitched beneath Emma's hearing. "There was a man on horseback on the ridge. At the edge of the timber, above the upper pasture. He was sitting there, watching us. He's gone now; he turned into the trees."

Adam looked past her toward the ridge.

"Did you recognize him?" he asked.

"I couldn't make out his features from this distance. But Adam, the way he sat there, the way he held himself—he was watching us on purpose."

Adam's gaze stayed on the ridge for a long moment. "Take Emma inside," he said. "I'll ride the ridge. See if I can catch sight of him."

"Be careful."

"I will, but it could've been anyone up there. A hunter, somebody passing through, maybe someone who got turned around on the mountain." He looked at her, and his voice was calm and practical. "I'll go and look."

Clair nodded and turned back toward Emma, who was pulling weeds with one hand and watching them with open curiosity.

"Come along, Emma. Let's go inside and see what your grandmother is doing. We'll come back to the garden later."

"But I haven't finished my row."

"The weeds will still be there, I promise you; they're not going anywhere."

Emma sighed and gathered her pail and followed Clair through the garden gate and across the narrow back porch. Clair opened the back door and ushered Emma through into the sitting room, her hand resting on the child's shoulder as they crossed the threshold.

Lydia sat at the kitchen table with a colander of green beans before her and a bowl at her elbow. She was stringing them with slow, careful movements.

"Grandma, there was a man on a horse on the ridge looking at us," Emma said.

Lydia's hands stilled on the bean in her fingers, and she looked up at Clair.

"Emma," Lydia said, her voice warm and unhurried, "fetch your primer and your slate from the shelf. Practice your letters for a bit, and when you've filled one side of the slate, bring it to show me."

"But Miss Clair said we'd do my lesson this afternoon."

"And so you shall. But a little practice beforehand never hurt anyone. Go on now."

Emma set her weed pail by the back door and crossed to the shelf in the sitting room.

Lydia folded her hands in her lap. She looked at Clair and tilted her chin toward the empty chair across from her. "Come sit. That man on the ridge frightened you."

Clair sat down and placed her trembling hands flat on the table. "Indeed he did," she said, keeping her voice low enough that it wouldn't carry past the kitchen. "But something about the way he sat there, Lydia, the stillness of him. He wasn't resting or hunting. He was watching."

"And that put you in mind of something," Lydia said.

"Yes."

"Something to do with why you left Helena."

"Yes."

Lydia studied her for a moment. "Tell me what you're thinking, Clair. You've kept a great deal close to your chest since you arrived in this house, and I haven't pressed you because I trusted you'd share when you were ready. But I'm looking at your face right now, and what I see there goes past ordinary worry."

Clair glanced toward the sitting room. She could hear the soft scratch of Emma's slate pencil.

"I told you when I first came here that I discovered circumstances involving my father's business that put me in danger," Clair said. "I haven't told you the particulars, and I owe you more than I've given. There was a man, Lydia. A man connected to the business. I found evidence that he'd been stealing from my father's accounts after my father died, and when I confronted him with the figures, he threatened me. He had two men in the room with him that day. They weren't company employees, and they most definitely were not good men. One of them stood by the door the entire time and never spoke a word, and the way he stood there, Lydia, the way he watched me without moving—that is what I saw on the ridge just now."

"You think this man followed you here? All this way?"

"I couldn't see his face from the garden. The distance was too great. But the way he held himself, the patience of it," Clair pressed her fingertips against the table. "I've seen that before. I've seen it up close."

Lydia reached across the table and covered Clair's hands with her own.

"Later that day, after I confronted this man about what he'd done, I walked home from the office. I turned the corner onto my street and looked behind me, and both of them were following me. They kept their distance, but they made no effort to hide."

"Goodness!" Lydia said.

"When I got inside my house, I locked every door and drew the curtains and sat in the parlor trying to figure out what to do. Each time I checked out the window, both men were watching my home. They never came to the door; they just watched."

"And that is when you decided to leave."

Clair drew her hands from beneath Lydia's and folded them in her lap. "Yes. I took care of a few things in the house and packed up a few things to bring with me. I sat in the dark for quite a long time and listened for footsteps on the porch, and when I had worked up my nerve, I saddled my horse in the back stable and rode east before first light."

Lydia was quiet for a moment.

"Clair, are you certain about what you felt today? Truly certain? A man on a ridge above a ranch such as ours could be any number of things. A hunter passing through, a traveler who had lost his way."

"I know that. And I've told myself every reasonable explanation I can think of." Clair met Lydia's gaze. "But I know with every-thing in me, Lydia. The moment Emma pointed, and I looked up and saw that figure sitting there, something in me went cold in a way I hadn't felt since the night I left Helena. I could be wrong, and I pray that I am. But I cannot dismiss what I felt, and I would rather tell you and be wrong than stay silent and be right."

"You did right to tell me," Lydia said as she picked up the bean she'd set down, turning it in her fingers without stringing it. "But I want you to hear me say this clearly. Whatever trouble might have followed you out of Helena, you are not facing it alone. You are in this house because God put you here, and the people in this house protect those we care for."

Clair's throat tightened.

"I should have told you more from the beginning," Clair said.

"You shared what you could when you could. Nobody asks a person to lay bare the worst day of their life over a first cup of coffee." Lydia set the bean into the colander and reached for another. "But Clair, I'll ask you this. Is there more to tell? Beyond what you've shared with Adam and with me?"

"There is. A great deal more."

Lydia nodded.

"Then you'll tell it when you're ready," she said. "And we'll listen. No need to borrow trouble when we have none on our doorstep for now."

They sat together at the table while Emma practiced her letters in the next room, and Clair picked up a handful of beans from the colander and began stringing them. She and Lydia worked side by side without speaking for a while, the bowl between them filling with trimmed beans.

Adam came through the front door nearly an hour later and hung his hat on the peg above the bench and stood by the kitchen door.

"I rode the full length of the ridge from the east timber to the old logging road," he said. "I never saw a soul. I found tracks along the game trail that cuts above the upper pasture. The tracks stopped where Clair said the man was sitting, right at the timber's edge where the ground opens up and you can see the whole property below. He sat there long enough that the horse shifted and stamped a few times. Then the tracks go back into the timber heading south."

Adam leaned his shoulder against the doorframe. "It could've been anyone. A traveler cutting through, someone scouting timber for the mill, or simply someone out for a ride."

He looked at Clair; her hands were still in her lap, the half-strung bean forgotten between her fingers.

She knew what her face was showing him because she could feel it in the set of her jaw, in the tightness across her brow that she couldn't smooth away, and in the way her lips were pressed together. Her chin was lifted as if bracing for a wind that hadn't arrived yet.

"I need to tell you both everything," Clair said. "Tonight, after Emma is in bed. All of it. The entire truth about why I left Helena and what I brought with me. I should have told you before now. I've been carrying this burden for far too long, and I am unable to carry it alone anymore. I need your help to decide what to do, because I don't know what to do, and the not knowing has been eating at me since the day I arrived in your barn."

She looked away from Adam and focused her attention on Lydia.

"But for now, let's carry on as if it's an ordinary day," Clair continued. "Emma doesn't need to be frightened. She and I will work on her reading this afternoon, and we'll have supper as usual, and tonight, when she's asleep, I'll tell you both everything."

Adam studied her from the doorway.

"Should I ride to town and bring the Marshal here?" he asked.

Clair shook her head. "Not yet. Please. Let me tell you everything first. Then we can decide together whether to go to the marshal or whether I need to leave your home so that you and your family aren't in danger."

The word left her mouth and landed in the kitchen like a stone dropped into still water. Leave. She saw it register on Adam's face before she finished the sentence and watched the stillness that came over him. His jaw set hard, the muscles beneath his ears pulling tight, and his shoulders drew back a fraction. The look in his eyes lost every trace of the calm he'd been offering and replaced it with something raw and unguarded and fierce.

"I'll be outside working near the house for the rest of the day. You all stay inside. I'll see you at dinner," he said as he put his hat back on his head. He opened the door without another word and was gone.

Chapter 21

The lamp sat at the center of the kitchen table with its wick turned low, the flame no taller than Adam's thumbnail. Emma had gone down easily, tired from the long day.

Clair sat across from Adam, her hands in her lap, and his mother sat to his left.

Clair looked at Adam, then at Lydia.

"I have so much to tell you both, and I'll do my best not to ramble through all that I've been keeping to myself. Harlan Greaves was my father's general manager." Clair said. "My father hired him twelve years ago, when the business was still growing from a handful of wagons into something substantial. Mr. Greaves knew the mining camps and the freight roads, and the men who worked them. My father needed someone to manage the operations side of the company while he focused on contracts and business strategy, and Mr. Greaves filled that role. He filled it well."

She spoke calmly, her voice measured and precise

"Over twelve years, my father gave him increasing authority. He hired and dismissed drivers. He negotiated with the suppliers. He managed the warehouse inventory. And eventually, my father gave him signatory authority on all the company's bank accounts so that Mr. Greaves could pay suppliers and drivers when my father was unavailable." She paused. "He ate at our table. He attended our church. He called me by my first name. My father trusted him. We both did. He was family to us in every way that mattered, except blood."

"My father died alone in his office," she said. "He was found sitting in his chair. The doctor couldn't say with certainty what took him, only that it was sudden and that he didn't suffer. I still question what took him from me. I believe with everything in me that something happened to him that day. He was fifty-four years old, and I had spoken with him that morning before he left for work, and by afternoon, he was gone."

"After the funeral, I stayed home. I grieved. I couldn't bring myself to go to the office, nor look at the ledgers, nor sit in his chair. The business had been running for years. I told myself it would continue running without me for a few weeks while I found my footing," Clair's chin was level, her shoulders square, but Adam could see the effort was costing her. "That was two and a half months. For two and a half months, I stayed home, trusting the company to manage itself. I was so foolish; I should have been more responsible."

"Edmund Holt, the company secretary, came every Friday during that time at the close of business to bring me a report and see how I was faring. He was a good and loyal man. He'd worked for my father for years. And then there was Mr. Greaves. He visited every week or so. He brought provisions. Flour, sugar, coffee, smoked meat. He sat at our kitchen table and told me everything was running well and encouraged me to take whatever time I needed. He was kind .... always so kind."

She stopped and drew a breath and held it for a count before she released it.

"I was grieving, and he used my grief the way a man uses an open gate. I should have been stronger. I should have forced myself back to work sooner. But the grief held me so deeply in the darkness that I felt as if I were drowning, and every time Mr. Greaves told me to take my time, I believed him because I needed to believe someone was minding what I couldn't."

"You were mourning your father," Lydia said. "There is no weakness in that."

"There was a cost to it," Clair said. "And I paid it."

She described her return. The morning she finally dressed and walked to the office and sat at her father's desk and opened the primary ledger. How the numbers had looked wrong before she'd finished the first page. Entries that didn't reconcile. Payments recorded to suppliers without matching receipts. Shipments logged in the books that she couldn't verify against the manifests. She'd spent several days working through the records, cross-referencing every entry against the correspondence files and the shipping logs, and the arithmetic had assembled itself with a precision that left no room for doubt. She spent weeks going over everything again and again, trying to figure things out logically.

"One day, I went to the bank," she said. "I needed to confirm the account balances against what the ledger showed. And that is when I discovered there were accounts I didn't know existed. A business emergency fund my father had established, separate from the primary operating account. And a personal account he'd been building for me, money he was setting aside for my future." Her voice held steady, but Adam watched her fingers curl against each other in her lap, the knuckles pressing white. "All three accounts were being drained. Steady withdrawals, all authorized under Mr. Greaves's signatory authority, began after my father's death. The primary account, the emergency fund, and the account my father had been building for me since I was a girl."

"How much?" Adam asked.

"Fourteen thousand two hundred dollars. Across all three accounts."

Fourteen thousand dollars. Adam knew what that figure meant in a territory where a good horse sold for forty and a working ranch hand earned thirty a month. It was a fortune. It was the accumulated labor of a man's lifetime, the whole of what Ezekiel Whitmore had built and saved and set aside for his daughter's future.

"How long had this been going on?" Adam asked.

"Only after my father's death. Mr. Greaves didn't steal while my father was alive. It was my absence that gave him the opportunity, and he took it. He then continued to take it even after I had returned to the office."

Adam's jaw tightened, and he could feel the muscles along his temples pulling.

"Eventually, after I had worked up the nerve, and I was certain, I confronted him," Clair said. "Privately, in the office, with the specific figures written out in my own hand. I laid the ledger pages across the desk and showed him every false entry, every inflated cost, every withdrawal that had no corresponding business expense."

"What did he do?" Lydia asked.

"He moved through a sequence of responses. The first was dismissal. He told me I was a grieving girl who didn't understand freight accounting and that the entries I was questioning were standard operational costs. When I showed him the bank records and the discrepancies between what was recorded in the ledger and what was actually paid to suppliers, he changed course. He told me that a territorial probate court could appoint a male executor to oversee my father's estate if I were deemed unfit to manage it, and that he knew people on the court."

Adam's fingers curled inward until his knuckles went white against the table where his hands rested.

"When intimidation didn't work, and I didn't back down," Clair continued, "he offered to buy the company. He framed it as practical advice for a young woman alone. A fair price, a clean transfer, a fresh start somewhere else. It was hush money dressed in business language, and we both knew it."

"And when you refused that?" Adam asked.

"When I refused everything and told him I intended to take the matter to the authorities, his composure dropped." Clair met Adam's eyes across the table and held them. "He said, 'Women such as you often go missing in the dead of night, never to be heard from again. And I know just the people to make such a thing happen.'"

Adam stared at her. His hands were still curled on the table, and the tension in his forearms was visible, the cords standing out beneath his skin.

"There were two other men in the room with us that day," Clair said. "Judd Sutter and Charles Rawlins. They weren't employees of the company. My father never hired them. There were no employment records for either man. Mr. Greaves brought them in from Helena's rougher circles after my father died, gave them a thin pretense of legitimacy, and used them as his eyes and his muscle. They frequented saloons and had been arrested before for theft. They were trouble through and through, and I'd heard talk of them among the women in Helena. When I first returned to work and saw them loitering near the warehouse, I knew something was wrong before I opened a single ledger."

"The day I confronted Mr. Greaves, one man stood by the door. The other stood near the window. Neither spoke. After I left Mr. Greaves' office, I took every piece of evidence with me and walked home," Clair said. "They followed me. When I reached my house and locked every door and drew the curtains, they took up a position across the road. They stood there for the rest of the afternoon and into the evening. Watching."

"I decided that night," Clair said. "I couldn't go to the authorities in Helena. Mr. Greaves had standing in the community. He sat on a merchant committee. He had connections I didn't have and influence I couldn't match. I was a twenty-two-year-old woman with no male protector and no legal advocate. Judd Sutter and Charles Rawllins, standing outside my home, watching, further threatened me. I was afraid for my life, so I made preparations."

She told them about the carpetbag. How she'd taken her sewing kit to the kitchen table after dark and worked by the light of a single candle, stitching a false lining into the bag. She'd wrapped all the documents she brought home with her from the office in oilskin and placed them flat inside the false lining. Then she'd gone to the safe her father kept in the study. She emptied it of every dollar, placed the money alongside the documents, and stitched the lining shut.

"I packed what I could carry," she said. "I saddled my horse in the back stable after midnight, after I had calmed my nerves enough to slip outside my home, and I rode east."

She told them about Livingston. Mrs. Garrett's Boardinghouse, where she stayed two nights and overheard two men at the midday meal talking about ranch country to the south and a small settlement called Providence Ridge. She asked the boardinghouse keeper about it that evening and learned it was remote and sparsely settled and a full day and a half's ride from the nearest railroad. She left before dawn the next morning, heading south with no real plan in mind.

"South of Livingston, my horse went lame," she said. "I walked for two days. I was exhausted, and I was running on nothing but fear and instinct."

She looked at Adam. "And then I found your barn."

Clair rose from her chair and walked into Lydia's room. Adam heard the soft sound of her footsteps crossing the floor, then the rustle of fabric, and then she was back. She carried the carpetbag to the table and set it down, and opened the clasp. Her fingers found the edge of the false lining and worked it loose, and she drew out a thick packet wrapped in dark oilskin and tied with cord. She laid it on the table between them.

"I've been checking this bag every night," she said. "Every night since I arrived. Before I go to sleep, I check that it's still there. I kneel beside my pallet in the dark and run my fingers along the lining of the bag, and I feel the edges of the oilskin through the cotton, and I tell myself it's still safe. I don't know why I do it. Perhaps to calm my nerves. Perhaps because it's the only thing I have any control over." She looked at her hands on the table. "I think about my situation every night when I lie down. I turn everything over and over in my mind. What I should do. What I could have done differently. Was leaving Helena the right thing? Because from this distance, what can I do now? I left my home because I feared for my life, and here I am without a single notion of how to move forward."

Adam stared at the oilskin packet.

"The Lord brought you to us, Clair." Lydia said. "I said it that morning you arrived, and I will say it as many times as it needs saying. He brought you here for a reason, and I do not believe that reason was so you could carry this burden alone."

"My being here puts your family in danger," Clair said. "If that man on the ridge is one of Greaves's people, they know where I am. The right thing for me to do is leave before they bring trouble to your door."

Adam looked at her.

"Where would you go?" he asked.

"I could take the evidence to the authorities in Livingston."

"Livingston is a full day and a half's ride. You'd be alone on an open road. You are safer in this house, Clair."

"Adam, if they come here, Emma and your mother are at risk while you're out working the ranch. I cannot bear the thought of bringing harm to this family. If I leave, they have no reason to trouble you."

"Clair," he said her name and waited until her eyes met his. "Please hear me. I don't want you leaving this house for fear of putting my family at risk. We all want you here."

Adam leaned forward with his forearms on the table. "I was already planning to ride into town tomorrow for supplies. I need a few things for the ranch, and you and Ma can put together a list of whatever you need from the mercantile. While I'm there, I'll talk to Amos Pemberton and find out whether any strangers have been asking questions around town. I'll check with Leora Hanscombe at the boardinghouse. I'll keep my eyes open while I'm in town and see if I notice anyone who stands out."

"And while you're gone?" Clair asked.

"Ma knows where Pa's shotgun is, and she knows how to use it." He glanced at his mother. "You'll be fine in the house. I don't believe any danger will come to you while I'm away. These men, if they are Greaves's people, aren't here to hurt anyone. They're here for what you're carrying and for a signature on a piece of paper more than likely. I imagine that Harlan Greaves might have sent these men to force you to sign a bill of sale for the business."

He looked at the oilskin packet on the table.

"Clair, there's a place in this house where we keep money and anything of value. My father built it, and only my mother and I know it's there. You're welcome to put your documents and your money there for safekeeping. It's more secure than a carpetbag lining."

Clair looked at him.

"Yes," she said. "I'd like that very much."

Adam pushed his chair back from the table and stood.

Clair gathered the oilskin packet and reached into the carpetbag's false lining and withdrew the rolls of cash, thick bundles bound with string, more money than Adam had seen in one place. She held them against her chest and followed him through the doorway into Lydia's room.

The room was dim, the lamp from the kitchen casting a wedge of light through the open door. Adam crossed to his mother's bed and gripped the iron frame and pulled it away from the wall, the legs scraping softly against the floorboards. He knelt beside the wall where the bed had been and found the board with his fingers, the one his father had cut to fit so precisely that you couldn't see the seam unless you knew where to look. He pressed the far end and the near end lifted, and he worked it free and set it aside. Beneath it was a shallow cavity in the floor joists, and nestled inside it was a wooden box with a hinged lid.

He lifted the box and opened it. Inside were several coins, a roll of money, a folded deed, and a gold pocket watch that had belonged to his father.

Clair knelt beside him and placed the oilskin packet into the box, then the rolls of cash. Adam closed the lid and set the box back into the cavity and replaced the floorboard, pressing it flush until the seam disappeared. He slid his mother's bed back into place.

He straightened and turned to face her. Clair stood an arm's length away, and in the dim light from the kitchen doorway, he could see her face clearly.

"You're safe here," he said. "I believe with everything in me that you have nothing to fear. I believe that if these men are here, they want those papers, and they want you to sign away your father's business, and as long as we are careful and we are wise, they will not get either one."

Clair's chin dropped a fraction. Her lips parted, and the breath that came out of her was uneven, and the tears she'd been holding broke past the line she'd drawn for them and ran down her cheeks in two silent tracks.

Adam stepped forward and drew her against his chest, settled his hands against her back, and held her.

"Please forgive me for being so forward," he said. "But I cannot take a woman crying. Please don't cry. You are fine."

Clair nodded. Her forehead rested against his chest, and he could feel the small motion of it. She pressed her face into the cotton of his shirt and let herself be held.

Chapter 22

Adam kept the team at an easy pace as he rode into town. His thoughts turning over in his mind.

Clair had sat at his kitchen table last night with her hands in her lap and her voice level. Her composure was held so tightly that when it finally broke, the single sharp breath she drew sounded like something tearing inside her.

He thought about the oilskin packet lying on the table, the physical evidence of everything she'd carried alone since Helena, and the steady, precise way she had laid out every fact as though she were reading figures from a ledger. The story she had told would have brought most people to pieces long before the end.

She hadn't fallen to pieces, though. She had told them about Harlan Greaves, a man who had eaten at her family's table and called her by her Christian name for twelve years. Then stood in her father's office and told her that women such as her often went missing in the dead of night. She had told them about walking home alone with two men following at a distance and about sitting in her house with the curtains drawn and the doors locked while they stood across the road and watched.

Adam's hands tightened on the lines until the leather creased against his palms.

Twenty-two years old and alone in the world, and a man she once trusted threatening to make her disappear.

He tried to envision Clair sitting at a kitchen table and stitching a false lining into her carpetbag by candlelight. Then, alone in a dark house, working up the courage to walk out of the only home she'd ever known and ride into the night, praying for safety.

The courage of that. The solitary, quiet, furious courage of a woman who had no one to call on for help, probably at that point not trusting anyone in the world, and yet she called on herself instead.

He thought about what he'd done afterward, in Lydia's room. The floor compartment his father had built, the documents, and the cash sealed inside it, the bed slid back into place. And then Clair, standing an arm's length from him with her composure finally broken open. The tears running down her face and the feeling that had moved through him when he stepped forward and put his arms around her and held her against his chest. The feeling had been simple and enormous at the same time, and it had told him something he already knew.

He loved her.

He loved the woman sleeping in his mother's room on a pallet on the floor, and he could no longer deny it.

The road curved east around a low rise, and the valley widened, and Adam could see the Yellowstone River in the distance, the cottonwoods along its banks standing pale and still in the windless air.

He straightened on the seat and let his eyes move across the countryside, reading it. The road ahead was empty. The benchland to the west showed nothing but grass and sage. The timber to the east climbed the foothills in an unbroken wall of lodgepole and fir.

He knew this ground. Every drainage, every tree line, every contour of the hills where they folded against each other and created pockets of dead space that couldn't be observed from the road. His father had run cattle on this land for years before Adam was old enough to ride, and Adam had been riding it since he was old enough to sit in a saddle. If Greaves's men were on this ground, they were on his ground, and the advantage belonged to the man who knew where every gate hung and every fence post stood.

He thought about what needed to happen. Clair needed to give her statement to Marshal Tom Callahan. The evidence had to enter the legal system.

The road dropped toward the river crossing, and the new bridge came into view, its timbers still pale against the darker wood of the cottonwoods on either bank. The wheels changed their sound when they left the packed earth and met the planking, a hollow drumming that the horses knew and didn't startle at. Adam held the lines steady and let them cross at their own pace, the river running fast and clear beneath the gaps in the planks.

On the far side of the bridge, the road followed its gentle curve southward, and the buildings of Providence Ridge began to show. The false front of the mercantile on the east side of the road. The boarding house across from it on the west. A few horses tied to the hitching rails, a dog lying in the shade beneath the boardwalk, and the distant ring of iron from the blacksmith's shop at the south end of town.

Adam pulled the team to the rail in front of Pemberton's Mercantile and set the brake. He wrapped the lines around the brake handle and climbed down. He stepped up onto the boardwalk and pushed through the mercantile door.

Amos Pemberton was behind the counter with a crate of tinned goods open before him. He looked up when the door opened, and the expression that crossed his face when he saw Adam was not the usual merchant's greeting.

"Adam," Amos said. He set down the can in his hand and came around the end of the counter. "I'm glad you're here. I need a word with you."

Adam stopped. "What is it?"

Amos glanced toward the front windows, then back. "Two men came in here yesterday evening, close to closing time. One of them did the talking. Medium build, decent clothes, well-spoken. The kind of man who smiles a great deal and wants you to think he's your friend. He asked me about a young woman from Helena. Light-brown hair, educated way of speaking, arrived sometime in early July. Said she was a relative they were worried about, that she'd left Helena in a state after her father died. They just wanted to make sure she was all right."

Adam's jaw set as he listened.

"The other one stood by the door the whole time," Amos said. "Never spoke a word. Harder-looking. The kind of man who doesn't smile, doesn't try to, and doesn't care whether you like him or not. He stood there and watched the room while his partner talked, and I'll tell you plainly, Adam, I kept one eye on him the entire conversation."

"Did you believe the story?" Adam asked.

Amos shook his head. "The story was rehearsed. Polished and practiced, the way a man practices a sales pitch before he walks into a negotiation. Every sentence came out too smoothly, and when I asked a question he didn't expect, there was a half-second pause before the smoothness came back. And the quiet one by the door was definitely not here for some kind of family reunion."

"You knew who they were asking after."

"I did," Amos said.

"What did you tell them?"

"Nothing. I told them I hadn't seen any new faces come through town that matched what they described. I told them Providence Ridge is a small settlement and that a newcomer would be noticed, and that I hadn't noticed one." Amos folded his arms across his chest. "I know a rehearsed story when I hear one, and I know the difference between a man who is worried about a relative and a man who is hunting someone down."

"Where did they go?" Adam asked.

"I watched them from the window after they left. They walked south along the boardwalk and went into the saloon. I didn't see them come back out, but I closed up shortly after and went home." Amos paused. "Margaret saw them yesterday, too. She'd noticed them pass the front window earlier in the day. She said they didn't have the look of mill workers or ranch hands, or Yellowstone travelers. I agreed with her."

"Have they spoken to anyone else in town that you know of?"

"I can't say for certain. But I'll tell you this: if they're still in the area, they aren't staying at the boardinghouse. Leora would have mentioned it to someone by now, and I haven't heard a word."

Adam stood in the mercantile aisle with the morning quiet of the store around him and the information settling into the structure of what he already knew. Two men. One who talked and one who watched. Sutter and Rawlins. The names Clair had spoken at his kitchen table matched the shapes Amos had just drawn, and the match was precise enough that there was no room left for coincidence.

"I appreciate you telling me, Amos," Adam said.

He looked at Adam with the direct gaze of a man who had weighed a situation and chosen his side. "Whatever is going on, Adam, I'm trusting your judgment on it. If there's anything I can do, you tell me."

"For now, keep your eyes open," Adam said. "If you see them again, I'd like to know about it."

"You'll know the same day, I promise. I'll drop everything and ride out to your place."

Adam pulled Lydia's list from his pocket and unfolded it on the counter, and Amos returned to the business of commerce. He measured coffee from the barrel into a paper sack and weighed it on the brass scale. He scooped salt into a smaller sack and tied it with twine. The flour he pulled from a fifty-pound bag behind the counter, portioning it into a cotton sack that Adam had brought with from the wagon. He counted nails from the bin and bundled them in a twist of brown paper. He measured a length of rope against the marks on the counter's edge and cut it.

The spool of thread he found on the notions shelf beside the buttons and thimbles. The bolt of cloth took longer. Amos carried two bolts to the counter and laid them side by side: a sturdy cotton in a dark blue and a lighter weight calico printed with small flowers.

"What's your mother after?" Amos asked.

"She said cloth for a dress," Adam said. "She didn't say which kind."

"The calico is better for a dress. The cotton's heavier, better for a work shirt or an apron." Amos tapped the calico. "I'd send this one home. Margaret picked the pattern herself from the Livingston wholesaler, and she has better taste in fabric than I'll ever have."

"The calico, then."

Amos measured the yardage against the brass tacks driven into the counter's edge at one-yard intervals and cut it with his shears. He folded it neatly and wrapped it in brown paper and set it with the rest of the order. He tallied the figures in his ledger with the pencil he kept behind his ear, his handwriting small and exact, each number aligned with the column above it.

He turned the ledger so that Adam could see the total. "I'll add it to your account."

Adam nodded. He gathered the supplies into two armloads and carried them out to the wagon, setting them in the bed behind the bench seat. When he'd finished, he crossed the street.

The boardinghouse sat with its wide porch facing the road, the two long benches flanking the door empty at this hour. Adam stepped up onto the porch and through the front door.

Leora Hanscombe was behind her desk near the foot of the stairs. She looked up when Adam entered.

"Adam Dawson," she said. "What a pleasure to see you."

"Morning, Leora. I was in town for supplies and thought I'd stop in."

"I see." She set her fountain pen in the ink tray and gave him her full attention.

"Have you had any new boarders this past week?" Adam asked.

"I haven't. My current guests are Mr. Hensley from the lumber company, who has been here since April, and Mrs. Carpenter from Livingston, who's visiting her daughter and will be here through the weekend. No one else."

"Noticed any strangers passing through town?"

Leora studied him. "Adam, what's this about?"

"I've heard there might be strangers in the area," he said. "Asking questions."

"What kind of questions?"

"The kind that doesn't quite match the reason given for asking them."

"If something is going on that I should know about, Adam, I'd appreciate hearing it sooner rather than later."

"If there's anything to tell, I'll tell you," he said.

"I'll hold you to that." She picked up her pen. "And I'll keep my eyes open meanwhile. Not much passes through this town that I miss."

"I know it," Adam said.

He stepped back out onto the porch and crossed the street to his wagon.

Adam climbed onto the bench seat and released the brake. He turned the team south along Main Street and let them walk at their own pace past the assayer's, past the open ground between the buildings. The saloon sat ahead on the west side of the road, its door closed, its windows dark. At this hour, the building held the shuttered quiet of a place that wouldn't open for hours yet. Adam let his eyes move over it as the wagon passed: the front, the side wall, and the alley beside it. Nothing stirred. No horses at the rail. No sign of occupancy at all.

He turned the team in the wide space in the road past the blacksmith's shop and brought them back north through town. When the last building fell behind and the road opened onto the valley again, he let the horses settle into their traveling pace and pointed them toward home.

Chapter 23

The front door opened while Clair was turning the ham slices in the skillet. Adam came through carrying a wooden supply crate and set it on the kitchen table.

She moved the skillet off the hot plate and wiped her hands on her apron. "Did you have any trouble?"

"None." He pulled a paper sack from the crate and set it beside the coffee tin on the counter. "I never saw a soul going to town nor coming back."

"Did Amos have everything?" Lydia asked.

"He did." Adam pulled the wrapped fabric from the crate and handed it to her. "Calico. He said Margaret picked the pattern from the Livingston wholesaler."

Lydia took the parcel and worked the paper open at one corner to see the print. She nodded once, satisfied, and set it on the counter.

"Amos told me something this morning," he said. "Two men came into the mercantile yesterday evening. One of them did the talking and asked about a young woman from Helena with light-brown hair. Said they were family and her father had passed away recently, and they were concerned about her welfare. The other one stood by the door and watched, and never spoke. Amos said the story sounded rehearsed and the man who wasn't talking had no interest in any family reunion."

"Did Amos tell them anything?" Clair asked.

"He told them he hadn't seen any new faces matching that description and left it there."

Lydia had moved closer to the table, her face grave and attentive. "Did Amos say where these men went afterward?"

"Into the saloon. He watched them from the window. He hasn't seen them since, and he said he'd ride out here if he spotted them again." Adam looked at Clair. "What would you like to do?"

She looked at him. "I don't know. I've turned this mess over so many times in my mind, and I just don't know what to do."

"Let's get the evidence," he said. "The wagon is already hitched and ready to go. I think we should go see Marshal Tom today."

"Are you sure?" she asked.

"It would help to get this off your mind," he said. "Tell Marshal Tom everything from the beginning. Hand him the evidence, give him your statement, and let him take it from there."

Clair looked at him and nodded. "All right, if you feel that's best. Would you like something to eat first before we leave?"

"No, I'm fine," he said as he turned to leave. "I'll give the horses a drink of water before we go. That gives you time to get the documents."

Clair walked into Lydia's bedroom and gripped the iron bed frame, and pulled it away from the wall. She found the board she needed, pressed the far end, felt the near end lift, and worked it free. The wooden box sat in its cavity. She left her money in the box and closed the lid and replaced the board and pressed it flush, then slid the bed back into place.

She walked back into the kitchen.

"When this is settled, Clair, I want you to hold on to something," Lydia said. "You didn't leave Helena because you were afraid. You left because you were brave enough to take the evidence with you when you could have burned it and walked away from all of it. You could have just signed the papers and sold the business, too. You could have shriveled up and kept quiet about the evil deeds you had uncovered, but you didn't. You stood your ground. Your father raised a daughter with a spine made of good iron, and right now you're proving him right." She paused and held Clair's gaze. "Be proud of yourself."

"Thank you, Lydia," Clair said.

***

Clair sat on the bench seat for a moment and looked at the building. It was a modest frame structure with a single window facing the street and a door that stood ajar against the afternoon warmth. A sign hung from the porch overhang, plain lettering on a plank that read MARSHAL in black paint. The boardwalk in front of it was swept clean.

Adam climbed down and came around to her side and offered his hand, and Clair took it and stepped down from the wagon. He reached beneath the bench seat, retrieved the oilskin packet, and handed it to her.

"I'll be right beside you. I'm not going anywhere," he said.

She held the packet against her waist and walked with him up the single step onto the boardwalk and through the open door.

The marshal's office was a single room, spare and functional, with a desk near the side wall. Two chairs faced the desk, a rifle rack on the wall behind it. A woodstove in the corner that sat cold and unused in the August heat. A corkboard on the wall beside the door held a few posted notices, their edges curled from humidity. The room had the scrubbed, orderly quality of a space maintained by a man who believed that a place of business ought to look like one.

Marshal Tom Callahan sat behind the desk with a ledger open before him and a fountain pen in his hand. He was a man of perhaps forty-five, solidly built, with gray threading through brown hair that was trimmed close and parted neatly. His shirtsleeves were rolled to his forearms, and a badge was pinned to his vest. He looked up when they entered.

"Adam," he said as he set his pen in the ink tray and pushed his chair back. "What brings you in today?"

"Tom, we need your help," Adam said. "This is Clair Whitmore. She has been staying with us for several weeks now, helping my mother around the house. Clair needs to speak with you, and I'd appreciate it if you'd hear her out."

Tom looked at Clair, then at the packet in her hands, then back at her face. He gestured toward the two chairs.

"Nice to meet you, Clair. Please sit down, both of you," he said.

"Nice to meet you as well, Marshal Tom," she said as she sat down. "My father was Ezekiel Whitmore, and he owned a company called Whitmore Freight and Supply in Helena. That is where I am from as well. My father died four months ago, and after his death I discovered that the company's general manager, a man named Harlan Greaves, had been stealing from the business."

Tom listened without interrupting. Clair told him about her father's company. Nineteen wagons at peak. Mining camps across the territory. She told him about Greaves's twelve years of service, the signatory authority her father had granted him on all three bank accounts, the trust that had been built over years of shared meals and shared church pews. She told him about her father's death and her retreat into grief and the months during which Greaves had sole, unsupervised access to the company's finances.

"When I returned to work," Clair said, "I found entries that didn't reconcile. Payments without matching receipts. Shipments logged without corresponding manifests. When I went to the bank, I discovered two accounts I hadn't known existed, a business emergency fund and a personal account my father had been building for my future, and both were being drained through withdrawals authorized under Greaves's signature as well as our larger main account for the business."

"How much money are we talking about?" Tom asked.

"Fourteen thousand two hundred dollars in bank withdrawals alone, across all three accounts," Clair said. "That figure accounts only for the direct withdrawals I traced through the bank records. The fictitious shipments he created in the ledger, freight runs that never happened with supplier costs that were never incurred, represent additional losses I was still calculating when I confronted him. The total theft is larger than what the bank records show. I honestly did not check the safe we had in the office, which normally held petty cash we would give our drivers to take with them in case of emergencies."

"Okay, go on."

"After I had gone over everything several times and knew that something underhanded was going on, I confronted Harlan Greaves. He moved through a sequence of responses, beginning with dismissal, telling me I was a grieving young woman who didn't understand freight accounting. Then he offered a veiled threat about the territorial probate court appointing a male executor if I were deemed unfit to manage the estate. He said he knew people on the court."

"And then?"

"He offered to buy the company outright. He framed it as the sensible course for a young woman alone. It was bribery disguised as a business transaction, and when I refused, his composure changed entirely. He told me that women such as myself often go missing in the dead of night, never to be heard from again, and that he knew just the people to make such a thing happen."

Tom's eyes went still and focused with precision.

"Were there witnesses to this threat?" he asked.

"Two men were in the room," Clair said. "Judd Sutter and Charles Rawlins. They're not employees of the company. They're men from Helena's rougher circles. Harlan Greaves brought them in after my father died and introduced them as associates, but they did no freight work. They stood in the office while he threatened me, and their presence was the reason I believed him."

"What did you do after the confrontation?"

"I walked home. Sutter and Rawlins followed me and positioned themselves outside my home for the rest of the day. That night, after dark, I sewed a false lining into my carpetbag and hid the documents and bank withdrawal records inside, wrapped in oilskin. I took cash from my father's household safe, left on horseback, and rode toward Livingston. I stayed two nights at Mrs. Garrett's boarding house in Livingston, overheard someone mention Providence Ridge, and came south. My horse went lame on my journey here, and I walked the last two days."

Tom sat back in his chair and looked at the oilskin packet on Clair's lap. "And those are the documents?"

Clair unwrapped the oilskin and laid the contents on his desk.

Tom leaned forward and turned the pages one at a time, his eyes moving across the columns of figures. He studied the withdrawal records the longest.

Tom set the last page down and placed his hands flat on the desk on either side of the documents.

"Miss Whitmore, I appreciate you bringing this to me," he said. "I want to explain what I can do from here, because Providence Ridge is a long way from Helena."

"That is what concerns me," Clair said. "I don't know how something like this could be handled from here."

"The first thing I need from you is a sworn deposition," Tom said. "That's a written statement, given under oath, detailing everything you've just told me. I'll write it out as you tell it, and you'll sign it in my presence. A sworn deposition carries legal standing in territorial court. It doesn't require you to be present in Helena for the investigation to begin."

"And the evidence?" Clair asked.

"I'll package everything together: your deposition and the documents, sealed and witnessed. I'll send it by dispatch rider to Livingston. From Livingston, it goes by rail to Helena, addressed to the Lewis and Clark County Sheriff's office. If the sheriff determines the case warrants it, and based on what you've shown me I believe he will, he can also bring in the U.S. Marshal's office for territorial jurisdiction." Tom paused and looked at her directly. "You don't need to return to Helena, Miss Whitmore. The deposition and the evidence are legally sufficient to initiate an investigation. Once these documents enter the legal system, they become government evidence. They belong to the territory, and no private party can retrieve or destroy them."

"What will happen to Harlan Greaves?" she asked.

"Based on what you've described and what these records show, the sheriff will probably open a formal investigation. If the evidence supports the charges, and I believe it does, Greaves will be arrested and charged with embezzlement. The threat he made to you may bring additional charges. The legal process is not fast, Miss Whitmore. I won't mislead you about that. An investigation of this kind could take weeks to begin and months to resolve. But once the machinery starts turning, it doesn't stop because the accused has friends on a merchant's committee."

"How long before the documents reach Helena?" Clair asked.

"The dispatch rider can be in Livingston by tomorrow evening if he leaves this afternoon. From Livingston, the eastbound train can have the package in Helena within a day. Allow a week for the sheriff's office to review it and begin its inquiry. You could see movement within a fortnight, though the full process will take longer."

Clair looked at the documents spread across Tom's desk. "I'm ready to give my deposition," she said.

Tom took a fresh sheet of paper from his desk drawer and picked up his fountain pen. He worked carefully, writing in a clear, legible hand, pausing to ask Clair to repeat dates and figures and names, confirming the spelling of Greaves and Sutter and Rawlins and Whitmore Freight and Supply.

The deposition took the better part of an hour. When Tom finished, he read it back to Clair, and she confirmed that the information was correct.

"Read it once more yourself," he said. "When you're satisfied it's accurate and complete, sign at the bottom. I'll witness the signature."

Clair read through the deposition. The facts of the embezzlement were laid out in the plain, sequential language of a legal document. The threat was recorded in words that carried no emotion but stated the truth with the specificity the law required. She picked up Tom's pen, dipped it in the ink, and signed her name at the bottom of the last page.

Tom signed beneath her signature as witness, dated it, and set the document beside the evidence. He gathered the ledger pages and the bank withdrawal records into a neat stack, placed the deposition on top, and folded the oilskin around all of it. From a shelf behind his desk, he produced a length of cord and a stick of sealing wax. He bound the packet with the cord, heated the wax over the small flame of a candle stub he lit for the purpose, and pressed his badge into the wax as a seal.

"This packet will leave Providence Ridge today," Tom said. "I'll have Paul Higgins send his fastest rider to Livingston with instructions to deliver it directly to the rail agent for the Helena line. The rail agent will log the package and ensure it reaches the Lewis and Clark County Sheriff's office." He set the sealed packet on his desk and looked at Clair. "Once this package leaves my hands, the evidence belongs to the territory. It can't be intercepted by anyone without authority."

"Thank you, Marshal Callahan," Clair said.

"You don't need to thank me for doing my job. This is exactly the kind of matter I'm here for, and I'm glad you trusted me with it." He looked at Adam. "You'll keep your eyes open out there?"

"I will," Adam said.

"If you spot these two men in the area, I want to know about it," Tom said. "I'll make some inquiries of my own, and I'll let you know what I find. If they come near your ranch or approach Miss Whitmore in any way, you come to me immediately." He stood and extended his hand to Clair. "You've done a brave thing today, Miss Whitmore. And you've done it the right way."

Clair shook his hand, and then they stepped out of the marshal's office and onto the boardwalk. The afternoon had advanced while they were inside, and the light along the street had softened, the shadows of the buildings stretching farther across the packed earth than they had been when they arrived. A horse shifted at the rail down the street, and somewhere near the south end of town a hammer rang twice against iron and went quiet.

Adam walked to the wagon and turned to Clair and offered her his hand. She took it and climbed up onto the bench seat. He walked around the wagon and climbed up on his side. He gathered the lines in his hands but didn't release the brake.

He turned to face her.

"You did the right thing today," he said. "And now we go home, and we live. Tomorrow I'll check the stock like normal and go about my business. You go about your normal day. The day after that, too. And the one after that. That's how this works, Clair. As long as you want to stay in our home."

Clair looked at him and smiled.

"Is that a promise?" she asked.

"It is," he said.

He released the brake and spoke to the horses, and the wagon pulled away from the rail and turned north along Main Street toward home.

Chapter 24

The bean plants had thickened since last week, their vines winding higher up the stakes and curling at the tips. Clair worked her way down the row, pulling weeds from the base of each plant and dropping them into the wooden pail beside her, and Emma moved along beside her.

"Miss Whitmore, this one has a caterpillar on it," Emma said, holding a leaf open with two fingers so Clair could see.

"Pick it off and put it in the bucket," Clair said as she reached for the next clump of crabgrass wedged between two bean plants.

Emma had moved ahead and was picking beans from the lower vines, placing each one into the colander Lydia had sent out with them. Her small fingers were quick and sure, pulling each bean with a clean snap at the stem.

Clair heard a sound that came from the far side of the garden. She turned to see two men climbing over the split-rail fence.

The recognition arrived like a door slamming shut inside her chest. One man settled his coat and brushed his trousers as he straightened; he was the one who had stood beside the office door the day she'd laid the ledger pages across her father's desk in Helena. The man behind him was the one who had stood by the window.

Clair reached for Emma, pulled her back, and stepped in front of her, shielding the child with her body.

"Stay behind me," Clair said.

Judd Sutter spoke first. He removed his hat and held it at his side, a gesture of courtesy so practiced it had the quality of a stage entrance.

"Miss Whitmore," he said. "Mr. Greaves has been very concerned about your welfare. We've been looking for you for some time now, and I cannot tell you how relieved we are to find you safe and sound."

Charles Rawlins said nothing. He stood a step behind Sutter and to his left, his hands at his sides, his eyes moving across the property with the slow, cataloging attention of a man reading the layout of a place he intended to remember.

"What business do you have here?" Clair said. "What do you want?"

"We're here on Mr. Greaves's behalf," Sutter said. "He'd like the documents you took with you when you left Helena. He's prepared to consider the whole affair settled once those papers are returned."

Clair's pulse was loud in her ears.

"I gave everything to Marshal Tom Callahan here in Providence Ridge. He sealed them and dispatched them to the Lewis and Clark County Sheriff's office in Helena by courier. The papers are no longer in my possession. They belong to the territory now. There is nothing for you to retrieve."

Sutter's expression shifted. The practiced warmth receded like water pulling back from a riverbank, and what replaced it was something flatter and colder: the expression of a man recalculating a sum that had come up short. He studied her face with focused patience.

"Is that so?" he said. "And why should we believe you, Miss Whitmore?"

"Because it is the truth," she said. "And because Marshal Callahan will confirm it if you'd care to ride into town and ask him."

Sutter held her gaze for a long moment. Then he reached inside his coat and produced a folded document. He unfolded it with the deliberate care of a man handling something he considered valuable and held it out toward her.

"This is also why we're here," he said. "Mr. Greaves is offering a fair price for Whitmore Freight and Supply. A bill of sale, drawn up and ready for your signature. He believes this would resolve the matter for everyone concerned and allow you to move forward with your life in whatever manner you choose."

Clair looked at the paper in his hand.

"No," she said. "I will not sign my father's business over to the man who stole from it."

Sutter waited, as if the refusal were a first offer in a negotiation that had not yet begun.

"Miss Whitmore, I'd encourage you to consider your position carefully," he said. "You're a long way from Helena, and Mr. Greaves has been more than patient."

"My position is clear," Clair said. "And my answer will not change."

Sutter folded the document and returned it to his coat, and then he glanced at Rawlins.

Rawlins stepped forward and to the side, and his eyes moved from Clair's face to the child pressed against her backside.

Every muscle in Clair's body tightened. She pressed Emma harder against her back with one arm and felt the child's fingers curl into the fabric of her skirt, small and gripping.

"There's something else you should know," Sutter said. "Your house in Helena burned, Miss Whitmore. The evening after you left. On Mr. Greaves's orders, we had the pleasure of seeing the deed through. Your cook and the housekeeper got out, but we were surprised to learn you weren't home. We'd expected you to be there. Imagine our confusion when we learned a horse was also missing from your stable as well."

Clair stared at him. Her house. The house on the quiet street where her mother had kept the china in a glass-fronted cabinet beside the dining-room window because she liked the way the afternoon caught the pattern on the plates. The kitchen where Clair had stood beside her mother and Mrs. Berger at the cookstove, the two women working side by side while Clair watched and asked questions and learned the feel of dough and the sound a skillet makes when the lard is ready. Her father's study, with the desk and the leather chair and the shelves of correspondence files that held two decades of the freight business in her father's handwriting. The front parlor with its settee and two chairs by the window where her mother used to sew in the evenings while her father read aloud from the Scriptures after the dishes were cleared.

Gone. All of it. Burned by the orders from a man who had sat at their table for twelve years and called her father his friend.

"Why should I believe you?" she said.

"Write to Helena and ask," Sutter said. "The fire made the paper."

Clair's vision narrowed at the edges, and the garden and the fence and the two men standing inside it pulled away from her as though the ground between them were stretching. Her mother's quilt. The quilt her mother had stitched by hand the winter before she died, a rose pattern on cream muslin, had been folded at the foot of Clair's bed for six years. She would never touch it again.

The back door of the house opened, and Clair heard the creak of the boards on the narrow porch. She turned her head to see Lydia. She held a shotgun in both hands, the stock braced against her shoulder, the barrel leveled at the two men in her garden. Her arthritic fingers gripped the wood and the steel, her swollen knuckles white and locked around the forestock.

"You are on my son's land," Lydia said. "And you will leave it now."

Sutter folded the brim of his hat between his fingers and placed it back on his head.

"We'll be back, Miss Whitmore," he said. "Mr. Greaves is a patient man. But his patience has limits."

He turned and walked to the fence. Rawlins followed without a word. They climbed the split rails and dropped to the other side. Clair watched as they walked into the timber at the edge of the property, their shapes thinning between the trunks until the trees took them.

The only sound was the creak of the porch boards shifting under Lydia's weight and Emma's breathing, quick and shallow, against Clair's hip.

Chapter 25

L ydia set the shotgun against the wall beside the back door. Clair came through the doorway with Emma pressed against her side, the child's fingers still twisted into her skirt. Lydia shut the door and turned the latch.

Clair's pulse was still beating high in her throat, and her hands hadn't stopped shaking.

She knelt in front of Emma and took both of the child's hands. Emma's face was pale and tight, her blue eyes moving between Clair and her grandmother.

"You are safe, and everything is all right." Clair said.

"Why were they in our garden?" Emma asked.

"They came to speak to me," Clair said as she squeezed Emma's hands. "I need to speak with your grandmother for a little while. Will you sit here on the settee and play with your doll?"

Emma nodded, and Clair guided her to the settee and settled her against the cushion. She found the rag doll on the floor beside Lydia's chair, where Emma had left it earlier, and placed it in the child's lap. Emma pulled the doll against her chest and tucked her chin over its yarn hair. Clair pressed her palm against Emma's cheek for a moment before she stood.

Lydia had already moved into the kitchen. She stood at the table with one hand resting on the back of a chair, her face composed. Her other hand hung at her side, and Clair could see the tremor running through her swollen fingers.

Clair pulled a chair out and sat. Lydia lowered herself into her own chair, and for a moment neither of them spoke.

"I heard some of what was said because I was listening through the open window before I stepped outside," Lydia said. "Please, start from the beginning and tell me what just happened."

Clair told her. She started with the first man climbing over the fence, and the recognition that had struck her instantly. She told Lydia about Sutter's rehearsed courtesy and his claim that Greaves was concerned about her welfare. She told her about the demand for the documents and that everything had been dispatched to Helena.

"He produced a bill of sale," Clair said. "Drawn up and ready for my signature. Greaves still wants me to sign Whitmore Freight and Supply over to him. I refused again."

"Good," Lydia said.

"And then he told me my house burned down . On Greaves's orders, the evening after I left. Mrs. Berger and the housekeeper got out. He said they'd expected me to be inside."

Lydia was quiet for a long moment.

"How can we be certain they burned your home?" Lydia asked. "Men who come onto another family's property uninvited and make threats are men who would also lie to frighten a young woman. They could be saying this to break your resolve and get you to sign those papers."

Clair shook her head. "I believe them. Sutter told me it had been reported in the paper. A man who is bluffing doesn't invite you to verify the bluff." She pressed her fingers against the edge of the table and felt the smooth grain of the wood beneath them. "Harlan Greaves sat at my family's table for twelve years, Lydia. He ate our meals and sat in our church pew with us. He called my father his friend, and when my father died, he stole from me while I mourned and then threatened to have me killed when I found the proof. He is not a man who would hesitate to burn a house. He is a man who has already proven there is nothing he will not do to protect the evil he has done."

Lydia listened without interrupting, her gaze steady on Clair's face.

"I have to leave," Clair continued. "I brought these men to your door. They said they would come back, and I believe that, too. If I stay, I'm putting your family in danger, and you all do not deserve that."

"Clair."

"If they are watching this property, and I believe they will continue to watch it, they could come back when Adam is gone again, or in the middle of the night. They could do something far worse than climb a fence and ask for a signature. I will not be the reason something happens to this family."

Lydia leaned forward in her chair. "Running alone is what brought you to this ranch in the first place. You arrived in our barn exhausted and half-starved because you had no one to help you and nowhere safe to go. Running alone again will not protect anyone. It will put you on an open road with no shelter and no one beside you, and those men will follow you there just as easily as they followed you here."

"So be it. If I leave, there is no reason for them to trouble your family further."

"And what happens to you?" Lydia asked. "On the road, alone... you think leaving this is safe? No child... it makes you easier to target."

Clair's jaw tightened. She knew Lydia was right.

"Adam would never want you to leave," Lydia said. "You know that."

"I know," Clair said. "That's why I'm leaving now before he comes home."

Lydia pressed her lips together and held Clair's gaze with fierce, unblinking steadiness.

"The Lord didn't bring you to this family so you could be driven out by two men with a piece of paper and a threat," Lydia said. "He brought you here because this household needed you, and because you needed us, and I will not sit at this table and pretend otherwise."

Clair stood. "I have to go, Lydia."

She walked through the doorway into Lydia's bedroom, and she heard the older woman's chair push back and Lydia's careful steps following behind her. The room was dim, the two windows letting in the morning's clear light across the bed and the washstand and the pallet along the far wall where Clair had slept every night since her first evening in this house.

She gripped the iron bed frame and pulled it from the wall, the legs scraping against the floorboards. She retrieved her money from its hiding place and slid the bed back into place.

Her carpetbag sat on the floor beside the pallet, and she opened it and tucked the money inside, pressing the rolls flat against the bottom. She reached for the few things that were hers and placed each item in her bag.

Her Bible sat on the pallet, and she picked it up.

For the love of money is the root of all evil: which while some coveted after, they have erred from the faith, and pierced themselves through with many sorrows.

Her mother had taught her that verse years ago after Clair had heard a tale at school about two men who worked at the bank, whom they knew personally, and who had been arrested for stealing. Clair had been fourteen, sitting at the kitchen table in Helena while her mother stood at the counter helping Mrs. Berger cook, and Clair had asked why people would steal money from their employers. Her mother had wiped her hands on her apron and come to the table and sat down and opened her Bible to First Timothy, and read the verse aloud. Then she had said, quietly and with the certainty of a woman who believed every word of Scripture, that money itself was not the sin. The love of it was. The coveting. The choosing of it over every other good thing God had placed in a man's life.

Clair held her Bible and thought of Harlan Greaves sitting at their table on a Sunday afternoon, his plate full and his manners careful, a man her father trusted with the daily operation of everything he had built. Twelve years. Twelve years of shared meals and holiday dinners and small kindnesses. Her father had trusted him because Greaves had earned that trust with patience and consistency, and then Ezekiel Whitmore had died, and the money was unguarded, and the love of it consumed what was left of the man.

Every threat. Every mile she had walked. Every night she had checked the carpetbag lining. Every hour of fear in this valley and before it. All of it traced back to greed. A good man who chose money over honor and pierced himself and everyone around him through with the sorrows the verse promised.

She placed her Bible in the carpetbag and closed it.

"Clair, please," Lydia said from the doorway. "Think about what you're doing."

"I have thought about it," Clair said. She stood and lifted the carpetbag by its handle. "I am going to Livingston. I can deal with the business from there, send telegrams, sell the company, and settle the affairs. I'll be near the train if I need to go to Helena. I am not staying in Providence Ridge, where my presence puts this family and possibly the entire community at risk."

"Wait for Adam," Lydia said. "He'll be back this afternoon once he's finished with the herd. Wait and talk to him before you decide."

Clair looked at her. She knew what would happen if she waited. Adam would come through the door, and he would listen, and he would stand in the kitchen with that quiet, absolute certainty of his and tell her she wasn't leaving. She would stay because she loved him, and the love made her weak in exactly the place where she needed to be strong.

She couldn't afford to wait.

"I can't," she said.

She walked past Lydia into the sitting room, where Emma sat on the settee with her doll pulled tight against her chest. Clair set the carpetbag down and knelt in front of her.

"Emma, I need to leave for a little while," she said. "Will you be good for your grandmother while I'm gone? Keep up with your reading and help her with whatever she asks."

"Are you coming back for supper?" Emma asked.

Clair's throat tightened. "No, sweetheart. I need you to know that you are the bravest, smartest girl I have ever met, and I am so proud of how hard you've been working on your letters."

Emma's arms came up and wrapped around Clair's neck, and the child pulled herself close. Clair felt Emma's small ribs beneath her hands and the quick flutter of her heartbeat.

She kissed the top of Emma's head and eased the child's arms from around her neck and settled her back against the cushion. She placed the rag doll in Emma's lap.

She stood and picked up her carpetbag and walked to where Lydia stood and put her arms around the older woman. Lydia's hand came up and pressed against the back of Clair's head.

Clair released her and stepped back. She turned and walked to the front door and opened it, and stepped out onto the porch. The valley stretched wide before her, and she began walking north.

"Clair," Lydia called from behind her.

She didn't turn. Turning would do nothing but make the next step harder, and the next step was the only one that mattered now. She tightened her grip on the carpetbag handle and continued walking.

Chapter 26

Adam rode the fence line where the lower pasture dropped toward the creek crossing, and the cattle he'd been moving since midmorning were spread behind him in a loose, contented line along the fresh grass. He'd pushed them off the upper range to the south pasture, and the work had taken the better part of four hours in the August warmth. His shirt was dark with sweat between his shoulder blades, and the leather of his reins had gone soft and damp in his grip.

He angled the horse toward the house and pulled up beside the front porch. He swung down and looped the reins around the top rail, and stepped up onto the porch, pulling his hat off as he crossed to the front door and stepped inside. He hung his hat on the peg above the bench and turned toward the kitchen.

His mother sat at the table, and Emma was beside her in a chair that had been pulled close enough that the child's arm pressed against her grandmother's sleeve. Emma's face was blotchy and swollen, her eyes red-rimmed, and her rag doll was crushed against her chest in both arms.

Lydia looked at him, and every line of her face was drawn tight.

"What happened?" Adam asked. "Where's Clair?"

"Sit down, Adam."

"Tell me."

"Two men came this morning," Lydia said. "While Clair and Emma were in the garden. They climbed the fence. Clair recognized them as the two men from Helena, the ones she told us about. Judd Sutter and Charles Rawlins."

Adam stood and listened as a cold chill ran through him.

"They demanded the documents," Lydia said. "Clair told them the papers had been sent to Helena. They produced a bill of sale for her father's business and tried to get her to sign it. When she refused, they told her that her house in Helena had burnedburned down . On Greaves's orders, the evening after she left. They said they had expected her to be inside."

Emma pressed closer against Lydia's arm, and Lydia's hand moved from the table to the child's back.

"They said all of this in front of Emma," Adam said.

"Emma was behind Clair the entire time. Clair put herself between Emma and those men and didn't move. I heard the commotion from inside the house and heard a lot of what was said. After I had heard enough, I went out the back door with your father's shotgun. I told them to get off this property. One of the men said they would be back, and then they left."

Adam's hands were clenched, and the muscles along his jaw had drawn so tight he could feel the pressure in his temples. The anger that moved through him had replaced the chill he had been feeling, and now he was boiling hot.

Two men had climbed his fence. Stood in his garden. Spoken threats in front of his child.

"Where's Clair?" he asked again.

"She packed her bag, and she told me she was leaving to protect this family. I tried to stop her. I told her running alone was what brought her here in the first place and that leaving would put her in more danger, not less. She wouldn't listen."

Adam's chest constricted. He could feel his pulse at the base of his throat, heavy and slow.

"She walked out the front door with her carpetbag and headed north toward Livingston," Lydia said. "She told me she would go to Livingston and deal with the business from there, send telegrams, sell the company, do what needed doing. She said she would not stay in Providence Ridge, where her presence put this family and possibly the community at risk."

"How long ago?"

"Not more than two hours."

Adam looked at his mother, and then he looked at Emma. His daughter's blue eyes were fixed on him.

He crossed the kitchen in three strides and knelt in front of Emma's chair. He put his hand on her arm, and her small fingers gripped his wrist.

"Are you all right?" he asked.

Emma nodded, but her chin buckled and her eyes filled again, and Adam pressed his palm against the side of her head and drew her forehead to his shoulder and held her there for a moment.

"You're safe," he said. "I need you to stay with your grandmother and do what she tells you. Can you do that for me?"

"Yes, Papa."

He stood and looked at his mother. "Lock the front door and the back door after I leave. Keep the shotgun where you can reach it. Do not open either door for anyone except me."

"I know what to do," Lydia said. "Go find her, Adam. Bring her home."

He was through the front door and off the porch before his mother finished speaking. He pulled the reins free from the rail and swung up into the saddle. Adam turned the horse north and pressed his heels into the horse's flanks, and the animal broke into a canter before they cleared the yard.

The road stretched ahead of him, a packed-earth track that ran north through the valley toward Livingston, the ruts baked dry in the August heat. The Absarokas filled the eastern sky, their peaks sharp against the blue, and to the west, the Gallatin Mountain Range held the afternoon light along its ridgeline.

Clair was on foot and had been walking for close to two hours; she could have managed three miles, perhaps four. Adam's horse covered ground at a canter in a fraction of that time, and the arithmetic was simple. He would find her.

But the simple arithmetic did nothing for the thing turning over inside his mind. Two men had walked onto his property and confronted Clair and frightened his child, and he had been under a mile away, pushing heifers onto fresh grass.

He thought of Clair packing her bag and leaving.

She had run from Helena because she feared for her life. She was running again because she feared for the safety of his family. The pattern was a circle, and Clair was inside it, and every time the fear arrived, she translated it into departure because departure was the only thing she could focus on.

The horse's stride ate up the road beneath them, the rhythmic beat of the animal's canter carrying Adam north. The valley unrolled ahead of him in a long, open corridor of grass and sage and the pale ribbon of the track. He passed the creek crossing where the cottonwoods stood thick on both banks, their leaves turning in the breeze with a sound like rain on canvas. He passed the fence line that marked the northern edge of his deeded ground, the posts his father had set still standing square and true. He passed the place where the road climbed a low rise and the valley opened wider beyond it, and he kept his eyes on the track ahead, scanning the long, straight stretch for the shape of a woman walking alone.

A mile past his property line, the road crested a gentle swell and dropped toward a brushy drainage where willows lined a seasonal creek. Beyond the drainage, the track climbed again and ran straight for a quarter mile before bending east around a stand of ponderosa pine. Adam's eyes moved over the landscape, and then he saw her.

He urged the horse forward, and the canter lengthened toward a lope. The distance between them closed in seconds, and Clair heard the hoofbeats and turned.

She stopped in the road and faced him. Her hair had come loose from its pins on one side, and the wind had drawn strands across her face. Her carpetbag hung from her right hand, the handle gripped in fingers that were white at the knuckles. Her dress was dusty at the hem from the road, and her shoulders were set in the rigid, braced posture of a woman who had been walking for two hours on anger and conviction and was prepared to defend both.

Adam pulled up a few feet from her and dismounted. He dropped the reins and let the horse stand, and he walked toward Clair and stopped close enough to see the brightness in her eyes and the flush along her cheekbones, and the set of her jaw. She had been crying at some point, and the evidence of it was there in the redness around her eyes, but she wasn't crying now. She was furious.

He had never seen her like this. In all the weeks she had lived under his roof, he had seen her afraid and witnessed grief break through the composure she held in place with such precision. He had never seen her angry. The anger changed the geometry of her face, sharpening the line of her jaw and the set of her mouth. Anger made her look less like a woman who needed protecting and more like a woman who had decided she would do the protecting herself.

"Go home, Adam," she said.

"Clair, listen to me."

"I am not going back. If those men come again, what happens then?"

"What happens is the same thing that happened today. My mother put a shotgun between them and our family, and they left. You will do the same if it happens again."

"Your mother should never have had to do that. Emma should never have had to see that. And I am the reason they were there. I brought them to your property. My situation brought them. I have no right to stay in your home and invite that kind of danger through the door."

She was breathing hard, and her words came faster than her usual cadence, the measured precision of her speech overrun by the anger that had been building across miles of walking. He could see it in her whole body: the way she held the carpetbag like a counterweight and the way her free hand had closed into a fist at her side. The way her chest rose and fell with the quick, shallow rhythm of someone who had been arguing with herself for two hours and had not won.

"They stood in front of a child, Adam. A six-year-old girl. They stood in your garden where your daughter was picking beans. They talked about burning a woman's home and expected me to sign away my father's life's work. They did it in front of Emma, who should never have had to hear a word of it. I have been walking this road for two hours, and every step I take I get angrier, and I cannot recall the last time I was this angry about anything in my entire life."

Adam let her speak. He let the words come because she needed to say them and because the anger was honest. Clair had spent weeks converting her fear into composure and had earned the right to stand on a road in the middle of Montana Territory and be furious.

When she had finished, when the last of it had come out and her breathing was the only sound between them, Adam spoke.

"You're right to be angry," he said. "What they did was wrong, and I would give a great deal to have been standing in that garden when they came over that fence. But running is not the answer, Clair. Running is what brought you to Providence Ridge in the first place, and I thank God for it, but it didn't keep you safe. It put you on an open road alone, and here you are on an open road alone again, and the only difference between this road and that one is that I am standing on it with you."

She looked at him, and the anger in her face didn't leave, but something beneath it shifted.

"You are safer with me than you are on any road in this territory. Those men are not going to drive you out of my home. If they come back, they will find a locked door and a family that is not afraid of them."

He took a step closer. "We are going to ride into Providence Ridge together, and then we will walk into Tom Callahan's office and tell him what happened today. Let the law handle this. That is what the law is for, and Tom is a man who takes it seriously."

Clair's jaw was still tight, and her eyes were still bright with the anger that had carried her this far, but she was listening now. The rigid set of her shoulders had eased by a fraction, and her grip on the carpetbag handle had loosened enough that the color was coming back into her fingers.

"Come home, Clair."

Two words and her face changed. The anger held for another moment, and then the tears came.

He wrapped his arms around her and drew her against his chest, and held her. Her carpetbag bumped against his leg where she still gripped the handle, and her forehead pressed into his shirt, and her shoulders shook.

"Please stop crying," he said, his voice low against the top of her head. "I can't bear it, Clair. Please. Let's just go home and deal with this together."

She nodded against his chest. He felt the motion of it, small and sure, and he kept his arms where they were and let her cry until the shaking eased and her breathing steadied and her forehead lifted from his shirt. She looked up at him; her face was wet, and her eyes were red.

"Let's go," she said.

Adam released her and stepped back. He took the carpetbag from her hand and carried it to the horse. He secured it behind the saddle, tying it down with leather strings, and then he turned back to where she stood.

"Give me your hand," he said, and she did. He helped her up into the saddle, her boot finding the stirrup and her hand gripping the horn as she settled onto the seat. He swung up behind her, and the horse shifted once beneath the double weight and then stood steady. Adam gathered the reins in one hand and turned the horse south.

The road opened ahead of them, and Clair leaned back against him. The gesture was small and unhesitating, and Adam felt the press of her shoulders against his chest and the steadiness that had returned to her breathing.

"We'll stop in town first," he said. "Marshal Tom needs to hear what happened today. Then we go home."

She nodded, and her hand came to rest on his forearm, where he held the reins.

Chapter 27

Marshal Tom looked up from his desk and set his fountain pen down as Clair and Adam entered.

"I sense something else has happened; have a seat," he said.

Clair sat and put her carpetbag on the floor beside her. Adam took the chair next to hers.

"Sutter and Rawlins came to the ranch this morning," Clair said. "They climbed the fence around the garden while Emma and I were weeding. Emma was right beside me, Marshal, and they came over that fence with no more hesitation than if they were stepping through their own front gate."

Tom pulled a clean sheet of paper from the drawer beside his knee, picked up his fountain pen, and looked at her.

"Start at the beginning," he said. "Take your time."

Clair told him how Sutter had spoken with polished and precise words that made his purpose all the more obscene. She told him about the demand for the documents and how she had informed both men that the evidence was already in the hands of the law.

"He didn't believe me," Clair said. "Or he chose not to accept it. He produced a bill of sale for Whitmore Freight and Supply, drawn up and ready for my signature. Greaves still wants the company. He sent these men across the territory with a piece of paper and the expectation that I would sign my father's business over to the man who robbed it."

"Did you sign anything?" Tom asked.

"I refused. I refused clearly and without hesitation, and when I did, Sutter told me my house in Helena had burned. On Greaves's orders. The evening after I left. He said that the cook and the housekeeper had escaped. He said they had expected me to be inside."

Tom's pen had stopped moving. He looked at her across the desk, and the stillness in his expression had shifted into something harder and more concentrated.

"He confessed to the arson directly," Tom said. "To your face."

"He stated it as fact. He told me to write to Helena and verify that the fire had been reported in the newspaper. He wasn't bluffing, and he wasn't ashamed."

"And this was said in front of the child."

"Emma was behind me. I had placed myself between her and both men the moment I recognized them. She heard every word."

Adam spoke for the first time since they'd entered the office. "My mother came out the back door with my father's shotgun and ordered them off the property. They left. One of them told Clair they'd be back."

Tom finished writing and set his pen down. He placed both hands flat on the desk on either side of the paper and looked at Clair, then at Adam.

"I have news of my own," he said. "Since I sent your evidence to Helena and took your deposition, I've been making inquiries. I sent telegrams through Livingston to every law enforcement office I could reach across the Montana Territory. The U.S. Marshal's network, the sheriff's offices in Helena, Virginia City, and Butte. I asked for any information they had on Judd Sutter and Charles Rawlins."

Clair's hands were folded in her lap, and she pressed her thumbs together and held them there.

"The responses came back this week," Tom said. "Rawlins is a wanted man, Miss Whitmore. There is an outstanding warrant for his arrest in connection with a violent assault in Deer Lodge County. The details are sparse in the telegram, but the charge is serious enough that the sheriff in Deer Lodge has been looking for him for the better part of a year. His description matches what you've given me, and the name is the same."

"And Sutter?" Adam asked.

"Sutter's record is thinner. No outstanding warrants came back in the replies I've received so far. But a clean record on paper doesn't make a clean man."

Tom stood and crossed to the corkboard beside the door, where he unpinned a folded telegram and brought it back to the desk. He unfolded it and laid it flat beside his notes.

"What you've told me today gives me what I needed," he said. "I had the deposition and the evidence before. Now I have a confession of arson delivered to the victim's face, witness intimidation, trespassing on private property, attempted coercion with a bill of sale, and threats made in the presence of a minor child. Combined with Rawlins's outstanding warrant, I have more than sufficient legal authority to arrest both men."

Clair felt the knot she had been carrying in her chest since that morning loosen.

"What happens now?" she asked.

"I'll deputize men from the community," Tom said. "Reliable men. I have three or four in mind already, men who know this valley and who won't hesitate when it matters. Sutter told you they'd be back, which leads me to believe they won't leave the area until they get what they want. Men like that need somewhere to sleep and somewhere to eat, and in a country this sparse, the options are few. The saloon, the timber camps on the mill road, the old line shacks in the foothills, or a camp along the creek north of town."

"I want to ride with you," Adam said.

Tom looked at him and nodded. "I was going to ask. You know this ground better than most men in the valley, Adam. I'd be foolish not to have you along. In fact, we should search your property first and then move outward from there."

"How soon?" Adam asked.

"Today," Tom turned to Clair. "Where will you be while the search is underway, Miss Whitmore?"

Clair looked at Adam. His dark eyes held hers, and she gave him a small nod.

"She'll be at the ranch with my mother and my daughter," Adam said. "I'll take her home now and come back to help find these men."

Tom pushed his chair back from the desk and stood. He reached for his hat on the peg behind him and settled it on his head.

"Go quickly, Adam," Tom said. "Get her home safe, see to your mother and your daughter, and meet me back here in two hours. I'll have men gathered by then."

Adam stood, and Clair rose beside him. She picked up her carpetbag and held it against her side. Adam put his hand against the small of her back as they turned toward the door, and Clair walked through the doorway onto the boardwalk with the press of his palm still warm against her spine.

Tom Callahan followed them out the door.

Chapter 28

They rode south through the timber in a loose line, six men on horseback. Adam kept his horse to the left of the trail while Marshal Tom held the lead. Behind them rode Amos Pemberton, Cal Stackhouse, Jesse Mayhew, and Dale Wilson, each of them carrying rifles across their saddlebows. Tom had deputized all of them, and the tin stars he'd pinned to their shirts were crude things, cut from sheet metal and stamped with the word DEPUTY.

The trail narrowed where the ponderosa gave way to thicker stands of lodgepole and Douglas fir, the ground beneath the horses' hooves going soft with accumulated needles. Adam knew this area well because it was part of his property. The rolling hills at the very southern edge of what his father had purchased years ago dropped through a succession of shallow draws and timbered ridges before flattening into open land a few miles farther on, and scattered through that country were the remains of homesteads that had been claimed and abandoned in the years before the valley had enough people to sustain them. Root cellars caved in on themselves. Fence posts standing without wire. Shacks built from rough-sawn lumber and left to the weather when the families who'd raised them moved on to ground that offered more.

Tom pulled up at a fork in the trail where a seasonal creek had cut a shallow channel through the clay, dry now in late August, its bed cracked into plates the color of old leather. He turned in his saddle and looked at Adam.

"How far to the first of those shacks you mentioned?" Tom asked.

"There's one about a half-mile ahead in a draw below the south ridge," Adam said. "Another farther on, maybe another half mile past that, set back in the timber on the east slope. The third one sits in a clearing a ways farther and has good sightlines to the north, and there's a spring nearby that runs year-round."

"We'll check them in order," Tom said. "Stay together. Nobody rides ahead."

They moved on. The trail climbed a low ridge and dropped into a draw where the grass grew thick and ungrazed; the seed heads dried to a pale gold that bent under the breeze. A pair of magpies lifted from a dead pine at the edge of the clearing and wheeled away to the south, their black and white feathers stark against the sky. The first shack sat at the far end of the draw, its door hanging from a single hinge and its roof collapsed on the east side where the ridgepole had rotted through. Adam could see from thirty yards that no one had been inside it for months. The grass in front of the door stood undisturbed, and no tracks marked the soft ground around the foundation.

Tom glanced at the shack without stopping and angled his horse toward the trail that climbed the next ridge.

The second shack was in worse condition than the first, little more than four walls and a pile of shakes where the roof had fallen in. They passed it without comment.

The third clearing opened below them as the trail crested a timbered ridge and dropped into a wide, shallow basin ringed with pine on three sides. Adam saw the shack first, a low structure built from squared logs with a plank door and a window opening covered with oilcloth that had gone yellow and stiff with age.

Two horses stood tied to a pine tree thirty yards east of the shack, their saddles still on, their heads low in the shade.

Tom raised his hand, and the column of men stopped. He turned his horse sideways on the trail and spoke low enough that his voice wouldn't carry past the treeline.

"I'd say that's them," he said as he looked at each man in turn. "Amos, you and Cal circle east through the timber and hold the far side. If they come out the back way, you turn them around. Jesse, Dale, hold this ridge. Adam, you're with me."

The men split up without discussion. Amos and Cal moved their horses off the trail and into the timber, angling east with the quiet, unhurried competence of men who had ridden rough country their whole lives. Jesse and Dale pulled up on the ridgeline and positioned themselves where they could see both the shack and the tied horses. Adam dismounted and looped his reins around a low branch, pulled his rifle from the scabbard, and followed Tom down the slope on foot.

The grass in the basin was knee-high and dry, and it whispered against their legs as they crossed the open ground toward the shack. Adam could feel the tension in his chest that came before work that carried risk, the same tightness he felt when a range bull turned to face him instead of moving with the herd. His hands were steady on his rifle. Beside him, Tom walked with the measured stride of a man who had done this before.

They stopped twenty yards from the door. Tom positioned himself squarely to the entrance and raised his voice.

"Judd Sutter. Charles Rawlins. This is Marshal Tom Callahan of Providence Ridge. I'm holding warrants for both of you. I've got men on every side of this building. Step outside with your hands where I can see them."

Silence held for a few seconds, and then a voice came from inside, muffled by the log walls.

"On what grounds, Marshal?"

"Witness intimidation," Tom said. "Trespassing on private property and outstanding warrants. The evidence Miss Whitmore provided has already been dispatched to Helena by rail. A formal investigation has been opened. Your employer's affairs are now a matter for the territorial courts, and your presence in this valley constitutes interference with that process."

Another silence. Adam listened for movement inside the shack, the scrape of a boot, or the shift of weight on a plank floor, and heard nothing.

"I'd like to discuss terms, Marshal," Sutter said.

"There are no terms," Tom said. "You can walk out that door on your own feet, or my men can come in and get you. Those are the two choices available to you."

Adam heard a low exchange inside, two voices speaking over each other in a register too quiet to make out. The conversation went on for a full minute, and when it stopped, the plank door swung inward, and Sutter stepped through.

He had his hands raised to his shoulders, his palms open and turned forward.

"Judd Sutter, sir. I'm cooperating, Marshal," Sutter said. "I'd like that noted."

Tom stepped forward. "Where's Rawlins?"

"Inside."

"Tell him to come out."

"Mr. Rawlins makes his own decisions," Sutter said. "I've made mine."

Tom looked at Jesse on the ridge and jerked his chin toward Sutter. Jesse came down the slope and took Sutter by the arm and walked him back toward the tree line. Adam watched Sutter go without resistance, his steps measured, and his head turning once to look back at the shack before Jesse steered him behind the cover of a thick-trunked ponderosa and pressed him against it and held him there.

Tom turned back to the shack.

"Rawlins," he called. "Last chance to walk out."

No answer.

Tom looked at Adam. "Stay here. If he comes through that window, hold him if you catch him. If not, take aim and fire."

Adam moved to the side of the shack and positioned himself where he could see the oilcloth-covered opening. He braced his rifle against his shoulder and waited.

Tom crossed the remaining distance to the door. He flattened himself against the wall beside the frame, drew his revolver, and went through the doorway in a single motion, low and fast.

Adam heard a chair overturn. A short, hard sound of impact, a body hitting a floor, and Tom's voice, sharp, carrying the authority of a man who would not repeat himself. The sounds lasted no more than a few seconds, and then there was a longer silence. Next came the thud of boots crossing the plank floor, and Tom came back through the doorway with Rawlins in front of him.

Rawlins's hands were behind his back, already cuffed. A thin line of blood ran from a cut above his left eye where something had caught him on the way down, and his expression held the flat, hard stillness of a man who had lost.

Tom walked Rawlins to where Jesse held Sutter and cuffed Sutter's wrists behind his back with a second pair of irons. He stepped back and looked at both men.

"You'll walk to Providence Ridge," Tom said. "My men will ride on either side of you, and I'll be behind you. I'd encourage you to keep your feet moving and your mouths shut."

Cal and Amos brought the two saddled horses down from the pine where they'd been tied. Dale took the lead on horseback, riding ten yards ahead. Jesse and Adam flanked the prisoners on either side. Sutter walked with his head down and his steps even. Rawlins walked with the stiff, upright carriage of someone whose pride had not yet caught up with his circumstances.

Tom rode behind them. His revolver was holstered, his hands rested on his saddle horn, and his eyes never left the two men walking ahead of him.

The trail climbed out of the basin and crossed the timbered ridge, and the country opened as they descended the north slope toward the valley. Adam's ranch was visible from the ridgeline: the house, the barn, and the dark line of the creek running through the cottonwoods.

Adam looked at the ranch as they passed above it. The house where his daughter slept. The porch where Clair had sat beside him in the evenings and listened to the stories he'd carried alone for years. The garden where two men had climbed his fence and stood in front of his child and spoken words that should never have been spoken in her presence.

Those men were walking in irons now, and the road ahead led to a cell.

<h1 style="text-align:center">Chapter 29</h1>

Emma had a smear of apple pie filling on her chin, and her cup of milk sat half-finished beside her plate.

"And then Sunrise ran all the way to the far fence and turned around so fast his back legs went sideways, and I thought he was going to fall over, but he didn't; he just kept running, and he came right back to me and stopped right here." Emma held her palms apart at the width of the kitchen table. "This close to my face, and I could feel his breath on my nose."

"That sounds like quite an adventure," Lydia said from her chair at the end of the table.

"He likes me best," Emma said. "Miss Clair said so."

Clair smiled. "I said he comes to you faster than he comes to anyone else, which is not exactly the same thing, but close enough."

"It's the same thing," Emma said.

Adam sat across from Clair with his coffee in front of him and the last bite of pie still on his plate. He'd been quiet through supper, the peaceful quiet of a man whose day had been long and whose body was settling into the relief of a good meal.

Clair had made the pie from the apples Lydia had been drying since midsummer, and the crust had come out golden and flaky enough that it broke cleanly under a fork.

"He's fast, Papa," Emma said, turning to Adam. "Really fast. When he runs in the paddock, his legs go so fast you can't even see them."

"He's got good conformation. He'll be a solid horse," Adam said.

"What's con-for-may-shun?"

"It means his legs and his body are built right. He's put together the way a horse ought to be put together."

"He seems put together just fine to me," she said.

A knock came at the front door, and Adam pushed his chair back.

He crossed the kitchen and opened the door, and Marshal Tom Callahan stood on the porch with his hat in his hand and a leather satchel under his arm.

"Tom," Adam said. "Come in."

"Thank you, Adam. I apologize for the hour." Tom said as he stepped through the doorway, and his eyes moved to Clair. "Miss Whitmore, I have news for you. A courier arrived from Livingston this afternoon carrying a dispatch package from the Lewis and Clark County Sheriff's office in Helena. I thought you'd want to hear what it contained."

Clair stood. Her pulse had risen at the word "Helena," a reflex her body hadn't learned to release, and she steadied herself against the table's edge before she spoke. "Please sit down, Marshal. Can I pour you a cup of coffee?"

"I'd appreciate that."

Adam walked to Emma, lifted her, and sat down in her place and settled his child in his lap. She leaned back against his chest, her small hands resting on his forearm where it crossed her middle, her attention fixed on Tom.

Clair set a cup of coffee in front of Tom, who had taken Adam's vacant chair. She sat back down across from him and folded her hands on the table in front of her.

Tom took a drink of his coffee and then opened his leather satchel. He withdrew a sheaf of papers and placed them on the table beside his cup.

"I'll go through these one at a time," he said. "The first is a receipt of evidence. The ledger pages and bank withdrawal records you provided arrived in Helena intact. They've been entered into the official record as part of the investigation."

Clair nodded.

"Second," Tom said. "Harlan Greaves has been formally arrested and charged with embezzlement. The amount documented in the records you provided is fourteen thousand two hundred dollars. The pattern of fictitious shipments and unauthorized bank withdrawals was sufficient for the charges. The sheriff's office has indicated that additional charges may follow as the investigation continues."

Clair heard Lydia draw a slow breath beside her and felt Adam's gaze on her face, steady and watchful.

Arrested. The man who had stolen from her father's accounts and threatened her in the office where her father had built a company board by board and wagon by wagon. Arrested and charged.

"Third," Tom said. "The Helena sheriff has confirmed the fire that destroyed your home. The investigation has ruled it arson. Kerosene was used as an accelerant, applied to the outside of the house in two locations: the front and the back. Your cook and your housekeeper both escaped without harm and gave statements to the sheriff. They confirmed you were not present at the time of the fire." He paused and looked at her directly. "The fire is now being investigated in connection with the Greaves case."

Clair's hands tightened on the table. Official words that the home where she'd learned to read, where her mother had taught her to sew and to pray, where her father had sat at his desk in the study and tallied figures by lamplight while she curled on the settee with a book, was gone. Burned on the orders of a man who had once sat in their church pew at First Presbyterian on Warren Street.

"Miss Clair?" Emma's voice came from Adam's lap, small and careful. "Did those bad men burn your house?"

Clair glanced at Adam. His jaw was tight, but he gave her the smallest nod.

"Yes," Clair said.

Emma was quiet for a moment. "Are you sad about your house?"

"I am, very much so," Clair said. "But I'm thankful that the people inside got out safely, and I'm thankful that I'm here with all of you."

Emma nodded as she settled back against Adam's chest and tucked her chin against his arm.

Tom continued. "Fourth. Edmund Holt, your father's secretary, has been cooperating with the sheriff's investigation. He's confirmed Greaves's position as general manager and your role in the business and has provided additional details about the company's operations. He stated that he personally witnessed a change in Greaves's behavior over the past several months, that Greaves had become more guarded and more volatile, and that Sutter and Rawlins were present in the building on multiple occasions, watching the other employees and spending considerable time behind closed doors with Greaves."

Clair pressed her lips together. Edmund. She could picture him at his desk in the front office, his ledger open, his spectacles sitting low on the bridge of his nose. He'd always been meticulous, careful, and loyal to her father. He was a quiet, unremarkable man who did his job well and expected nothing grander than the satisfaction of a balanced column and a paycheck at the end of the week. He'd stayed on after she fled, and now he was doing the only thing he could do from his position, which was to tell the truth. The thought of him sitting across from the sheriff and confirming what she'd carried alone for months was a kindness she would find a way to thank him for when the time came.

"Fifth," Tom said. "The territorial law enforcement network has confirmed an outstanding warrant for Charles Rawlins, and they've provided criminal history on both Rawlins and Sutter."

"Are they still in your jail?" Adam asked.

"They are," Tom said. "My authority as town marshal is for Providence Ridge and the surrounding area, but the investigation into Greaves is being conducted through the Lewis and Clark County Sheriff's office in Helena. Sutter and Rawlins are wanted in connection with that case, and my jail isn't built for long-term holding. I've sent word to the U.S. Marshal's office requesting a deputy be dispatched to take custody and transport them back to Helena, where they'll answer for their part in the Greaves matter along with the local charges I've filed for trespassing and witness intimidation."

Adam shifted Emma on his lap and rested his hand on the table beside his coffee cup. "And until the deputy arrives?"

"They stay in my custody. I've got Jesse Mayhew and Dale Wilson taking turns on watch at night."

"The sixth item," Tom continued, turning back to Clair. "Your status. You are no longer listed as a missing person. My deposition, which confirmed your location and your safety, has been received and entered into the record. As far as the Territory of Montana is concerned, you are accounted for."

Clair nodded. "What happens next, Marshal?" she asked.

"The criminal case against Greaves proceeds through the territorial courts," Tom said. "That process belongs to the government now, Miss Whitmore. You've provided your evidence and your sworn deposition. The sheriff's office may contact you through me if they require further testimony, but you won't need to return to Helena for the investigation to continue. The prosecution doesn't require your presence." He took a sip of his coffee. "As for the fire, the arson finding strengthens the case against Greaves considerably. It establishes a pattern of criminal behavior that extends beyond the embezzlement. His attorney will have a difficult time arguing that a man who stole fourteen thousand dollars and then burned his employer's home wasn't acting with deliberate intent."

"Will they come back?" Emma asked. "The bad men who came to our garden?"

Tom looked at Emma. "No, young lady," he said. "Those men are locked up, and they're going to stay locked up. They won't bother you or your family again."

Emma studied him, and then she nodded once, a brisk, satisfied motion, and turned her face against Adam's shirt.

Tom gathered the documents and placed them back in his satchel. He fastened the buckle and stood, and his chair scraped softly against the floorboards.

"I appreciate the coffee," he said. "And I'm glad to be the one delivering this news rather than the other kind."

Lydia rose from her chair and crossed to him and took his hand in both of hers. "Thank you, Tom. You've been a steady hand for us, and we're grateful. I pray every day for your protection."

"Just doing my job, Lydia."

Adam set Emma on her feet and stood. He shook Tom's hand. "Thank you, Tom. You went above and beyond for us all."

"I went where the evidence led and did what the badge requires," Tom said. "Miss Whitmore did the hard part. She's the one who carried those documents out of Helena and put them in my hands. Everything that's happening in that courtroom traces back to her courage."

Clair stepped forward and extended her hand. Tom took it; his grip steady and brief.

"Thank you, Marshal Callahan," she said. "For believing me. For acting on what I brought you. For everything you've done."

"You don't need to thank me, Miss Whitmore. But you're welcome just the same." He settled his hat on his head and touched the brim. "Goodnight, all of you. Get some rest."

Adam walked him to the door and held it open, and Tom stepped out onto the porch and down the steps.

Adam closed the door and turned back toward the kitchen.

Lydia stood near her chair with her hands folded in front of her, and the lamplight from the sideboard caught the silver in her hair and the lines of her face that a lifetime of prayer and patience and loss had written there. Clair looked at her and felt the fullness of what this woman had done for her since the morning she'd come to her in the barn. Lydia had fed her. Clothed her. Taught her to cook various items and tend a garden, and care for a child.

Clair crossed the kitchen and put her arms around Lydia and held her. Lydia's hand came up and rested on Clair's back, warm and sure.

"Thank you," Clair said. "For taking me in and teaching me and standing by me through every bit of this mess."

"You were never a burden in this house, Clair," Lydia said. "You were an answer to a prayer I'd been praying for years."

Clair released her and turned to Adam, who stood by the closed door with Emma leaning against his leg, her small hand wrapped around two of his fingers. He watched Clair with the quiet, unhurried attention he gave to everything that mattered, and when she stepped toward him, he opened his arms, and she walked into them and pressed her forehead against his chest.

His arms closed around her, and she felt the solid, certain strength of him. She held on, and he held on, and for a long moment neither of them moved.

"Thank you, Adam," she said.

Emma tugged on his trousers. "Are we all done being serious now?" she asked. "Because I didn't finish telling you about Sunrise."

Clair stepped back from Adam and looked down at Emma and laughed, and the sound of it filled the kitchen, reaching into every corner.

"Yes, Emma," she said. "Tell us about Sunrise."

The child took Clair's hand in one of hers and Adam's in the other and led them both back toward the table.

Chapter 30

Adam turned the horse into the yard and swung down before the animal had fully stopped, looping the reins twice around the porch rail. He crossed the porch in two strides and opened the front door.

The kitchen was warm and busy. Green beans filled the colander in the dry sink, trimmed and cut to uniform lengths, and a row of glass canning jars stood along the counter, each one already packed tight with beans.

Clair stood at the counter with a jar in her hand, pressing beans into the glass with her fingers. His mother sat at the table beside her, stringing beans.

"Good, you're here," Lydia said. "We need the copper boiler brought out from the barn. Clair and I are ready to start processing these jars, and we'll need firewood gathered and the fire pit set up outside. Can you get all of that ready for us?"

"I will," Adam said. "In a minute. There's something I need to do first."

Adam crossed the kitchen to where Clair stood at the counter. He reached for her left hand, and his fingers closed around hers.

He lowered himself to one knee on the kitchen floor and reached into his vest pocket with his right hand and drew out a small cloth pouch. He worked it open with his thumb and forefinger and held it toward her so she could see what was inside.

Two gold bands.

"Clair. I love you. I have loved you for longer than I've had the courage to say so, and I am asking you to marry me."

Beside him, Lydia's hand went to her mouth. Her eyes filled, and the tears came fast and silent, running over her fingers where they pressed against her lips.

Emma sat with her slate and her primer open before her on the kitchen table. She had been copying a letter when her father walked in, and now she watched him kneeling on the floor with Emma's hand in his, her brow drawn.

"Papa, why are you on the floor?"

"I'm asking Miss Clair to marry me, sweetheart."

Emma set her pencil down on the slate. "What does marry mean?"

"It means she'd stay with us forever."

Emma's eyes went wide, and her whole body straightened in the chair. "Forever?"

"Forever."

Emma looked at Clair. "Does that mean Miss Clair would be my mama?"

Clair looked at Emma and smiled.

"Yes, sweetheart," Clair said. "If you'll have me."

"I'll have you," Emma said. She slid from her chair and came to stand beside her father, peering into the cloth pouch he held open. "What are those round things, Papa?"

"They're wedding rings," Adam said. "When two people marry, they each wear one, and it tells the world they belong to each other."

Emma reached into the pouch and lifted one of the bands between her thumb and forefinger, holding it up and turning it slowly. "It's small," she said.

"It's meant for Miss Clair, and she has tiny, delicate fingers," Adam said.

Emma placed the ring back in the pouch and looked at Clair again and smiled.

Adam looked at Clair; her eyes were glistening, and the color had risen along her cheekbones.

"Yes," she said.

Adam stood. "When?" he said. "When do you want to get married?"

The color in Clair's face deepened, spreading from her cheeks to the bridge of her nose. "Right away," she said. "I don't want to wait."

Lydia lowered her hand from her mouth and looked at her son with eyes that were bright and streaming with tears.

"Go get the preacher, son," Lydia said. "Reverend Hale should be in town by now. He and Eunice always arrive by midweek before Sunday services. They'll be at the boarding house or visiting their daughter. Go find him and bring him here."

Adam nodded, and he looked back at Clair and smiled. Then he turned and walked out the front door.

Clair looked at Lydia, and Lydia looked at Clair, and neither of them could speak.

Lydia bowed her head. "Thank You, Lord, for Your faithfulness. Thank You for sheltering this family through the storm and for bringing this precious woman to our door. You are good, and Your mercy is without end."

<h1 style="text-align:center">Chapter 31</h1>

Clair rose from the porch chair where she'd been sitting with Lydia and Emma. She stepped to the railing as Adam came into view at the top of the rise, and behind him a wagon followed, its canvas bonnet swaying gently with the road's contour.

Her pulse climbed, and she pressed her palms against the porch rail and watched Adam ride into the yard. He swung down and looped the reins around the porch rail in two quick turns, and when he looked up at her, he smiled like a schoolboy.

Adam walked to the wagon and offered his hand to Eunice as Webb set the brake and climbed down on his side.

Lydia rose from her chair.

"Webb... Eunice," Lydia said. "Thank you for coming."

"My pleasure, Lydia," Webb said. He took her hand in both of his and held it.

Eunice came up the steps and went straight to Clair and took both of her hands and squeezed them. "My dear girl," she said, and her eyes were already glistening. "When Adam came through the boardinghouse door and told us what he was there for, I nearly dropped the coffeepot. I said to Webb, 'Webb Hale, you get your Bible and you get in that wagon, because I know for a fact that Lydia has been praying for this for weeks now, and the Lord is not going to wait for you to finish your coffee.'"

"She did say that," Webb said. "Word for word. I didn't finish my coffee, and it was mighty good."

Clair laughed. "Thank you for coming, Mrs. Hale. Reverend Hale. It means more than I can say."

"Eunice, dear. I've told you before." Eunice patted Clair's hands and released them and turned to Emma, who stood beside Lydia with her fingers hooked through her grandmother's apron ties. "And there is the prettiest girl in the valley. Emma Louise, did you know your papa is getting married today?"

Emma nodded. "Miss Clair is going to be my mama," she said.

Webb stepped forward and shook Clair's hand. "Miss Whitmore," he said. "Adam tells me you'd like to be married today."

"Yes, sir," she said.

"Then we'll see to it." He looked around the yard and then at the front door. "Where would you like the ceremony?"

Adam had come up the porch steps and stood beside Clair.

"The creek. Where Pa and I used to fish," Adam said as he looked at Clair. "Is that all right with you?"

"Yes," she said. "That's perfect. "

They walked south through the lower pasture together, all six of them. The September afternoon spread wide around them, the sky a deep, hard blue above the valley.

Clair looked down at the dress she wore and smoothed her hand across the front of her skirt. Her dress. The dark blue one with the tailored waist and the covered buttons running from collar to bodice. She had arrived in it, soaked and muddied and stiff with road dust, the night she'd stumbled into the Dawson barn with nothing but a carpetbag and the last of her courage. Lydia had cleaned it, and Clair had mended the torn hem with small, careful stitches one evening while Emma slept on the settee beside her. It was the only dress that was truly hers in this house, and she had chosen it for a reason: it was the dress she'd worn when she walked into this family's life, and it was the dress she would wear when she legally joined it.

Emma ran ahead, darting off the path and into the grass, collecting wildflowers from the meadow. She found black-eyed Susans standing in a cluster near a fence post. She found wild asters, their petals a pale purple that looked almost blue in the afternoon light. She gathered late-summer blooms that had no names Clair knew, yellow and white and small enough to disappear in an adult's hand but perfectly scaled for a child's.

The cottonwoods stood tall along both banks of the creek, their trunks thick and pale, their leaves broad and beginning to turn color. The creek ran clear and steady over its bed of smooth stones, the current breaking white through the upper riffles before it slowed and deepened into the pool.

This was where his father had spoken the words that had carried Adam through the hardest years of his life. This was where Adam had brought her in August with two cane poles over his shoulder and a tin of worms in his back pocket. This was where he had looked at her and said the creek meant something different now.

And now he wanted to marry her here.

Webb stepped to the bank's edge and looked at the water and the trees and the mountains standing above the timber, and he nodded once as if confirming something. He opened his Bible and held it in one hand.

"I've performed a good many weddings in my years of ministry," Webb said. "In parlors and churches and once in a barn during a rainstorm that wouldn't quit. But I don't believe I've ever stood in a finer sanctuary than this one." He looked at Adam and Clair with a steady, kind gaze. "Shall we begin?"

Adam turned to Clair. He reached for her hand, and his calloused fingers closed around hers, and the grip was warm and sure. She looked up at him and found his dark eyes, and what she saw there was the man she had come to love across a summer of meals, silence, labor, and conversation, and one August afternoon on this very bank.

Emma positioned herself between them, pressing close against Clair's skirt on one side and Adam's trouser leg on the other. She handed the wildflowers to Clair, the stems bent and the petals slightly crushed from the walk.

Lydia stood beside Eunice, and Eunice had looped her arm through Lydia's, and both women were crying tears of joy.

"Dearly beloved," Webb said. "We are gathered here in the sight of God and in the company of this family to join this man and this woman in holy matrimony, which is an honorable estate, instituted by God, and not to be entered into lightly, but reverently, soberly, and in the fear of God."

"Adam Dawson," Webb said. "Will you have this woman to be your wedded wife, to live together after God's ordinance in the holy estate of matrimony? Will you love her, comfort her, honor and keep her, in sickness and in health, and forsaking all others, keep yourself only unto her, so long as you both shall live?"

"I will," Adam said; his voice was low and steady.

"Clair Whitmore," Webb said. "Will you have this man to be your wedded husband, to live together after God's ordinance in the holy estate of matrimony? Will you love him, comfort him, honor and keep him, in sickness and in health, and forsaking all others, keep yourself only unto him, so long as you both shall live?"

"I will," she said.

Webb looked at Adam. "Have you a ring?"

Adam reached into his vest pocket with his free hand and drew out the two rings.

"Place the ring on her finger," Webb said, "and repeat after me. With this ring, I thee wed."

Adam took Clair's left hand and slid the band onto her finger.

"With this ring, I thee wed," Adam said.

"Clair, place the ring on his finger," Webb said, "and repeat after me. With this ring, I thee wed."

Clair took the second band from Adam's hand.

"With this ring, I thee wed," she said.

Webb closed his Bible. "For as much as Adam and Clair have consented together in holy wedlock, and have witnessed the same before God and this company, and have pledged their faith each to the other, and have declared the same by the joining of hands and the giving and receiving of rings, I pronounce that they are husband and wife, in the name of the Father, and of the Son, and of the Holy Spirit. Those whom God hath joined together, let no man put asunder."

He looked at Adam and smiled. "You may kiss your bride."

Adam lifted his hand and touched her face. His thumb rested against her cheekbone, his fingers curving along her jaw. Clair leaned into his hand and looked up at him as he bent his head and kissed her.

The kiss was tender, his lips were warm against hers, and she felt his hand steady against her face. She closed her eyes, and the world contracted to the specific, astonishing fact of Adam Dawson's mouth against hers and the sound of the creek and the breeze in the cottonwoods and the small, hitching breath Lydia drew behind them. The kiss held for a moment that belonged entirely to them, unhurried.

Adam lifted his head, and he looked at her, and she looked at him, and they both smiled.

Emma tugged on Clair's skirt, and Clair looked down.

"Can I have my flowers back now?" Emma asked. "I want to throw them in the creek and see if the fish like them."

The laughter came from everywhere at once. It came from Webb, who tipped his head back and let it roll through him. It came from Eunice, who pressed both hands against her cheeks and laughed through her tears. It came from Lydia, whose laughter was quiet and deep, the sound of a woman whose prayers had been answered so completely she had no words left and could only let the joy of it move through her. It came from Adam, open and unguarded.

"They're your flowers, sweetheart," Clair said as she handed them back to Emma. "You can do whatever you like with them."

Emma grinned and ran to the bank's edge and flung the bouquet into the creek with both hands. The flowers hit the water and scattered, the black-eyed Susans spinning in the current and the asters floating wide, and the creek carried them into the deep pool, where they drifted in slow circles.

<h1 style="text-align:center">Epilogue</h1>

Adam climbed down from the wagon and came around to Clair's side. He reached up and took her hand, and she stepped down from the bench seat. When her boots met the packed earth, he didn't release her. He drew her closer, his free hand settling against the small of her back, and she looked up at him in the fading light.

"Ready for this?" he asked.

"More than ready," she said.

He bent his head and kissed her. When he lifted his head, he was smiling, and Clair pressed her palm flat against his chest and felt his heartbeat through the wool of his coat.

"Let's go in," he said.

She tucked her Bible under her arm, and Adam offered his elbow, and they walked together up the boardwalk and through the front door of the boardinghouse.

The dining room was full. The long tables had been pushed against the walls, and the chairs arranged in rows facing the front of the room. The people of Providence Ridge filled many of them, and Clair recognized every face.

Adam guided Clair to two open chairs near the end of the third row, and they sat. His knee rested against hers, and she folded her hands over her Bible in her lap and waited.

Marshal Tom Callahan stood at the front of the room. He wore his vest and his badge, and his shirt was pressed. He held a small ledger open in one hand with the composed attention of a man who conducted these meetings the way he conducted everything else in Providence Ridge: with competence, brevity, and a complete absence of pretension.

"Evening, everyone," Tom said. "Let's get started. If you'll bow your heads."

The room settled. Hats came off. Heads bowed.

"Lord, we thank You for the gathering of this community and for the work You have given us to do in this valley. Grant us wisdom in our decisions and generosity in our dealings with one another. Watch over our families and our homes as the season turns. Amen."

"Amen," the room answered.

Tom looked down at his ledger. "A few items before I turn things over to Amos. First, the Hendersons' milk cow got through a fence again last Tuesday and spent the better part of the morning in Mrs. Carpenter's garden. She ate most of the late cabbage before anyone noticed. Mrs. Carpenter has asked that the Hendersons repair their fence, and the Hendersons have agreed, and I consider the matter settled unless someone objects."

A low ripple of laughter moved through the room. Clair saw Mrs. Carpenter press her lips together and shake her head, and Mr.

Henderson, seated three rows back, raised one hand in a gesture of surrender.

"Second," Tom continued, "the new bridge has a plank on the east side that's splitting rapidly. I've asked Paul Higgins to take a look at it this week and determine whether it needs replacing or can be shimmed and reinforced. If it needs a new plank, we'll need someone to donate the timber or agree to a cost split. I'll have more on that at the next meeting."

He closed his ledger. "That's all from me. Amos."

Tom stepped to the side, and Amos Pemberton rose from his chair and walked to the front of the room.

"Thank you, Tom," Amos said. He faced the room and clasped his hands behind his back. "I have two matters to bring before the committee this evening. The first is the mining operation at the southern end of town. As most of you know, the surveying company that assessed the mineral deposits earlier this year has broken ground. Prospect shafts are being sunk into the hillside, and adits are being driven into the lode. The assay results on the initial ore samples have confirmed what the surveyors suspected. There is viable silver and gold beneath the ridge, and the company intends to develop it."

He paused and let the room absorb this. Several men leaned forward in their chairs.

"A company office is under construction near the mine site," Amos continued, "along with a bunkhouse for the men who will be hired to work the operation. The company expects to begin bringing on workers within the month. Some of those men will be single and will board at the bunkhouse. Others may bring families. Either way, it means new commerce for Providence Ridge, new customers at the mercantile, and new faces in this room before long."

A murmur passed through the room, the sound of a community absorbing the fact that it was about to grow.

"The second matter," Amos said, "is the school and church building. Margaret has been working on this effort for well over a year now, and I want to acknowledge that work publicly because it has been considerable."

Margaret sat with her hands in her lap and her chin level.

"The funds are not where they need to be," Amos said. "The lumber is expensive, the labor would need to be donated or paid for, and the cost of furnishing two purposes inside a single structure has proven larger than our initial estimates. We have not made progress since the last meeting, and I would rather not misrepresent our position. The building remains a priority for this committee, but I cannot tell you tonight when construction will begin."

Adam touched Clair's arm, and he nodded once.

Clair stood, and Adam stood beside her.

"Pardon us, Amos," Adam said, "but we'd like to propose something to the committee, if we may."

Amos stopped. His brows lifted, and he looked at the two of them standing together at the end of the third row. "Certainly," he said. "Go ahead."

Adam looked at Clair and nodded again, and she stepped into the center aisle and walked to the front of the room. The faces on either side of her turned as she passed, and she felt their attention the way she had felt it the first Sunday she worshipped in this very room. She had been a stranger then, wearing the only dress she owned.

She turned to face the room, and Adam stood beside her.

Clair held her Bible in both hands. She opened it to the page she had marked with a thin strip of ribbon, and she read aloud.

"For the love of money is the root of all evil: which while some coveted after, they have erred from the faith, and pierced themselves through with many sorrows."

She closed her Bible and held it against her waist.

"First Timothy, chapter six, verse ten," she said. "My mother taught me that verse when I was fourteen years old, sitting at our kitchen table in Helena. I had asked her why people steal, and she opened her Bible and read those words to me, and she told me that money itself was never the sin. The love of it was. The coveting. The choosing of it above every other good thing God has placed in a person's life."

The room was still, and Clair looked at the faces she had come to know across months of Sunday worship.

"Most of you know something of what brought me to Providence Ridge," she said. "I came here because a man my father trusted for years chose money over honor. After my father died, this man stole from the company my father built, and when I discovered what he had done and confronted him, he threatened my life. The love of money turned a trusted man into a thief. The love of money sent two men across the territory to find me. The love of money burned my childhood home to the ground in Helena."

She paused.

"I arrived in this valley with a carpetbag that held very little. I was frightened and alone and running from everything I had ever known. And this community took me in. Lydia Dawson opened her home to me. Adam gave me his protection." She looked at her husband, and the steadiness in his face was the same steadiness that had carried her through every trial since the night she stumbled into his barn. "Emma gave me her trust before I had done anything to earn it. Marshal Callahan took my evidence and sent it to Helena through proper legal channels. Amos, you protected me when strangers came asking questions at the mercantile. Other people in this room stood with us when the danger came to our doorstep; I owe you more than I will ever be able to repay."

"Adam and I have something we'd like to share with you," Clair said. "We have put my father's company, Whitmore Freight and Supply, up for sale through an attorney in Helena. Last week we received word that a buyer has been found and the terms have been agreed upon. Adam and I will be traveling to Helena next week to sign the final papers and close the transfer."

She drew a breath and felt Adam's hand settle against the small of her back.

"We have decided to donate a portion of the proceeds from the sale to the town of Providence Ridge," she said, "for the construction of two buildings. A proper schoolhouse. And a proper church. Not one building serving both. Two."

The room was silent, and Clair could see the stunned expressions on every person's face in the room.

"We also want to give Providence Ridge the funds to furnish both buildings completely," Clair continued. "Church pews, Bibles, hymnals, whatever is needed for the church to open its doors for worship. Desks, slates, primers—whatever is needed for the schoolhouse to open its doors for the children of this valley.

The town will have the money to provide everything that is required to make both buildings ready."

For a single held breath, the silence was absolute. Then the room broke open.

The sound that rose was not just applause. It was something closer to a wave lifting, voices and movement arriving together, chairs scraping, and hands reaching for the hands beside them and words spoken to spouses and neighbors in the rushing, uncontainable way of people who have just been told that the thing they had prayed for and worked toward and nearly given up on was coming. Clair saw Jesse Mayhew turn to Dale Wilson with his mouth open and no sound coming out. She saw Leora Hanscombe close her eyes and press her fingertips together beneath her chin.

Margaret Pemberton stood up from her chair. The tears were already running down her face, and she crossed the room with the unsteady, purposeful stride of a woman whose legs were not entirely under her control. She reached Clair and wrapped her arms around her and held on. Her shoulders shook, and the sounds she made were small and broken and carried more gratitude than any complete sentence could have held. Then she turned to Adam and put her arms around him, too, and he placed one hand gently against her back.

Amos waited until the room had settled enough that his voice could reach the far wall.

He looked at Adam and Clair.

"My goodness," Amos said. "The both of you have brought such joy to this room tonight." He shook his head slowly. "Bless the both of you, Adam and Clair. But I need to ask you directly. Are you sure about this?"

"We're sure," Adam said.

Clair nodded. "The money from this sale is not evil in itself," she said. "But we want it to do good. We want it to honor my father's memory and serve the community that we both love. Money that evil tried to claim can be turned toward something that builds instead of destroys. My father built a freight company that supplied the camps and towns of this territory for years, and the best use of what remains from his labor is to build something permanent for the people who showed his daughter what it means to belong."

Amos looked out into the room.

"Well then," he said. "I believe we need to take a vote. All in favor of accepting this generous donation for the construction and furnishing of a schoolhouse and a church in Providence Ridge, raise your hands."

Every hand in the room went up. Some went up fast, shooting toward the ceiling with the force of people who had waited a long time for this moment. Others rose slowly, lifted by hands that trembled, and Clair watched them all, every one, and the sight of those hands rising together was the most complete and beautiful unanimity she had ever witnessed.

Clair turned to Adam while the hands were still raised and the room was still alive with the sound of voices and laughter and Margaret Pemberton crying openly against her husband's shoulder. She placed her hands on either side of his face, her palms against the rough warmth of his jaw, her fingers resting along the line where his dark hair met his skin.

"I love you, Mr. Dawson," she said.

She kissed her husband, and his hands came to her waist and held her, and someone in the back of the room let out a whoop that drew laughter from every corner.

When she stepped back, Adam's eyes held hers, and his thumb traced a line along her jaw before his hand fell away and found hers and closed around it.

Clair turned toward the room with her husband's hand in hers and looked out across the faces. The people had not sat back down. They stood in clusters, talking and embracing. Margaret was moving through the room, hugging everyone. Webb Hale had his arm around Eunice, and he caught Clair's eye across the room and nodded, slow and sure. Cal Stackhouse stood near the back wall with his hat in his hands and his eyes red, and when Clair's gaze reached him, he dipped his chin and held it there.

She looked down at Adam's hand around hers, at the gold band on her finger and the matching one on his. She felt the press of his calloused palm against her own, the same hand that had pulled her onto a horse on a dusty road and brought her home.

Her mother's voice moved through her, quietly: *the love of money is the root of all evil.*

Clair smiled, and she held her husband's hand as she watched the celebration going on around her, and she thought to herself:

The love of God and his people was the root of everything good.

Leave A Review

If you enjoyed this book, please consider leaving an honest review on Amazon

Visit Our Website:

www.vivianbelle.com

Visit Our Amazon Author Page HERE

Find Us On Social Media:

Facebook

Instagram

Scan the QR code above to sign up for our newsletter!

Afterword

Writing historical fiction invites us into a world shaped by different customs, language, and ways of life than our own. In striving to portray these stories with authenticity, I have sought to remain faithful to the speech patterns, expressions, and cultural realities of the time in which the story is set. At times, this may include phrasing or perspectives that feel unfamiliar by today's standards, yet they are included with care to preserve the integrity of the historical setting and the voices of the characters who inhabit it.

It is never my intention to offend, but rather to tell stories that feel honest, immersive, and true to their time. More importantly, it is my prayer that every page reflects something far greater than history alone—the unchanging truth of God's love.

Scripture reminds us in Genesis 1:27 that "we are all created in the image of God" and in Acts 17:26 that "He has made every nation of mankind." These truths anchor every story I write. No matter the era, the heartbeat of each novel is the same: grace extended, redemption offered, and love that endures.

Thank you for stepping into this story with me.

With gratitude,

Vivian Belle

About Vivian

Vivian Belle is a talented author known for her sweeping **Historical Christian Romance** novels set against the untamed beauty of the American frontier. With a deep love for history and storytelling, she brings to life **resilient heroines, steadfast heroes, and faith-filled journeys** in the vast, rugged landscapes of the past.

Nestled in the **majestic mountains of northern West Virginia,** Vivian finds endless inspiration in the rolling hills, winding rivers, and boundless sky that mirror the spirit of her stories. When she's not writing, she enjoys **kayaking on tranquil waters, hiking through breathtaking mountain trails, and, of course, getting lost in a good book.**

Vivian's novels capture the heart of **faith, love, and perseverance**—where strong women and honorable men overcome life's trials to find hope, home, and happily-ever-after. Whether she's exploring the great outdoors or crafting her next frontier romance,

Vivian's passion for adventure and storytelling shines through in every word she writes.

Visit Vivian on the web: www.vivianbelle.com

Also By Vivian Belle

<u>Stand Alone Novels</u>

Where the Heart Finds Home

Faith on the Frontier

Love in Hopewell Creek

Abigail's Promise

Beneath Montana Skies

Rocky Mountain Promise

Hearts Unbroken

Beneath the Oregon Pines

Journeys of the Heart

<u>Providence Ridge Series</u>

A Bride Worth Keeping

Stronger Than the River

Tender Mercies

Sanctuary in Providence Ridge